The Lives
of Cat

The Lives of Cat

TIME PASSES AND LIFE CHANGES

BARBARA JEAN RUTHER

Disclaimer

This is a work of fiction. Names, characters, places and incidents either are products of the author's imagination or are used fictitiously. Any resemblance to actual events or locales or persons, living or dead, is entirely coincidental.

Also, I took liberty when stating that The Team purchased the USAF Base in the desert of Arizona. I was thinking of Thunderbird, a decommissioned WWII Air Base in Glendale, Arizona, which became The Thunderbird School of Global Management. I don't know how that came about, so I invented the base and the circumstances.

The military helicopter given to Joe was an act from my imagination. I doubt the USArmy would just abandon one of their expensive helicopters, but Joe loved it, so I gave it to him.

ISBN # paperback: 978-0-578-94547-7

Printed in the United States of America

Cover and Interior Design: Creative Publishing Book Design

This book is dedicated to the three loves I carry in my heart —
Kathryn, Molly, Jessica

Contents

THE ACADEMY TEAM
EIGHT SKILLED SPECIALISTS

Xander Xavier—Administrative Director of The Bodyguard Academy. Father—American Ambassador to Russia. Childhood friend of Nikolai Ivanov, President of The Russian Federation, and Zack Andrez, from Mexico.

Zach Andrez (Second Passport, André Zackery)—Principal Accountant of The Bodyguard Academy, entrepreneur, CEO of his private hedge fund, investment specialist. Father—Wealthy Mexican business executive. Childhood friend of Xander Xavier and Nikolai Ivanov.

Geoff—Martial Arts Champion, known as "Cheetah" in World Tournaments for his quiet, quick, powerful actions. Academy physical trainer, instructor of martial arts and languages—Russian, French, Spanish, English. Mother—Russian, divorced, professor of languages at St. Petersburg University, friend of Nikolai Ivanov, who recommended her son to Xander.

Hitch—U.S. Army Special Forces retiree—munitions expert, planner of schemes to ambush, extinguish the enemy. Accomplished Ground Control operator for drones carrying Hellfire Missiles. The President of The Russian Federation frequently requests his help with projects and recommended him to Xander as an instructor at The Academy.

Joaquin—Authority on knives, from stilettos to machetes to switchblades, instructor for use as protection, defense, and quick elimination. Ex-gang leader from the streets of LA, recruited by Xander.

Joe—Psychiatrist and veteran U.S. Navy pilot, expert trainer of aircraft carrier landing discipline, retired to join The Team at The Bodyguard Academy. Flying instructor and individual psychiatric therapist. Longtime friend of Xander.

Oso—Gun specialist and arms instructor—cleaning, rebuilding, and the use of handguns, rifles, and other artillery. Studies psychiatry, assists Joe with therapy. In prison for killing his father, rescued by Xander.

Sarge—Retired U.S. Army sergeant—breeder/trainer of dogs for attack and locating hidden drugs or ammunition. With his hand signal, one of his dogs attacked the general, who had called him and his dogs useless and stupid. After retirement, Sarge trained dogs as bodyguards for wealthy executives, friends of Xander's. Head of security at The Academy.

CHAPTER I
The Value Of Self-Esteem

C at wrote the date in the empty space. *People who sign important papers never know the date,* she thought, *as if promising to pay millions of dollars is an everyday occurrence.* The Intent To Purchase document lay on the round table for two, pushed to the other side of thick frosted holders of lighted votive candles, all on starched, flawlessly ironed white linen. The last page glared strangely on top, out of order. The flickering candles seemed to spark on the empty signature line, causing Cat to blink as if a camera flashed, recording the scene.

The bottle of Pinot Noir on the table was the exact shade of her new silk, burgundy blouse, bought to wear at dinner with this client. She never spent $300 for a blouse, but the sale at the outlet mall brought the cost down to her price range of splurges for special occasions and important work-related events like this.

Cat worked for ME Commercial Real Estate, her first job out of college, moving her way from assistant agent to agent in charge of office rentals. After three years she requested another move to commercial sales. A primary broker with twenty years' experience agreed to take her on as an aide and teach her the fundamentals. He was representing the seller of a vacated shopping mall and had been courting a buyer. He found Cat helpful, diligent, courteous, and dependable.

It was time for the buyer to sign his intentions and give a deposit. He requested to be allowed to treat the young trainee to a sumptuous dinner where he would sign the Intent and present her with a check for $50,000 deposit. She wouldn't get a share of the commission, but at least would be wined and dined. Also, the primary broker had deemed her helpful, and recommended a modest bonus. Her boss, the owner, agreed.

Cat had chosen giant Australian shrimp with buttery orange sauce and thought, *Wouldn't it be wonderful to have this dinner, in this elegant restaurant with a caring, handsome boyfriend?* She knew the wine was expensive because it didn't have that bitter aftertaste like the wine her sometimes-boyfriend brought to her apartment with a barely warm pizza. She reached for the balloon glass, almost large enough to need two hands, held it to her perfectly shaped mauve lips, and took a small sip, meeting eyes with Bradford Ayers. A builder who bought vacated shopping malls, President of Bradford Ayers Construction Company, his name was found on the signs of developments throughout California, always a big flashy sign with an architectural drawing of the future site. His company demolished everything around the skeleton steel structures and rebuilt with a theme: Tuscan Village, Plum Tree Creek, Orange Grove Promenade, all with extensive landscaping. Of course, he never bought the property until he had commitments from popular restaurants and fancy stores that would rent space designed especially for them.

He emptied the bottle of wine into his own glass. "What kind of name is Cat? Short for Catherine, Catlyn, Catalane, Caterpillar?" An impressed-with-himself smirk gleamed across his flushed face.

Cat calmed herself, inhaling, exhaling. *There it is,* she thought, *the inevitable question.* Sometimes she lied or just showed her impatience.

It's short for something, or maybe it's shortsightedness, shortchange, shortcut, shortstop. Sometimes she would leave the question hanging, unanswered, annoyed. People usually continued to another subject and she decided they weren't really interested in the drama behind her name. The drama was in Cat's mind. Any mention of her name brought painful memories of when her mother told her the truth behind her naming. Her friends told her it was a delightful name and, in fact, suited her personality.

In the working world, friends told Cat she had the qualifications of a fashion model, should go to New York City, find an agent. She was five feet nine, over six feet in heels, thick, blond-streaked hair that moved like a drape, gemstone eyes encased in hedges of eyelashes. The starlet face caused people to turn and stare, which she was never aware of. She attended exercise classes, ran two miles several times each week, kept a moderate diet, but allowed herself two pieces of fudge each week. "It's inspiration for my soul," she justified to girlfriends.

Cat's green eyes steadily gazed at Bradford. She pronounced each word slowly. "It's not short for anything, it's my name."

He smiled, put his elbows on the table, leaned toward Cat, his jowls hanging even more prominently, his protruding stomach pressing against the edge of the table. "I like your name, Cat, and I like your pretty face. You've worked diligently on this sale: weeks spent helping me study the architect's preliminary designs, the engineer's proposals, the landscaper's drawings. As you know I have also been considering another site a few miles further down the coast and these properties are too close to each other for me to be interested in both."

Why is he telling me about another site for his project? She interrupted him, a slight panic in her voice. "But this is the perfect setting, the perfect location."

"Cat, when I build a shopping/dining center, it's the perfect place to be seen. It's where women brag they shop, wear their wide-brimmed hats, sit under umbrellas, and gossip over iced lattes. The two locations are the same for me. I need a little incentive to make that final decision. Let's go up to my suite, I'll order Dom Pérignon for our celebration and you'll go home with signed legal papers for an impressed boss who will reward you with a bonus."

She felt her heart beating, vibrating her head, shoulders, arms. She wondered if he noticed her shiver. The promised signing bonus from her boss would mean a helpful addition to her meager salary. She thought frantically, *Can I do it—go to his room, have sex? Would it be debasing, repugnant? Would the signed contract negate my self-disgust, invalidate the fact I've dismissed my principles and traded sex for a bonus?*

She stood. "Excuse me, I'm going to the ladies' room."

"Take your time, powder your nose, I'll get the check." Behind his grin she heard elated arrogance, his voice thickened with egotism.

The foyer of the ample ladies' room held several French boudoir-style chairs upholstered in rose brocade, small round tables topped with pink granite. She sat, got her cell phone from her huge inappropriate-for-fancy-dining shoulder bag, and pressed her employer's number. He had told her to call, no matter what time it was, and assure him that Bradford had signed the papers her mentor had given her. He answered on the first ring.

She took a deep breath. "He's not going to sign unless I have sex with him." Her voice was hoarse, gloomy, dejected.

The answer was loud, impatient. "Cat, this is a business deal. In business we have to make concessions. Think about it, you need to bring me those papers—signed."

The flat, impersonal response contained an underlying threat. She felt overwhelmed, frightened, like being close to the edge of a cliff. Cat thought, *My job is on the line here.* She tried to hang on to the rope. "I've rented office spaces that bring the company commissions for the length of the leases."

"That's peanuts! This is Big Bucks. You wanted to move into sales and I gave you this opportunity to work with our largest-grossing broker, learn from the best, because I had confidence in you. Our primary broker is depending on you, did you a big favor. Without this Intent and deposit, you're in trouble. You're one of the lowest producers in the office. It's as simple as that." He clicked off.

She slouched into the elaborate fabric. *I have given three years of my life to the company, working until I'm exhausted: phone calls and meetings lasting into nights, twelve-hour workdays, weekends given up to meet a renter's schedule. And for what? A success that lasts only until the next signature?*

Cat took a few more minutes to digest the situation. She stared at the luxurious, silky, pink and green striped wallpaper, not seeing it, her thoughts being written somewhere on a chalkboard. *Can he erase my self-esteem and self-respect? With the stored-up guilt, will I feel my worth has been measured by a signature and then have to live with that knowledge? Have I been set up, to make this buyer happy? He may have already agreed to sign the Intent To Purchase, but is using me for his bonus.*

Dizzying thoughts made the room swirl. *Do I lower myself into the grime of daily existence? Life will go on, but will I be disappointed by my careless actions? I've always believed that taking a definite stance, right or wrong, for or against, is better than indifference. Indifference can kill your soul. I am a strong woman, I will not be used!*

Cat walked with determination through the elegant dining room of beautifully dressed people, women coiffured, not a hair out of place, well-groomed men wearing silk ties, reserved laughter, clinking crystal. She stood at the table and looked at Bradford Ayers: overweight, conceit on his face, the sparse comb-over still obvious in the soft light of chandeliers.

Her shoulders went back, her posture straight, the smile of a winner as she picked up the five-page agreement, tore it in half, put the pages together, tore them in half again. With a firm hand, she placed the pile of papers in front of him. "Thanks for dinner, Mr. Ayers."

CHAPTER II

The Uninvited Visitor

Her too-high heels clicking on the white Carrara marble floor, Cat sauntered carefully through the hotel lobby, out the etched-glass double doors where the uniformed doorman offered a cab. "No thanks." She lifted her chin and with collected poise, informed him, "I'm going to walk."

He smiled as he glanced at the narrow beige straps holding her feet to stiletto heels that almost kept her on tiptoes. She crossed the street, not seeing the stopped driver who was scowling, palms up to express his annoyance for another jaywalker. Cat was thinking, *I'm unemployed, but people lose their jobs and still go on with life. So will I.*

Only a few minutes ago, from the elegant restaurant on the top floor of the ritzy hotel, she had seen the full moon reflected on the foam-edged surf and remembered the boardwalk was across the busy street and down one block. One short block of singles bars on both sides, the blatant eyeing of cleavages and crotches, the negotiations and where the outcome would take place. The preprogrammed music was loud. Conversations were made with lips close to ears, sometimes revealing the dreaded bad complexions underneath the growth of the supposedly masculine-looking unshaven face, beer breath, perfumed necks, and many layers of mascara accenting enticing eyes. Usually these transactions resulted in sex, ended before morning, and were seldom followed up with a phone call or even a text. If there was effort on both sides to give a satisfying performance, recognition in another bar, on another night, might lead to an encore, the possibility of even remembering each other's names. This was the California Beach Scene, beautiful young people biding their time. Were they waiting for a callback from a film audition, a check from parents, an offer to model, a payout from a trust fund, a publishing contract? Being chosen for sex proved attractiveness, boosted the confidence, relieved stress.

It was in a similar bar where Cat had met Shane, her sometimes-boyfriend. She frowned at the memory of how easily she had accepted his suggestion. *Loneliness,* she thought, *causes people to make erroneous decisions.*

When she was alone, she yearned for easy, shared, personal conversations with adoring eyes, the slow caress of caring hands, the warmth of an attentive lover. Shane offered none of these traits, she wasn't even sure it was his real name. *Shane! Isn't that a name from a movie?*

In bars he sat on a barstool to give him a few inches more height. Shane was one of those short men who felt inferior among the bare-chested volleyball beach guys, their bicycle seats elevated to the highest notch to keep their long legs from cramping as they cycled up and down the boardwalk.

Some short men are surrounded by a proficient air of confidence, height not being an issue with them or anyone in their company. They are comfortable with taller women, perhaps looking beyond height to intelligence, pleasing personality, honorableness.

Shane seldom asked Cat out to dinner, but the few times they walked to the local Trattoria, he noticeably looked at her shoes to make sure she wasn't wearing heels. Once she had worn a pair of low wedgies and, annoyed, he'd asked her to change shoes. Even in flats she was two inches taller and felt herself stooping and bending her knees to please him. Cat didn't mind being taller than Shane; he was handsome, a nice build from working out, looked good in jeans and a tucked-in polo. Lots of movie stars married taller women. She wished he would be more relaxed about their difference in height. Otherwise, Cat liked his personality. He made her laugh and she enjoyed rare evenings of Pinot Grigio, which she would buy on the way home from work, Chinese Sesame Chicken, which she suggested he pick up, and long talks. They would take on controversial issues like religion, politics, relationships, the meaning of love. It was refreshing to have conversations with an intelligent person and perhaps that's what Shane enjoyed, also, but it seemed he didn't want a serious relationship. From gossip she heard, he liked having lots of girlfriends. *I don't want to be just one of somebody's girlfriends, I want someone who is interested in me full time.* He wasn't a caring boyfriend who tried to please her with a loving touch, a little gift, a drive up the coast, or even movie tickets. She knew their relationship would never be more than their discussions and occasional sex and wanted to break up, but she just kept saying, "Okay."

Cat left the narrow street of singles bars and the disappointing memories of them. She took off her uncomfortable shoes, held them with one finger by the heel straps, and stepped up to the boardwalk. *That's enough of those for one day,* she thought, as she walked the few steps across to the beach side, sat on the edge of the worn surface, putting her bare feet on the warm sand, then digging in with her toes to find the coolness. Her condo building was about one mile south, then east a few blocks, off the main street. She had walked here many times. The familiarity of the ocean smell, the feel of the fine grainy sand, the moon showing the outline of palm trees, all relaxed the core of her being. *I am going to find one positive item in my life right now and when I feel depression will take over, I will think of that absolute bright spot.* She stared toward the horizon, searching the index in her memory, her spine straight, shoulders back, eyes squinting. Then, a slight smile formed, half happy, half sad. *I'm grateful to be in California instead of Ohio. I will go forward. There are other jobs and I will find the right one. Friends talk about networking, so I will call everyone I've met the past three years while employed at ME Real Estate and get recommendations and referrals and send out my résumé.*

Cat's mind became a busy machine, purring, running smoothly, thinking of job possibilities until she slumped, overtaken by the realization of her financial responsibilities, the mortgage and expenses on her condo, monthly payments on her Chevy, groceries. Since getting her first job out of college, Cat had scrimped and sent small amounts every month to her sister, May, in Toledo, Ohio. She felt obliged to repay the money May had sent her while she was in college. May finally convinced her to stop when she received another raise, telling her sister to put the money toward her condo, a good investment. Six years older, May had been both sister and mother, and Cat was grateful to her. She appreciated the scholarship, but the jobs around school paid barely enough to survive.

During her senior year in college, May and Cat's mother had fallen on the back steps, lain there passed out until morning when a neighbor called 911. She had broken her hip. After surgery the hospital sent her to rehab for physical therapy and then she had fallen twice more, trying to leave the facility. May and Cat thought, *Probably looking for a bar and a free drink.* She died in her sleep. Both girls searched for sorrow, dug deep into their souls, but there were no good memories to bring up. They continued their life without even missing her.

Cat stood on the boardwalk, slung the strap of her heavy purse over her narrow shoulder, and picked up her shoes. *I will walk to the end where the beach houses begin, then east a couple blocks to my condo.* The fiery-coal moon had gotten covered by dark clouds leaving a pale glow, giving just enough light to walk the path. *I have enough money in my savings account to pay next month's mortgage, and some bagels and soup in the freezer. I will get through this one day at a time. I am a resilient woman and after I have a good cry, I will spring back.*

As Cat looked ahead to find the end of the boardwalk, she noticed the first house extended out to where the beach started. There was a sea-worn board fence all around and many strings of tiny lights on the fence and inside, emitting a festive atmosphere.

She was now close enough to hear music, not disco-loud music to drown conversations, but sensuous instrumental music, creating a mood for crystal wineglasses, pool-party flowery dresses, and best manners. Cat had never been to a party like this. She didn't even have a fancy summer party dress. *I've just gone through a terrible experience. Maybe, just once, I could hang on the edge of this party.*

Cat stepped down from the boardwalk to the sand, walked to the fence, stood on tiptoes, and barely got a view of an oblong swimming pool, a huge Jacuzzi, and a gate on the other side. Stepping carefully, as if someone might hear her, she walked around the fence and found the gate locked. A large flower pot next to the gate provided a precarious step, and reaching her hand over the top she felt the latch. *I have lost my mind. I am entering private property, these people will call the police and I will spend the night in jail. Does that mean I will have a record that will prevent me from getting a job?*

The latch released, she stepped down from the flower pot and pushed the gate open a few inches, then more. It seemed the self-absorbed partiers didn't notice an uninvited, curious, beautiful young woman entering the enclosure, carrying her go-with-everything beige blazer and stylish, very high-heeled shoes she had bought when a girlfriend dared her, so she wouldn't continue being so conservative. Cat looked around the softly lighted area—so many beautiful people at one party. Some were vaping, the breeze sending cherry-scented vapors around the slate-tiled pool area. On the tables were several hookahs, glass cylinders of bubbling water with tubes protruding, ready for partiers to sit and inhale. Cat thought, *They are so perfect, they could have just stepped from a magazine, but the smokers don't look glamorous like pictures of the slim-hipped women of the '20s in a pose, holding the long cigarette holders in the air.* The E-cigs, battery-powered devices that vaporized nicotine, were clumsy, too heavy to hold with two fingers, they looked like fat, black, permanent markers. Cat had observed vaping outside the singles bars, the leaning against each other, the sharing of puffs. She wanted to try it, but thought it might be addictive. She didn't want to become addicted to drugs. *I have to support myself and I can't afford the luxury of being part of the in-crowd.*

A movie-star-pretty girl was sitting on the top step of the spa in the warm bubbly water, fully clothed in a yellow sundress, so bright it seemed like she had been sprinkled with sunflowers. A wide-chested brawny male sat on a canvas chaise above her.

In the back corner, on a cushioned lounge, Cat placed her shoulder bag, jacket, and shoes. She unfastened her skirt, slipped it off, unbuttoned her lustrous blouse and carefully laid both on top. Wearing a practical black, cotton bra with a bit of lace and matching hipster panties, she sat on the smooth, tiled border of the pool and slid into the water holding on to the edge. Cat didn't know how to swim; she copied a friend she had watched who didn't want to get her hair wet: head above the water, both hands reaching out to paddle, kicking her legs like a frog. It wasn't glamorous, but it moved her across the pool through cool water, soothing her body, refreshing her mind. She got to the shallow end, stood up, and observed the clusters of elegant people: men wearing freshly ironed button-down shirts with initials embroidered in front, and alluring women, holding wineglasses and flipping their long shiny hair around their shoulders.

She walked across the pool to the spa, put both arms on the edge, and looked up at the lovely but somber face. "Why are you wearing that pretty dress in the spa?"

A bright daffodil sundress with tiny straps tied behind her neck lent no sunshine to the girl's disposition. The soft linen fabric, which undoubtedly was tagged with a "Dry Clean Only" label, had shrunk out of shape. Her hair hanging wet, makeup half washed away, the rest smeared, she turned to Cat. "My boyfriend, declaring, 'Why isn't anyone in the pool?' decided it would be great fun to pick me up and toss me into the deep end for his party entertainment." She suppressed more tears that had already streaked her cheeks.

"Where is your boyfriend?" Cat asked, curious to know what a person looked like who would do this to his girlfriend.

She silently pointed her chin to a blond Adonis, white narrow-cut slacks, white designer polo with the arms of a white cardigan on his shoulders, casually looped across his chest. Three women, their breasts barely covered by skimpy summer dresses, necklines dipping front and back, were laughing too loud, talking animatedly, touching his shoulder, arms, pushing back strands of hair falling on his forehead.

Cat turned back to her. "You need a new boyfriend." *And I need a new boyfriend, also.*

A slight smile appeared as the girl fully turned toward Cat, remembering she had just watched Cat dog-paddle across the pool. "Why are you swimming in your underwear?" She was not judgmental, not criticizing, just puzzled interest.

"It's a depressing story." All the words came out crowded together as if they had been in her mouth, waiting to be spit out. "Basically, I was fired from my job tonight because I wouldn't have sex with a powerful man who wanted me to go to his hotel room before putting his signature on a business agreement. I decided to keep my self-esteem, so thanked him for dinner and left the restaurant." Cat inhaled the chlorine-filled air. It felt good, almost uplifting, to tell someone her thoughts.

The defeated yet alluring young woman in the shrunken dress looked confused. "If it was going to cost you your job, why couldn't you have sex with him and forget about it? People have sex for lots of reasons and most of the time love isn't involved." She looked into the space above Cat's head, as if she was thinking about her own life. She looked back at the determined face in the pool. "Do you have a boyfriend?"

"This is another upsetting subject. I have a sometimes-boyfriend who fits me into his schedule between other girlfriends. I enjoy his company, but there are no deep feelings between us. Every time I have sex with him, I am thoroughly disappointed with myself." Cat thought, *I've never admitted that to anyone. I guess I want her to know lots of us have boyfriend problems.*

A petal-pink knit polo shirt stretched across a muscular chest and shoulders turned toward Cat, a question on his handsome face: *I'm looking at a beautiful woman who is concerned about principles, morals, and is struggling for her self-esteem. Who is she?*

The aura of faded sunshine perked up as she turned to look at the bulk of muscles next to her, sitting upright on the lounge. "Xander, this is the perfect girl for you." She leaned down to the pool to whisper to Cat. "Xander doesn't like any of us 'party girls,' he calls us. He is only here because he's a childhood friend of Rodney, my boyfriend." She motioned with her chin again, then added sarcastically, her face expressing pain, "As you can see, Rodney doesn't have time to visit with an old friend." She hesitated a moment, looking at Cat, her new friend, and quietly continued. "You need to get yourself some bigger boobs."

Cat giggled. She liked the open, honest, wanting-to-be-helpful advice. "Nope, this is all there is. I'm not going to have a boob job or puff up my lips. Well, maybe I'll get puffy lips when I'm forty, if I don't have a real boyfriend by then." Cat looked down at her body, seeing she was almost nude. Still, she had only received quick glances, people too self-involved to give her a thought.

A chilling breeze lingered at the party and Cat realized she needed to get dressed and find her small, safe, warm condo. "It was good—no, it was helpful—talking with you. I hope your boyfriend doesn't mind that I crashed his party and I'm sorry about your pretty dress. I'm going to walk home now, have a good, loud cry, and tomorrow I'll check the want ads in the *L.A. Times.*"

With one hand, she held on to the side of the pool and walked, then paddled to the deep end and hoisted herself up, into the darker corner where she had piled her clothes. She slipped into her skirt, took off the wet panties, all in one motion. Cat was holding her new silk blouse, wondering if it would get ruined over a wet bra, when she felt a fluffy towel being draped around her shoulders. She looked up at a leading-man-handsome face smiling at her.

"This is not a dilemma. I'll hold the towel while you take off that wet bra and put on your jacket. I promise not to peek. You can wrap your wet things in a towel, Rodney will never miss it."

A little half-laugh escaped from her throat. *Obviously there's nothing left unseen.* Cat slung the bag over her shoulder, held the heel straps with two fingers, tucked the bundled towel under her arm, and picked up her prized burgundy blouse. She murmured, "Thank you," and walked toward the gate, conscious of a tall, broad figure beside her, who bent to unlatch the gate.

"How far are you going to walk barefoot?" He was much taller than Cat. She looked at his face again, fixed on his eyes, now reflecting the party lights, emitting a strange combination of midnight blue and sky blue. His gaze was so intense, it made her take a step back.

"I live only a few blocks down this street."

"My car is here in Rodney's driveway. Let me drive you home. Reny will vouch for me."

He followed her a few more steps, and as they passed in back of a white Porsche SUV, he stepped to the passenger side, opened the door, and motioned toward the leather seat. "I won't even ask your name or talk at all. This is just help from a Good Samaritan."

Cat felt the rough cement under her feet. *I'll never make it three blocks. I know I'm too trusting.* She closed her eyes. *After this distressing day, if I can just have a safe ride home.* A wish, a longing, a prayer?

The smooth-riding luxury car was filled with quiet. Cat could hear herself breathing, a little too fast. She forced her eyes to look straight ahead, thinking of the too-handsome face next to her, not wanting to seem interested.

Xander did not talk, waited for her directions, but thought, *I don't want to scare her with questions, I will find her name. She stopped at that party because it was in the cards, fate. She doesn't know it yet, but she came there to meet me.*

Cat directed him into the half-circle driveway of her condominium building. He stopped at the modest front entry, the part-time doorman stepped to the car and opened the door for her.

The condominium association could only afford his services six to midnight, but he knew every owner's name. "Good evening, Miss Donley."

Xander smiled. *Name and address. Good night, Miss Donley.*

CHAPTER III

Friends Go Through The Storm With You, Stay Until The Sun Comes Out

Cat spent the weekend copying want ads with a black ballpoint pen that advertised ME Commercial Real Estate, Inc. *I will dispose of this distressing reminder from a bit of my past, which I am totally eliminating, and I'll buy a new pen for myself with a plastic rose on top—a professional woman with a sense of humor.* She made a list of phone numbers and email addresses, jotting notes beside them that detailed the jobs, then worked on several résumés, steering each one toward the jobs advertised.

In the late afternoon she decided a run would get her blood circulating and give her some energy. Off with the pj's, on with the sweats and headband as she checked her image in the full-length mirror on the back of the bathroom door. *It would be interesting if a white Porsche SUV drove by.* She held up her arm and sniffed. *Not today, these sweats need to go in the next wash.*

After her run, Cat went in The Pit Stop for an iced chai-to-go and sipped it on the way back to her condo. She showered, put on her fluffy pink robe, and sat on her small sofa going over her notes to begin job hunting tomorrow morning. The intercom buzzed and Leo's voice came through the speaker. "Miss Donley, there's a package for you. Shall I bring it up to your apartment?"

Leo, the doorman, also had a day job. He was a carpenter, worked for a friend who bought run-down houses, remodeled, then sold them. He had broad shoulders and big, rough hands with a gentle touch. Leo met the cars with a dance in his walk and had a way of bowing when he opened the door that made everyone feel special. He seemed proud of his uniform, straightened the lapel, smoothed the fabric. It made one think it was the only suit he ever owned.

"Yes, thank you, Leo." *May probably sent me a box of cheer-up chocolates. I didn't want to tell her about losing my job, she worries so about me, but I could never keep anything from May. It would be nice to have some sweet, creamy truffles right now.* The doorbell chimed and Cat peeked through the tiny hole before opening the door. Leo's arms were hugging a huge basket of cellophane-wrapped fruit. He placed it on the tiled counter, smiled, said, "Good evening, Miss Donley," and returned to his doorman job.

Cat had seen baskets like this in costly gift catalogs. A small envelope with "Miss Donley" written on the front contained a gold-bordered card, a thick black X, and no name. *Is this a kiss from sometimes-boyfriend Shane or did he accidentally send it to the wrong person? I'm keeping it. Thank you, Shane.*

She pulled the end of the satiny, purple bow, releasing the wrap, revealing plump, picture-perfect grapefruit, apples, pears, oranges, bananas and other fruits, mangos, guavas, kiwis that were too expensive to make it on her grocery list. *For dinner I'm going to make the most exotic fruit salad. What's this?* A small box contained a loaf of banana-nut bread, chamomile tea, and a jar of honey. *Shane, I didn't know you had it in you. I might fall in love with you.* (A small giggle.) *How did you find out I lost my job?*

The next day Cat was on her laptop from 7:00 to 4:00, intent on sending résumés to companies she had found in want ads on the internet. The intercom buzzed. *Oh, no! If that's Shane, I don't want to be ungrateful, but I don't want to see him, maybe next week. I won't answer.* The intercom buzzed again. *Okay, suck it up. Say thank you, but not right now.* "Yes?"

The response came through the speaker in a low, pleasant voice. "Miss Donley, this is Xander. Would you like to meet me in the coffee shop across the street? If you're still looking for a job, I have a lead for you."

There was a long hesitation. She let the invitation wander through her mind. *It's the middle of the day, lots of people around, he could have abducted me when he drove me home from the pool party—a late, dark night. A lead?* A hesitant answer went to the lobby intercom. "Okay, I'll be there in ten minutes."

A guy who had just walked out of the elevator heard Cat's positive reply and gave Xander two thumbs up. He waited in the lobby for her.

"I hope you had one of those Florida grapefruits for breakfast," he said as they walked to The Pit Stop.

Cat felt embarrassed. If she had known, of course, she would have thanked him in the lobby. To make sure she knew who it was from or that she received it, he had to mention it. *In the back of my mind, I knew that fabulous basket couldn't have come from Shane. X for Xander, but he doesn't even know me. I don't trust him.*

He carried the cups of chai and plain coffee to a café table on the sidewalk under a red awning, then pulled a chair out for her. His smile was too perfect, it made her nervous. Whatever Xander was doing, whoever he was with, all his attention was there, as though he was unaware of the surroundings. People passing looked at him, never received a return glance.

"I didn't get your first name, unless you would rather I call you Miss Donley. The building directory says C. Donley."

Here we go again with the name. A little defensively, expecting a comment, she sat up straight and stared into his eyes. "C is for Cat. That's my name." She gave him a serious, no-nonsense look.

Xander got to business. "I don't know if this is something that might interest you. I was at my accountant's office this morning, at tax-time they work every day. It's a big firm, lots of CPAs, phone lights going on and off incessantly, people in the waiting room with boxes of papers. I asked if they needed help. He said he needed ten people, but right now they are looking for someone to help with invoicing, sending bills to clients, and keeping track of the payments."

He barely had finished talking when she said, "I could do that. I'm organized and good with numbers. I took bookkeeping and accounting, I thought about being an accountant."

He smiled inside his face, so she wouldn't see how pleased he was with her enthusiasm. From the back pocket of his jeans he gave her two cards: his personal card and one from the accounting firm with a private number bluntly written on the back and the name Arthur, printed neat, like a schoolteacher writes on the chalkboard. "Just call that number and tell Arthur that Xander told you to call."

"What is your last name?"

"My name is Xander Xavier. My father thought it would be amusing for me to sign my name XX. I don't think he realized I would go through life never getting anything monogrammed." His stare was intense, sending the message—*Many of us live with our parents' humor.*

Cat met his gaze and felt a rush through her body. She hooked her hair in back of her ear, remembered she hadn't put on any makeup and only had some Chap Stick in her pocket. She ringed it around her mouth and smiled at him. "Thank you for the much-needed basket of delicious fruit. Last night I made a fruit salad like I've never had and even tried the banana-nut bread and tea with honey. It was so thoughtful of you. Also, I want to thank you for asking your accountant about a job for me. I appreciate your help." *There—I thanked him for everything.*

"I'm happy to be of assistance. I was thinking of how we met. I eavesdropped on your conversation with Reny, drove you home, thought you were a nice person, and here we are. It's interesting how people come together. Unfortunately, I leave for Mexico tomorrow and will be gone two weeks. I live in California and Mexico and go back and forth. In the hills of northwestern Mexico, I manage a school that teaches men to be bodyguards." Then seriously adding, "We haven't had any women apply yet." A smile, a hesitation, he was studying her face. "May I take you to dinner when I return? I'll tell you more about my job and I want to hear the story of Cat. And could I have your phone number?"

She relaxed, felt comfortable. On the night they met, she had glanced at him, but hadn't given him a good look. Now, while he was talking, Cat was making mental notes: *About six feet three—I can wear high heels. Thick deep-brown hair in a short, practical cut, shaved face, hypnotic intense eyes that command one's attention, a wide square brow with matching jaw and sensuous lips that promise something.*

The Arthur Blake Accounting Firm was not as chaotic as Xander made it seem. It was busy, but subdued, organized, orderly and run efficiently. The phones didn't ring, red lights quietly signaled calls and two receptionists answered in low, calm voices.

Cat was hired as assistant to a gray-haired woman who had worked at her job for twenty-five years when the fathers of the now accountants started the firm. She had trained several young assistants, but they didn't stay long. The offices were too boring for them, all the men married and not interested in breaking up their families for a pretty face. Cat was content with the generous salary, no commission worries, and gave full attention to her new job. She settled into a comfortable routine: up early, forty-five minutes on the gym machines, shower, arriving before 8:00 a.m. at the office. Mrs. Gabriel was already at her desk, her steaming coffee mug painted with "Mrs. G" in a flowery script.

"Get yourself a cup of tea, dear, and help yourself to a granola bar. On your desk is a stack of checks for you to post."

The four girlfriends usually met on Saturday mornings for a group run along the boardwalk, lunch at one of the fashionable cafés looking out at the ocean, and a good catch-up, including gossip. Cat's favorite was Amelia, bushy red hair, naturally curly in every direction, that matched her personality. She was always excited about something, started talking before she sat down, her freckles emerging from the foundation meant to cover them. Cat met the other two girls through Amelia. All four girls lived in the same condominium building, each investing their money in a mortgaged apartment, hoping to build equity.

Mona was a quiet, sweet girl, a loyal friend, didn't offer much news, but would shyly respond to questions. Amelia asked, "What happened with that new guy you had a date with last week? Come on, fess up." Mona seemed to sink into music only she could hear, a pleasant expression on her face. "Mona, where are you?"

Geena stood out from the group like a weed among daisies. She was unpleasant, unhappy, criticized their shoes, and interjected nasty comments into their stories. "Why would you go out with a guy that has nothing to offer, can't even carry on a conversation?" or "He sounds like a total loser" or "He took you to that crummy place?" Still, they seemed to dismiss her interruptions and go on talking. She had nothing positive to contribute and Cat wondered if she was the only one that Geena irritated.

Cat had texted Amelia to relate meeting Xander, and her new job. Now she reported the whole story. "He calls or texts almost every night. I feel we're getting to know each other through our phone conversations. He's coming in town next Saturday and we're going out for dinner. I'm wearing my halter-top black sheath dress, and the black pashmina stole May gave me for Christmas."

Amelia leaned toward the girls, lowering her voice. "Do you think this guy is for real? We need to be careful. Cat, I want you to take a picture of his driver's license and forward it to us. What if something happens to you? He might kidnap you, take you to Mexico, and sell you. And when we run back on the boardwalk, I want you to point out the party house where you met him."

Cat laughed. "I love you, Amelia."

CHAPTER IV

A Man Who Can Only Be Described In Superlatives Is Worrisome

Cat woke early Saturday morning. Her mind still in work mode, she reflected on her new job. She had quickly learned the accounting process, concentrating to make no errors. The hour lunchtimes were staggered among the office staff, who went to nearby cafés. Cat brought a salad from home, ate in the lunchroom, and was back at her desk in fifteen to twenty minutes. The lunchroom was abuzz during the two half-hour breaks, but Cat took a cup of tea to her desk and checked her entries. *Am I insecure or efficient? I check and recheck.*

This commitment to her job was not lost on Mrs. Gilbert, who reported it to the principals of the firm during the weekly management meetings.

Thoughts of her date with Xander tonight had kept a nervous smile on Cat's face all day. She again inspected her hardly worn black dress and strappy very high heels. She retrieved a small, square velvet box hidden in the back of her scarf drawer. May had said, "Every girl who goes on a job interview needs pearl earrings," and gave her pearl studs when she graduated. She wore them every day and told May, "I am surely going to wear them out." On her next birthday, May presented her with a short string of pearls. Even though she never saw other young women wearing pearls, Cat told her, "They're old-fashioned, just like me. My perfect jewelry. I don't want to wear the jewelry everyone wears, I want to be my own person."

Xander said he would come for her at 6:30. As usual, Cat was ready early, walking around her apartment, straightening sofa pillows, spraying lavender mist in the bathroom. *If he asks to come up, he probably will check out my housekeeping. He is so well-groomed, I bet he wouldn't like a girl who lives messy.*

The lobby intercom buzzed. "Yes?"

A smiley voice. "It's Xander."

"Shall I come down?"

"May I come up?"

"Okay." A quiet hesitant answer.

Her doorbell chimed. She suddenly felt nervous, checked the hole in the door and saw the too-handsome face. Opening the door she blurted, "I shouldn't have let you come up, I don't have wine or liquor to offer."

He held out one hand clasping a bottle of Veuve Clicquot and two cut-crystal flutes in the other, eyes smiling, freshly shaven, dressed as if he had stepped out of the Saks Fifth Avenue show window.

She thought, *Oh, no, I never have carbonated drinks, I might burp.* Cat took the flutes, held them out to take a good look, said "So beautiful!" and set them on the coffee table.

"I have a bunch of them. My mother always bought in bunches."

Cat saved that comment to discuss with Amelia. "I have some Brie and crackers." She had bought them to serve for girlfriends' discussion night. She put the small wheel of cheese appetizer on a glass plate, while Xander popped and poured champagne. He handed her a glass and held his up for a toast. "To our beginning."

She smiled, meeting his eyes, not knowing how to respond. He talked about himself, detailed, as though he wanted her to fully know him: growing up in California, an older brother, Wray, who lives in their parents' penthouse, travels often and writes books and articles about historic figures from the sixteenth and seventeenth centuries. "Right now he's very involved with poets of that era: Wordsworth, Coleridge, Shelley, both Brownings, and even the American, Edgar Allan Poe. He says poets are like politicians. Even with all those metaphors, you can't be sure what they're saying. I have a condo on the floor below Wray's and we get together when both of us are in town at the same time."

Xander wanted to hear about her life in Ohio, where she and May were born. He removed his suit jacket, laid it across the back of the stuffed chair, sat on the sofa next to her, not close, so he could turn toward her, look into her eyes as she spoke. "First I want to hear about your name."

She remembered middle school was the worst time to have the different, peculiar, uncommon name, teachers thought it was her nickname and asked, impatiently, for her real name. It was fun for the boys. "Here Catty, Catty," or "Lick your paws, Cat-girl." Finding out the truth about why she was named Cat was a wound that never healed. She was sixteen, a junior in high school, had brought a girlfriend home for a sleepover, to talk about boys, fasten their long, straight hair up into a topknot, apply a five-minute mask, giggle at each other.

The girls ran the three blocks from the bus stop in the steady rain without an umbrella, shook themselves in the narrow foyer, and removed wet sweaters and sneakers. Instead of continuing to her room with her friend, something made her stop. It was the familiar sound of her mother's laugh, a high-pitched, mocking laugh she'd heard many times. "The Cat got caught in the rain." Then more jeering laughter. Cat usually walked away, but she was cold and wet and embarrassed. She longed for a loving mother to cover her with a towel, blot her sopping hair, give her a warm hug.

Cat became more and more aware that damage inflicted throughout childhood affected one's self-confidence. Through life she was determined to fight that problem and countered it with determination to be capable, independent, strong.

Because her name had caused people to laugh and ask questions, she had felt insecure, unsafe, feelings she would do battle with. How could she tell them the disgraceful truth? She thought about changing her name, but eventually decided it would take a secure, competent person to deal with the name and the comments it caused. She promised herself she would become that mentally powerful person.

That long-ago afternoon Cat stared at the disheveled mess of a mother: vodka soaked, over-made-up, smeared mascara, bleary eyes, slurred words. She could have hissed at her mother, but she held her head up to rise above the scene and calmly, with a quiet voice said, "I'm not 'The Cat,' Mom, I'm Cat, that's what you named me." Her mother tried to stand, as if she had something she wanted to say close to Cat's face, then fell back against the sofa cushions. Her face formed into an expression of disgust, loathing emanated from low in her alcohol-fueled stomach.

"You—I didn't want you. My beloved Panzy died, my companion, the only one who really loved me. I was pregnant with you and I thought if I named you Cat, you would take her place. But you were a needy baby instead of a lovable cat." Resentment of an unwanted child filled the air between them with venom. Cat's eyes burned with tears as her friend took her hand, led her to the small bedroom Cat shared with her sister. She had been lucky enough to be born when the precious cat was alive and therefore got a normal name—a wonderful name that brought to mind a maypole with ribbons and laughter, full-leafed trees, and daisies woven into wispy hair.

May, six years older, just out of college, heard the stinging words and put her arms around her sister. "Soon as I get a job, I will rent a small apartment for us. Just keep thinking of that, only a few more months."

Xander had listened quietly, watching her face. The memory brought tears to her eyes, she turned away. He put his arms around her. "Thank you for bringing up this difficult time in your life. Now you've told me and we can go on and leave it behind us." He put his hand on her cheek. "I love your name."

They sipped champagne, she cut some Brie, placed it on a cracker. He opened his mouth, she nervously put the cracker on his tongue.

"Before we leave, tell me one more thing, about the evening you lost your job, when we met. We have plenty of time. For a while longer, let's just relax in this comfortable room that tells me so much about you."

The apartment was sparsely furnished: no bookcase, stacks of books in a corner on the floor, a love seat, one chair, an oval glass coffee table, one end table with a lamp, a framed poster of pink ballet slippers, left over from her dorm room, no cluttering knickknacks.

She decided to recount the whole episode with ME Real Estate and Bradford Ayers, then the walk down the boardwalk, the house with music and lights and beautiful people, her nervy swim when no one noticed, the sadness of Reny, fully dressed, sitting in the Jacuzzi, and the ride home. "I've talked to one of the girls who still works for ME Real Estate. She said I wasn't the only one Bradford used his sex ploy on, but I was the only failed attempt. She said it was good office gossip for weeks. Thank you so much for helping me get out of there and start over."

"You got out of there by yourself, Cat. You're strong, you held on to your principles even though you knew your job was on the line. I'm proud of you for that. Bradford Ayers is a predator and soon he is going to prey on the wrong person and find himself drowning in deep water of his own grimy repugnance."

She wanted to tell him the story she rarely told, about her father. Xander was attentive, interested to know about her life. "My sister May is six years older than me, and when she was twelve and I was six, our father took us to the park near our house." He often took Cat to the playground so May could visit her girlfriends without her young sister tagging along. "Instead of going to the playground area, he took the picnic blanket from under his arm, spread it on the grass, and said he needed to talk seriously to us." Cat knew what serious meant. When May's friend got pains in her stomach, had to go to the hospital and have her appendix taken out—that was serious.

Cat wasn't sure she could finish the story without crying. *I need to say this, so I won't keep holding on to it.* "My father's eyes teared, saying many times he was sorry that he could not live with us any longer. We walked back home, he made a big pot of macaroni and cheese, and left." He had given them instructions to go to their neighbor, the bent, wrinkled widow, Mrs. Grant, on the first of every month and she would give them the money he promised to send. May would buy food, and whatever was left over they could spend for themselves. They learned to save money to buy new jeans and tees and gym shoes.

Xander was quiet. *Her life story includes May, who obviously took the role of mother/sister.* "Let's continue this story on our way to Tierra Encantado. I can't listen and talk and drive at the same time, so I borrowed my brother's car and driver."

Cat picked up the cheese plate. "We didn't drink half the champagne. I'll put foil over the top and save it."

"Empty it into the drain. It doesn't last and I have more."

Cat turned toward him, deciding to ask her question, even if it annoyed him. "Would you mind if I drop it off at my friend, Amelia's?"

He didn't let her see his smile and quickly answered, "I think we should drop it off at Amelia's. Do you want to take the flutes to her, also?"

"Don't you want to take them back home to go with your set?"

"No, I brought them for you, for us." It intimated future times together.

"I'll save them." They looked at each other and smiled.

Tierra Encantado was an exclusive resort, situated high, overlooking the ocean, an hour south of LA. The large scrolled gates were opened by a guard. The maître d', Mediterranean-looking with an attitude, thick gray hair, a perfect razor cut, tailored black suit, smiled when he saw Xander. "Someone in the kitchen will be happy tonight." He led them to a back corner U-shaped booth for two. No menus were given. After ordering a bottle of French Sauvignon Blanc, Xander turned to Cat, gave her his full attention.

"Would you like Chilean sea bass, cooked to perfection and an interesting sauce made with the peel and juice of blood oranges? Chef insisted I taste it when I was in the kitchen last month."

She looked at him with confused questions on her face.

He explained. "Chef Ramón is an old friend of mine from Mexico. I wanted him to cook at The Academy, but after graduating culinary school, he wanted to work in a fancy restaurant." Xander didn't mention that Ramón's mother, Marta, was their cook at the family home in Mexico. She taught Ramón to cook, he read cook books, attended classes in person or online, became creative, inventing recipes of his own. Xander paid for him to attend culinary school. "I talked to the chef who was here, he took Ramón as his assistant and quickly became aware of his talent. He then stepped up to management and Ramón became Chef. He's quite popular with the regulars."

"The sea bass sounds wonderful." Cat liked fish if it wasn't fishy-tasting, the way it smelled at fish markets. She didn't like raw anything, especially fish. She said it was the consistency in her mouth she objected to. Cat never joined her friends at the sushi bar. "You're out of it," Geena would say. "Everyone loves sushi."

Cat watched him as he leaned toward her, observing his attentiveness, the clear, low, news-announcer voice. They talked through dinner.

His suit was the same Grotto-blue as his eyes, as if they reflected off each other. The deep-blue silk tie had flecks of pink and lime green, a contradiction to the conservative suit, but perhaps it revealed the hidden spark of Xander's personality. *He is the most handsome man I have ever known, movie-star-handsome.*

He was staring at her face. "I'm entranced by the shape of your lips. Did you draw them on?" The attentive way he looked at her made her feel glamorous, alluring.

He made her laugh and it seemed the nervousness was escaping. He encouraged her and she wanted to continue their life stories. "Ohio isn't an exciting place to grow up and I didn't live in a penthouse."

"I think Ohio produces beautiful women and sends them to California."

Xander put the back of her hand to his lips, their eyes met, and he had questions behind them. He wanted to know everything about her. "Cat, did you and May ever see your father again?"

She sighed, took a deep breath to help her get through the answer. "The ending to this story is sad. The money we received, faithfully, was cash with no return address, but three years ago, May finally saw a post office stamp that wasn't smudged and with persistent digging on the computer, she found him. He answered the phone and cried through their conversation. She thanked him for his help, assured him both of us were well, graduated college, had good jobs, and asked him to stop sending money, not wanting to be a burden any longer. May and Marco have a little girl and she told him he could see his granddaughter anytime. The next envelope she received contained a small obituary notice and a sticky note. 'Thought you would like to know—it was suicide.'"

When they got in the car for the ride back to LA, he put his arm around her shoulders, her head cozy, tucked into the warmth of his neck. He liked the feel of her as she slept and spent the hour planning to himself more together time. *Yes, she's the one.*

Cat had three glasses of wine, which was two over her limit. She was horrified with embarrassment when they arrived at her condo building and Xander woke her.

"I'll walk with you to your apartment."

She got nervous, the words came out rushed, all connected together. "I wanted to hear about your school I'm so sorry I fell asleep the restaurant was beautiful the fish was perfect thank you for . . ."

Xander put his finger on her lips. "Now, I'm aware you're not a drinker." He smiled to let her know he was joking and kissed her lightly where his finger had been.

As Cat opened her door, she asked if he would like to come in.

"I would like to step inside if you will let me give you a kiss." He waited for her approval, but she didn't know how to answer and stepped closer, looking up at him. He held her face in both hands, kissed her forehead, her nose, her lips, all so easily, so gently. "I can't see you tomorrow until the afternoon, but would you like to have dinner in Palm Springs? We could leave about 2:00, walk around the old part, take in some art galleries, have dinner at a casual café, no wine."

She nodded and they laughed together. She, because he didn't seem to mind her unsophistication, he, because he now knew how love felt.

"Don't forget to lock up. Oh, and tell the sometimes-boyfriend your real boyfriend doesn't want him to call you." He looked into her eyes and smiled.

Cat stared at the door, the tingling from his kiss lingering in her body. *He is the smoothest of the male population. A man who can only be described in superlatives is worrisome.*

CHAPTER V
To Love Is To Be Seized By Mystery

"The Girlfriends," as Amelia called them, met early for their run and quick breakfast. Cat needed extra time to prepare for her date this afternoon. Amelia, Mona, and Geena heard the details of the fancy dinner date with Xander the previous evening. Then each gave their critique and advice. Geena was in a particularly bad mood. "He's a phony! If he was real like he comes on, what would he want with you? Unless he's looking for a naive girl to abuse. I'm sure you would cower before him."

Cat valued her friends, but severe criticism like Geena's barbs left her quiet, hurt. A sad expression covered the usual positive attitude. *Perhaps I am naive.*

Amelia jumped to her defense. "Geena, you can be horribly rude. We're supposed to be happy when good things happen to our friends. I think you're jealous."

Mona put her arm around Cat. "He chose you because you're beautiful, intelligent, and a good person. It's because of you the men swarm around us when we have 'girls' night out.' Xander realizes you are a rare woman."

Cat loved Amelia and Mona. She recognized that Geena judged and censured. Cat thought, *I will not allow this rude person, unhappy in her own life, to tear away my elation. She is the one with a problem. I'm fortunate to have friends who support me.*

Xander borrowed his brother's car and driver again. He wanted to sit next to Cat, his arm around her, not having to think about the highway, traffic, directions. Decker had been with the family for thirty years. Xander remembered him as a friend growing up, who secretly let him in the kitchen door and helped him sneak up to his bedroom after curfew. Numerous times, Decker backed up his excuses, explanations to parents for the late return home of girlfriends. Cat and Xander sat in the back, focused on the life stories they entrusted to each other.

"Tell me more about May. You were so close, yet you left to live in California and she stayed in Ohio."

"It was May's suggestion that I leave Ohio. I have always been distressed about the guy she married. He takes advantage of her, lies, cheats, steals from her. She tries to hide it from me, but when I visit her, I see what is happening. He and I are like two clashing cymbals. And I am troubled for her safety."

May had earned a scholarship to the University of Ohio. After graduation she was hired by a local law firm, assisting in the office, answering the phones to give the receptionists a break, being a right-hand aide to the secretaries. She was efficient and never complained about the long hours. The firm awarded her with raises and a promotion to Office Manager. She ordered a new white BMW, doubling up on the payments to repay the bank loan faster. She obtained a mortgage to buy her own townhouse. All while sending small checks to her sister, Cat, in college. May developed into an independent, intelligent, beautiful woman.

Then the unfortunate happened. May met Marco when she and girlfriends went to happy hour at a local bar. He was an only boy with seven older sisters. Handsome, with full, black, wavy hair, dark eyes, he was charming in a polite Latin way and talked impressively about his privileged life growing up in South America, a famous father and Greek mother.

He told May he was between jobs, but was handy around the house and would do repairs around her townhouse, while he was waiting to begin his new job as an engineer for a large aeronautical company. May's calls to Cat brimmed with excitement.

May and Marco were married six months after they met. He had moved into her townhouse the previous month. For the evening before the wedding, Marco reserved a private room in their favorite Italian restaurant for May, her sister, and their old friends to meet Marco's family. May assumed they would share the expense of both this dinner and the wedding lunch. But when the check for the dinner lay enclosed in a black folder on the table, he pushed it over to May. His mother, sisters, and their families starting leaving, thanked them profusely, and talked about the Big Day tomorrow. May placed her credit card in the folder.

Marco had chosen to be married in the only country club in Toledo, which allowed nonmembers to use the restaurant for special occasions. His family made up most of the guests: mother, seven sisters and their husbands or boyfriends and children. In addition to Cat, there were a few old friends of May's from growing up who hadn't moved out of state and her new friends from work.

Then, the introduction of Marco's chronic late problem. It started on their wedding day. He and his mother and two of his sisters came to the wedding one and one half hours later than the photographer asked them to be there. For the ceremony on the terrace overlooking the golf course to be on schedule, there was no time for wedding pictures of the bride and groom and his family. After the ceremony lunch was served and a few casual pictures were taken of Marco, May, and his family. There were lots of beautiful pictures of the bride and her sister and their friends. The wedding album would always be an unhappy reminder to May and Cat of Marco's inconsiderate behavior. Cat already sensed her sister was drowning, but didn't know how to save her.

May had given her credit card to the manager of the country club restaurant, for the fifty percent deposit, earlier when she chose the menu and told him the balance would be paid by her fiancé. He asked Marco if he wanted to pay by check or credit card. Marco looked at May, smiled. She handed her credit card to the manager.

May had told Marco it was her fantasy to honeymoon in Tahiti. "That's where we will go. Make the reservations," he said. She took the money from her savings account to pay for the trip. May, who had lived a gloomy life avoiding her mother's alcohol-fueled rants, had been fooled by his good looks and glamorous tales. She would learn about deceit thick as mud beneath the smooth, guileful charm.

Holding hands, Cat and Xander walked the streets of Old Palm Springs, inspecting art galleries, imported men's silky-soft Italian sweaters, enviable women's designer dresses.

He knew she liked ice cream. When they were at The Pit Stop, she casually looked at the dessert menu and exclaimed, "Raspberry chocolate chunk ice cream."

"Palm Springs is famous for their date shakes, would you like to try one?"

"Yes, only one for both of us."

On the drive back to LA, they continued sharing more of their lives. Cat still hadn't gotten over the stings from Geena that morning.

They kept appearing inside her mind and the thoughts brought back previous hurts that were adding up. She couldn't seem to let them go and decided that telling Xander about them would help. She knew he would be her defenseman.

He quietly gave his opinion. "Geena is an unhappy person, carelessly offensive. Meanness and jealously make up her personal identity. She likes hurting people and doesn't know how to be a friend. Her tongue is a weapon and someday she is going to go too far with her painful stings and someone will leave her without a stinger."

He made her feel the problem with Geena wasn't her fault. Tired, Cat slumped into the leather contoured seat as Xander caught the yawns. "I don't mind if you sleep on my shoulder." He put his arm around her and reached for the alpaca lap robe to ward off the chilly air conditioning. She felt warm, shielded.

Inside Cat's apartment Xander wrapped his arms around her. She slipped her hands to his back, feeling raw strength, electricity, his intensive, gentle hold. When he kissed her, it was firm, soft, easy, sending a sensation through her body that kept her wanting more. Her eyes stayed closed for a few more seconds after he raised his head and it made him smile. *How will I last two weeks without seeing her?* "Three guys from our team want to take some personal time. I won't be able to leave The Academy until they return. After that, would you like to spend the weekend at Tierra Encantado, the resort where we had dinner?"

Cat was quiet. She needed to think about it, roll it around in her mind. The thought of spending the night with Xander was exciting, but she was apprehensive, nervous. What if he was disappointed, didn't like her?

Xander picked up on the deep thoughts going on. "Think about it, just a couple lazy days lounging by the pool, walking the track around the property, having afternoon tea and watching the seagulls. I'll call you and we'll discuss it. Meanwhile, Cat, you will be on my mind all day, every day." He kissed her forehead, her nose, her lips, then turned and opened the door. "Don't forget to lock up."

I'm not going to tell Geena about him. I refuse to let her storm up my good feelings. Amelia and Mona will be happy for me. I'm moving Geena out of my life. Didn't Oprah say, "One shouldn't be around people who bring you down?"

At work the next week, Cat received a call from the secretary at ME Real Estate whom she stayed in contact with. "Have you read the *L.A. Times*? Bradford Ayers was robbed and killed in the garage of his office building. I hope his wife gets some condolence cards. She deserves sympathy, not for his death, but for her trials in tolerance."

Cat was shocked, but couldn't bring up any sorrow from her soul. *It's wrong to not have some compassion for the family of someone killed, even if the victim was a wretched person.* She wanted to discuss this with Xander, but the card he had given her didn't have a cell number, only an email address. When he called, she mentioned this to him.

"But I know your schedule and call you every day." All return calls were blocked. If someone wanted to call Xander, they needed his private number.

"Why don't I know your schedule and have your cell number so I can call you whenever I want?"

"I will correct that immediately." He gave her his private number. "Call me anytime, day or night. I look forward to your calls." Xander liked her feistiness when she felt she had been wronged.

Cat repeated the story about the murder/robbery of Bradford Ayers. Xander didn't know him, but he listened attentively when she had told him about her episode with Bradford, and Cat remembered his comment, "He is a pollutant on the earth." She felt protected, like the Bradford Ayers of the world couldn't reach her.

He said, "Yes, I read the article in the *L.A. Times* online. I was going to ask if you had seen the write-up, but I was afraid it might upset you. I'm so sorry for his family, even though I didn't like the circumstances he tried to force on you."

Xander didn't want to linger on this and bring back difficult memories for her. "When we get together next week, I want to tell you about each member of my Team and The Compound where I live in Mexico. Now, tell me some good news. Are we going to spend the weekend at Tierra Encantado? I would like very much to be with you, lie together, tell more of our lives to each other, share our feelings. But you must want it all as much as I do. Cat, the weekend is not about sex, it's about us. I don't want to make love to you until you're ready. We have plenty of time, we have the rest of our lives."

Cat decided to get trusted advice from Amelia and Mona. Amelia said, "We have discussed this and decided that you have good feelings for him and you want to be with him—you should go. We will be on call if you need us to drive out there and get you. We're thankful he didn't invite you to Mexico."

Xander called. Cat told him she was looking forward to spending the weekend at the lovely resort with him. After work she went to Gisela's, an expensive lingerie shop.

Friday, he was waiting for her in his Porsche SUV, outside the accounting firm. She came out the front door carrying a garment bag containing Amelia's black dress, in case he remembered hers and would think she only had one dressy dress, which would be true. A duffel bag was neatly packed with a one-piece bathing suit, sweats, and tee shirts, jeans, and gym shoes, her black strappy heels and the new purchases from Gisela's. A small makeup bag was stuffed down the side.

"Our suite has a Jacuzzi and we will be sitting in it one hour from right now," Xander said. "I called and asked to have it filled with hot water and soothing bath balm, and a bottle of champagne chilling next to the tub. That will remind me of our first date, we drank half and took the rest to Amelia." He chuckled at her.

Cat was quiet. *This is much too romantic for a girl from Toledo.*

"Also," he continued, "Tomorrow we'll have dinner in the resort restaurant, but tonight we will have room service."

They soaked in the ample hot tub for two, placed in an alcove of the white marble bathroom, the Jacuzzi jets massaging their bodies. She had averted her eyes as he stepped in nude across from her, talking nonchalantly, as if it was their weekly occurrence, about life in Mexico. She didn't see him smile at her turned head.

Sitting in the living room of their suite, Cat was a little overwhelmed. The suite was bigger than her apartment. She was wearing the fluffy white terry robe she found hanging next to the tub, had quickly wrapped it around her wet body after scurrying out of the tub. Xander watched and fell more in love. As he sat next to her in his matching robe, she asked him to tell her about The Academy and The Team.

Room service set dinner on a small table, a wine stand held a bucket of ice cooling a bottle of Perrier-Jouët. Salads were placed on the table, the warming oven contained their dinner of lobster tails on beautiful Rosenthal plates.

This is a fancy dinner to be wearing a robe, barefoot, and no makeup.

Xander described the walled-in Compound built on a ridge, which had been whittled down to make the building site wide and flat like a mesa. The main house where the previous Manager lived, he had taken for himself. There were seven houses, for each of the other Team members, including Zack, a close friend he grew up with. Also, a large training building with dorm rooms for the students, guardhouses with offices at the gate, and two helipads, one inside the walls. Outside The Compound was a landing strip, the other helipad and hangar, a golf driving range, and one tennis court. "All were on the property when I took over as Manager, but needed reconstruction on some buildings and personalizing on The Team houses, some sprucing up other places. It took almost three years, but The Academy is in the fourth year of producing bodyguards." He showed her an aerial view taken with his cell phone.

Cat studied the picture. "It looks like a small town in itself. I see big trucks parked by the gate. And are those golf carts?"

"We use the carts inside the walls. The SUVs and trucks are for driving to nearby towns, the helicopters are for going to farther places, the small airplane gets us to cities in the U.S., and our new Gulfstream takes us to Europe."

"Where are the people who were in charge of the school before you came?"

"The Manager, his wife, and team were Russian. They were called back to Russia. There was a problem with finances. The complex was built by Nikolai Ivanov, President of The Russian Federation. His father was chairman of the KGB, then President of Russia, and a friend of my father, who was the American Ambassador to Russia. Zack's father was a friend of Nikolai's father, also. Zack and I would accompany our fathers to Russia, and that's where we met Nikolai when we were six years old. The three of us went to private boys boarding school at ten years old through high school, then college together. When my father's terms were finished, Zach, Nikolai, and I took turns visiting each other until Nikolai became President. Now, we visit him at one of his country houses. He rarely comes to Mexico, it's difficult bringing the Secret Service and his entourage. I would like you to meet him if you will go with me to Russia." *That's something we can talk about later. A change of lifestyle should be introduced slowly.*

Cat was quiet. *Is he inviting me to Russia? I've never been out of the United States. I'm not going to think of that now. As May says, "Stay poised and take each day as it dawns."*

They had been sitting, eating, talking through the evening. He had told her much to digest, the load made her slump. She needed some quiet, thinking time. Room service cleared the remains of dinner. Xander put his arms around her, felt her tense as he kissed her.

"Cat, you prepare for bed. I'm going to work on my computer and I'll tuck you in when you're ready."

She wasn't surprised that he didn't hover or suggest sex with actions. After all, he had told her there wouldn't be sex until she was ready. As Cat brushed her teeth, she was again aware of the tingling from his kiss lingering through her body. *He gives me feelings I've never known. I've never been in love, is this how it feels? Whatever, it's a wonderful sensation.* She took off her comfy robe, put on the new floor-length silky nightie she had bought at Gisela's, dabbed on some moisturizer, giving her face a lovely glow, and looked at herself in the mirror. *You silly girl!* She walked out of the bedroom, Xander was sitting with his back to her looking at his computer. She leaned, pressing her body against his back, her cheek to the side of his face, and slipped her hand inside his robe, slowly rubbing his chest, feeling the hard nipples, the coarse hair.

Xander lifted his head, closed his eyes. "If you do that, you're going to be in trouble."

"I'm looking for some trouble."

CHAPTER VI
They Called Themselves
A Team Of Brothers

Xander relaxed into the quiet, serene, peacefulness of flying his Learjet back to Mexico. The weekend with Cat was the beginning of his new life. *She is the sun above the clouds, giving brightness to my consciousness.* She had asked about how The Academy was started and wanted to know The Team who were the instructors.

His thoughts went back to the beginning of The Academy. He was visiting his childhood friend, Nikolai Ivanov, the new President of The Russian Federation. They were at his secluded mountain dacha, skied all day, then stretched their legs out in front of the massive stone fireplace and praised the private-label vodka.

Nikolai had the build and attitude of the Commander-in-Charge. In his offices, his face never strayed from stern, serious, his posture was uncompromising. He had two friends, the men he knew since they were six years old. Only with them did he relax, shucking the outer layer.

"As President of this country, with a substantial cabinet of mostly toxic men, I need someone like you, Xander. You are my most trusted friend. I know you better than my brother and love you more. I must impose on you. I need your help. At my Bodyguard Academy in

Mexico, some difficult problems have arisen. The ambitious Russian businessman I hired to build and manage it sent padded bills to my accountant and kept the excess payments for himself. I relieved him from his position."

Xander looked into the ice-blue eyes that emitted anger and understood the meaning of the statement.

Nikolai continued. "He also became friendly with El Torbellino—The Whirlwind—head of the Mexican cartel and delivered some heroin for him to a customer in Iowa. After the last delivery, he made the big mistake of keeping the money. El Torbellino came to kill him, take over The Compound, and set up his headquarters. There was much damage. I need you to reconstruct the training building, hire your own specialists, and train bodyguards for me."

Nikolai often furnished bodyguards for leaders of friendly countries, as a gift or perhaps a bribe.

"I can't help you, Nikolai. I have no experience in business and I don't know anything about running a school. You need a university dean or president and a good construction foreman."

Nikolai laughed. "My friend, at twelve years old you would take on any dare, any challenge, just to prove that incredible, adept ability. You haven't changed. Right now that brain is planning your methods, stimulated by the new adventure."

He was right. Xander smiled at him. "I don't want to get relieved of duty like my predecessor."

"You won't steal my money, you have more than I do. This will be a challenge for you. Get our math genius roommate to keep the books. Last time I heard from him he sold his hedge fund company and was traveling around Asia. He's taking Mandarin lessons to impress a Chinese actress. The latest interest in his love life."

When they were together, the men enjoyed reminiscing about their childhood and the years growing up. All three remained close throughout their lives. The math genius was their friend since six years old, their roommate at the Swiss boys boarding school through university, Zack Andrez, from Mexico City.

Xander sent a message: *Nikolai and I need your help. Come home. I'll meet you in LA in two weeks.*

Vadim Ivanov, father of Nikolai, when President of Russia, enjoyed the company of the U.S. diplomat Xeno Xavier, Xander's father. They had similar personalities: both egocentric, intelligent, self-absorbed, and self-indulgent. President Ivanov inherited the leadership position, power and wealth that came with it.

The Xaviers' abundance of money was passed from generation to generation, multiplying as if the dollars were breeding. First the funding of U.S. cross-country railroads, then investments in oil fields pumping up the dollars every second.

The boys communicated by email and text when they weren't together. Before starting Swiss boarding school, Xander accompanied his parents to Russia during school holidays and two months in summer. President Ivanov, his wife, and sons visited the Xaviers at their second home in Baja California, on a cliff overlooking the Pacific Ocean, accompanied by Russian Secret Service. The Xaviers' primary residence was the penthouse floor of a posh LA apartment building.

President Vadim Ivanov, Nikolai's father, allowed the CEO of a steel export company in Mexico City to ship his product to Russia. Carlos Andrez often brought his son, Zack, who became close friends with Nikolai and was often in Russia at the same time as Xander.

The three boys, at six years years old, formed a secret pact, pledging to be lifelong friends.

The boys thought of one another as brothers and when, at ten, President Ivanov and Ambassador Xavier suggested the boys attend a prep boarding school in Switzerland, they excitedly agreed, having spent the previous two years in separate private boarding schools in their own countries.

Nikolai and Xander asked if President Ivanov would propose to Señor Andrez the possibility of Zack attending the boarding school with them.

The three boys arrived in Lausanne, escorted by a Russian bodyguard, who left them at their new school after they were settled into their triple suite. The bodyguard would live in a nearby apartment, driving them and keeping watch when they left the gated campus. The pledge they made at six years old was reinforced and they vowed to stand together, support one another, forever.

They quickly added French to their list of languages, Russian, Spanish, English, but thought it was fun to communicate in Russian. No one understood Russian and they laughed, talking about boys standing next to them. The students were intimidated and insulted at the rudeness of being left out of their conversations. The three boys were called frequently to the Headmaster's office.

Zack Andrez (aka André Zackery—
Two passports, Mexico and USA)

At sixteen years old, Zack's father, CEO of C&Z Steel Export Company, Mexico City, taught him the principles of investing money: research above all, buying short, corporate raiding, and secret insider trading. Starting with $25,000, canny research, and astute intuition, he registered a stock market account that had ups and downs, wins and losses, but showed a huge profit at the end of each quarter.

Throughout college, homework time was divided equally between scholastics and his investment business. At six feet three, a strong, muscular body and athletic, he could have played football or basketball, but team sports with practices and socializing, he felt, took too much time. He opted for gym workouts and tennis. Dating was easy. He never looked for a girlfriend, just picked from the many that followed him, hanging around the courts watching him play tennis, begging his roommates for a fix-up. He was exotically handsome: thick black hair cut short, dark eyes framed by bushes of eyebrows and lashes, pronounced lips that were always slightly open in a sexual way.

His roommates, Xander and Nikolai, would each grab a powerful upper arm and drag him away from whichever computer he was engrossed at.

"We are now going to play three-man basketball, before you become a total wimp," Nikolai teased.

"I am in the middle of investing our money in a very iffy stock and need to keep watch."

They pooled money for an investment account. Zack's astute and shrewd research served them well, though the three would become wealthy heirs. His investment business was a challenge for Zack. After attending several graduate schools with his two best friends, he started his own hedge fund company, managing capital from Nikolai's, Xander's, and his own trust fund.

"After our game, we're going to the pub for a beer," Xander informed.

"I hate beer."

"How did we end up with this deadbeat?" Nikolai laughed.

They walked shoulder to shoulder—three strong young men linked together in brotherhood, laughing, teasing, grateful for genuine friendship.

* * * *

Decker, the Xaviers' family driver, still worked for Wray, Xander's brother. He had known Xander's friends since they were ten years old and would come home with Xander during a break from their Swiss boarding school. He picked up Zack at LAX and delivered him to the front of the elegant building where Xander and Zack maintained condominiums. Xander's parents had owned the penthouse where Xander's brother, Wray, now lived. The brothers could have shared the luxurious apartment that spread across the entire story, but Xander carried painful memories of that residence and preferred his own space.

They were deep into the discussion of The Academy when Zack's computer beeped, signaling time for streaming from Russia. Nikolai's face appeared on the giant screen built into the wall.

"I'm angry at both of you for meeting without me. You should have met here in Moscow."

Zack frowned. "Don't say that in front of your bodyguards. They will send a shooter to get rid of men who displeased their boss."

Nikolai smiled, leaned back in his soft leather desk chair. "I miss you two, my life is boring without you."

Zack stood. "Instead of organizing this Academy, I'll help you start war with another country."

Xander was quick to his feet. "Stop! No politics! Nikolai, you send the money and furnish the students. Zack, you keep the books. I will be the Manager. I'm meeting with some prospective instructors next week."

* * * *

During reconstruction of The Compound, Xander and Zack took turns overseeing the progress, each staying a month or more and sometimes meeting together to discuss The Academy's curriculum and instruction experts. They met with a graduate of the previous Academy, now one of Nikolai's private bodyguards, to get information about the instructors and the teaching methods. The graduate was also the President's informant while attending the year of training.

He filled in the details of the day The Academy was attacked. President Ivanov was informed by the accountant that the Manager and his wife were buying expensive cars, jewelry, custom-made clothes, and paid for them out of The Academy expense account. Also, it was known in The Compound that they partnered with El Torbellino's cartel and delivered shipments of drugs to a private landing strip at a farm in Iowa. At the last known delivery, the Manager and his wife accompanied three cartel soldiers. As usual, The Academy pilot would get a small extra payment. On arrival, the Manager killed the three soldiers in the airplane and after opening the door, killed the three men who met them and were to put the money in the airplane hold and collect the drugs. The pilot helped them load their luggage and the drugs, packed in large suitcases, into the drug buyer's Range Rover. The money to be exchanged for the drugs was in duffel bags. With the pilot no longer useful to him, the Manager shot him in the back of the head. They drove to a small airport where he had made arrangements to be picked up in a chartered plane and flown to their secret, sprawling island home. He planned to sell the drugs on the Caribbean islands, stash the money in an offshore bank on a nearby island, known for keeping secret accounts from all over the world.

When the Manager and his wife left The Compound with the drugs and their personal possessions, the informant called his President who instructed him to tell the local employees to leave for their safety, suspecting El Torbellino would invade The Compound, and to accompany the newly graduated class and the Russian staff on commercial flights to Moscow.

Soldiers of the cartel stormed The Academy, carelessly destroying much of the instruction building, then headed for the main house to capture the Manager and his wife and deliver them alive to El Torbellino. They were shocked to find The Compound empty.

El Torbellino decided it was his chance to check out The Compound, his pilot landed the helicopter in the courtyard. He was impressed with the main house and facilities and planned to move there. He would use it for his second headquarters, installing some of his army.

However, he luckily left before President Ivanov sent Russian Special Forces to oust the cartel soldiers, secure The Compound, and protect it from further assaults. He then called Xander, asking him to come to Moscow.

Xander began planning his new venture. Zack would have his office at The Compound, hire an assistant, and set up the bookkeeping. Money from Russia would go into an account in Banco de Republico in Mexico City, where expense payments would be processed.

* * * *

Colonel Lawrence West of the U.S. Air Force, in command of the base in the Arizona desert across the Mexican border, was an old friend of Xander's.

While flying from New York to LA, Xander's private jet had a mechanical malfunction and he landed on an Air Force strip. In the office of Colonel West, Xander said, "You can have the plane, a personal gift for the trouble I've caused you. I'm getting a new one."

Through the years they met, usually at the Xavier family second home in Baja California, where Xander and Wray spent many vacations growing up and had inherited.

Xander visited Colonel West again. *If I'm going to live in Mexico, I need a safe landing place in the U.S. If the drug cartel decides to invade us again, we may have to leave quickly and I don't want to explain to Immigration and U.S. authorities.*

"Colonel, I'm rebuilding The Bodyguard Academy in Sonora. We will refurbish the landing strip and helipad. You can use them for your pilots and your private jet if we can land on one of yours."

The Colonel smiled. *I knew there would be strings attached to that extravagant gift.*

* * * *

News was passed to select friends in law enforcement, hoping for their help in finding expert instructors for The Academy. From recommendations, Xander selected men to interview. Two were caught in a web of self-destruction, biding their time until the poisonous bite.

Oso (Bear)

Oso grew up in a small village on the outskirts of Mexico City. At birth, a huge baby, his back, arms, and legs were covered with dark hair. His mother laughed and called him her baby bear.

His father was a farmer with strong, rough hands and demeanor. He had learned to drink tequila and roll cigarettes at nine years old. He talked in a growl. The children and their mother were quiet and subservient when he was in the house. Laughter was saved until he was out of sight.

Wealthy families from Mexico City brought au pair girls from Russia to care for their small children. The girls stayed, got jobs in offices and shops, married, sponsored cousins and friends, bringing into Mexico a flow of lovely young Russian women.

Veronika, a former au pair, was Oso's mother and taught her two children to speak, read, and write in the Russian language. There was no mention of the lessons to their father, who told Veronika she must only speak Spanish in his house. To their father, kids that were too smart were not respectful. They were careful to hide the workbooks, dictionaries, history books, which would provoke his temper. They remembered the time Oso left the classic Russian novel, *The Brothers Karamazov,* lying on his bed when his mother called to get help in the kitchen. After dinner his father walked past Oso's room, glanced in, saw the book, and a tirade shook the small house. Not that he knew the content, but the strange writing on the cover infuriated him. He had banned such books and was disregarded, disobeyed. He picked up the heavy tome and began slamming it against Veronika's head, knocking her against the wall, continuing the barrage until Oso grabbed his arms, then held a threatening, oversized fist in front of his father's face. Oso was bigger and stronger than his father, who usually hit Veronika when Oso wasn't at home.

The father didn't mind the meager English taught at school, not aware that Oso also studied English alone in the school library, listening to teaching CDs. His father thought that children speaking some English would be helpful to him at the market where he sold freshly picked vegetables to chefs and maids. Oso was up at sunrise, gathering the produce, helping sell at the market before going to school.

Since ten years old, Oso was ordered to shoot coyotes and wolves who stole their chickens. He was curious about the operating method of guns and taught himself to dismantle, clean, repair, and put them back together. It became Oso's responsibility to keep his father's guns in flawless condition. Word of his expertise passed through the village to surrounding towns and larger cities. He skillfully turned any old rusted firearm into a perfectly sighted killing machine.

As the years passed, his father sank further into an irritable, sulking, mean grouch, aided by the local tequila, which was too available. Oso loved his mother and sixteen-year-old sister and hated his father. He observed the bruises on his mother's arms, legs, shoulders and watched as she limped from the counter, where she rolled out the tortillas, to the stovetop grill. He was angry and frustrated, not knowing what to do or say, afraid to cause more of his father's wrath. One day when he came in the house from working in the fields, he found his mother and sister holding each other, both sobbing. He saw puddles of blood on the well-scrubbed kitchen floor. Bruises were difficult to look at, but blood was a different source of concern.

He asked gently, "Why is blood here?"

His sister broke away from her mother's arms. The distraught child screamed, releasing feelings of crazed helplessness. "He raped me!" She sobbed and hung on to her brother, convulsing with anger, pain.

Oso calmly removed her arms and placed them on their mother's shoulders. In his tiny room, barely big enough for a bed and dresser, the rifle was propped in a corner. As he came back through the kitchen of moans, the defeated young voice whispered, "Kill me also, *mi hermano*." (my brother)

"No, no, *mi hermana*, this will be the end of bruises and blood."

The rifle shot was loud like thunder, echoed off the walls in the modest house, the noise lingering in the air, then a calm after the storm, as if the breeze stood still. The mother and daughter sighed, freed from bondage. There was no more fear, no more tears.

Oso, now a boy of nineteen, intelligent, fluent in three languages, a tree-trunk body, thick arms of powerful bear strength, with the demeanor of politeness, respect, kindness. The Mexican law enforcement knew him. For years he had kept their weapons in factory-new condition.

After a year in jail, the Policía Federal still didn't know what to do with him. No one wanted to start the process of prosecution. Oso sat against the wall in a caged cell. His mother brought food and the teachers, librarians, friends, all brought books and binders of ruled blank paper. He requested works on ancient history, the practice of medicine, psychology, the art of cooking, advanced language books of Russian, Spanish, English, and beginning French. Oso was engrossed in his own school, grateful for uninterrupted time, yet worried about his mother and sister. They had moved in with his aunt, Veronika's sister, her gentle-mannered husband, and teen daughter. Veronika sold her house and farm. *How long will that money last?* he often thought. *I need to get out of here, find a job to help them.*

The dirty walls of jail were splattered with dried food, smashed flies, vomit, from years before Oso arrived. The walls could tell of so much frustration, so few ways to vent. Oso ignored them, oblivious to smells, cockroaches, and the rants of other prisoners.

The Captain of Policía Federal, in charge of the villages on the outskirts of Mexico City, a friend of Xander's, related Oso's story—the abuse, the father's murder, the obsessively intelligent boy, the uncertainty of his future. "Xander, take him, send him to school, hire him to teach about guns in your Bodyguard Academy."

"It's going to take me several years to get that school going again. The main house where I live is in good shape, but the work started on the rest of The Compound is a slow process. I hired a military architect to design a multi-use structure for the training, using the old foundation and walls, but a stronger, more functional building. I've hired many local men to help the foreman and construction crew from LA. The experienced foreman has made a work schedule to avoid mañana time."

They both grinned. "We don't like to move too fast in the heat of Mexico," the Captain joked, but was seriously interested in a future for Oso. "Xander, he could be sentenced to prison and rot there. Get him in school, he's a vessel for learning and a good kid. Please talk to him."

The lock on the cell door clicked. Oso looked up and saw a smiling, tall, muscular gringo, speaking Spanish.

"Is this the jail library or are you in here for stealing all the books from your school?" Xander sat on the floor at the end of long brawny legs attached to thick bare feet.

"Are you the prosecutor?"

"No, I'm your mentor, here to offer you a contract." Xander noticed that the piles of books were orderly, stacked by subjects. *He has a drive to learn. It will be my pleasure to send him to school.* "If you accept, you will have three years before starting your job. You can spend that time in school. How about a year in medical school, a year in law school, a year of mixed subjects: history, literature, science, and at the same time three years of advanced lessons in reading, writing, and speaking Russian, English, and correct Spanish?"

Oso gave him a serious face, full of suspicion, doubt, like a big dog backing away from tainted meat. "What's the hitch?"

"When I have my Bodyguard Academy ready, you will be the arms instructor, teaching students to use weapons and how to keep them in perfect working condition. You will receive a high salary and have your own house within The Compound, a member of The Team of Eight Skilled Specialists."

"It sounds like I would be selling my soul, like Faust."

Xander smiled. "Something like that. I may need you to use your weapons for me." *He's smart. He'll think it over, but hopefully choose The Academy over prison.*

Oso hesitated, let his brain absorb the conversation. "I don't think I could be a sniper."

"You will be giving bodyguards the capability of eliminating the enemy, protecting their boss. You would be expected to do the same for your Team. Think about it, we'll talk in a few days."

They stood at the same time, eye to eye, Xander turned to leave. Oso made another comment, strong and loud. "There's a problem. According to these medical books, I am manic-depressive."

Xander stopped, took one step closer to him. "Oso, you and millions of us share that disease. A psychiatrist will be on our Team, counseling each student and Team member. He's good at his job, very helpful. I've known him for fifteen years."

Joaquin

The leader of an LA street gang for five years, the twenty-two-year-old Joaquin contained an embodiment of entangled characteristics. Knives were his specialty, everything from stilettos to machetes to switchblades. He spent hours practicing, reshaping his instruments, inventing new ones, then studying the body, finding the most vulnerable places. He honed his skills at the poker table when he caught a cheater. Anyone who wouldn't hand over a wallet or purse was introduced to his knife. Members of opposing gangs avoided Joaquin, respecting his reputation. His mother's boyfriend carved his initials on her stomach. She was saved by a layer of fat. Joaquin, wiry, silent, strong as a jaguar, waited for him to visit again. He dragged the bound, struggling bundle into the dark alley and carved "REVENGE" in neat, close letters across his chest. The sharp, stinging blade went deep, there was no fat to save him. He bled to death in the trash-filled alley, leaving a feast for the rats.

Joaquin dropped out of school at seventeen. Teachers and counselors sent messages, begged the kid with unlimited potential to return. He didn't mind wearing used jeans and tee shirts from The Salvation Army store or eating rice and beans and tortillas daily, but when his mother had surgery, could no longer clean houses, needed months of recuperation, Joaquin knew it was his responsibility to pay the rent and buy the groceries. He joined a gang and soon became leader, planning the robberies, intimidating with his knives. His share of money from selling the stolen goods supported him and his mother like a trust fund had kicked in. Their quality of life climbed to top-floor apartments and rooftop restaurants.

For years he had been sneaking into large classes at California universities, sitting in the back, taking notes. He accumulated piles of textbooks and hired a tutor.

Young boys from the streets, wanting to join gangs, were swept up by Joaquin and taken to Christian organizations that housed homeless boys, feeding and schooling them. He often rented a bus and took forty boys to sit in the bleachers at a Dodgers game. *I want to show them another life that is out there waiting for them to work toward.*

Joaquin's gang, *Los Hombres Águila*, The Eagle Men, refused to be associated with drugs. They didn't sell or avail themselves of that self-destruction, having witnessed too many lives it destroyed. Joaquin was like an unofficial undercover informant, reporting the lair locations of drug dealers to the DEA.

Los Hombres Águila were thieves, swooping down on mansions of the wealthy, stealing outdoor sculptures and fancy cars, breaking in and hauling away treasures to sell.

When a drug dealer kidnapped an Eagle Man, filled his veins with heroin, the entire drug gang was found in different areas of the city, each with lethal throat wounds. While fleeing, each was stopped in flight with a stiletto thrown like a dart to his neck with force and accuracy. When the knife was retrieved, it sliced across the throat.

The law enforcement knew Joaquin, they nodded at each other when passing, acknowledging his help. The unknown was how long he could keep up the robberies, killings, until he was caught in the net of higher authorities. An old friend, now in charge of the LA DEA, talked to Xander about a possible candidate for his school.

Xander and Joaquin met in the back corner of the restaurant at Tierra Encantado and Xander explained the concept of experts in their field, training men to be bodyguards. He had talked to professors, detectives, policemen, and knew what would get Joaquin's attention. "We'll be ready in three years. You have that time to attend university, take graduate classes of your choice."

Disappointment grabbed Joaquin. "I didn't graduate from high school." Rare defeat showed in the onyx eyes, a slight drop forward of the matching, long hair that fell in waves to his collar, down his forehead, mixing with thick, shaggy, black eyebrows.

In Spanish, Xander said, "Sure you did, I have your diploma. You even graduated from UCLA, with honors."

Joaquin understood. *If anyone could produce those papers, have the information planted in the proper computers, it would be this clever, innovative, strange man.* His face smiled, spreading to midnight eyes.

They bumped knuckles, laughed, high-fived, did the street hand-touch routine. "I like you Xander, you're crazy."

CHAPTER VII

When True Friends Are Together, Each Feels The Gift

President Nikolai Ivanov of The Russian Federation, Xander Xavier of The United States of America, and Zack Lorenz of The United Mexican States lounged on oversized cordovan leather sofas in the President's private library. They were celebrating their fortieth birthdays.

Nikolai looked at his friends from childhood. He had known them most of his life, depended on their advice, trusted them. These were the friends he could confide in. "I'm too young for this responsibility. It's making me old, my hair is turning gray. My father started grooming me to be President when I was a teenager, my life was geared toward this job. I was too young to be an officer in the KGB—FSB as we call it now—but I had no choice. I married the girl my father picked for me. Love was not involved, she was poised, educated, had the right background. When he suggested who would be my friends, where I would go to school, what I wore, I knew from childhood it wasn't a suggestion, it was authoritative direction. I'm grateful he approved of both of you."

Xander wanted to relieve his friend of gloomy recollections. "I liked having a bodyguard drive us to the girls school to watch their tennis matches, then take us all for Swiss hamburgers, drive the girls back to their dorms and pretend he wasn't watching us kiss. Nikolai, let's not forget the good memories."

In the offices of the President, Nikolai never reminisced aloud or spoke of feelings, good or bad. It would be taken as a sign of weakness, so he projected the stoic demeanor of strength. He was popular, a people's president, but in silence he was resentful of the absence of self-choices in his life. He confided to his friends about his resentments. "I suppose everyone harbors feelings of indignation. As we get older, these feelings are like enemies, always nearby, looking for a fight."

Zack agreed. "We have each other to release our feelings to. That makes life easier."

As if he had received permission, Nikolai went on. "Xander, your father turned you loose. You were untethered, traveling the world with that diplomatic smile, corralling people into your life. You don't have friends, you possess people."

Nikolai continued, "And you, Zack, quiet, reserved, no antics to get attention. You just stand like a beautiful statue and people swarm around you, pulled like a magnet to subdued charm. All the women and some of the men, from the cooks and servers to the officers in this administration, continually want to know when Zack is returning. If I didn't love you so much, I'd be jealous."

Zack filled the Czechoslovakian cut-crystal tumblers and felt the sentimental air. "This is our birthday celebration. Remember with me our thirty-four years of brotherhood. Let's think of the time we secretly schemed to run away from home and meet in Istanbul, to watch the belly dancers." They laughed, thinking back on the shared magazines Zack had found in a tutor's briefcase. Looking at one another, they wanted to hold on to this moment. "To thirty-four years of intertwined friendship. *Boodiem*." (To us, let's drink.)

Xander had been waiting to make his announcement. He stood, looked at his friends, and they knew this was the moment he had chosen to share with them. "I want to add my happy news to our celebration. Cat Donley and I will be married in three months, on the one-year anniversary of when we met."

Throughout the courtship friends received email photos, descriptions of each detail of her face, and explanations of how and why love transported him to paradise. The announcement wasn't a surprise.

He told them about the way she made him laugh, many times using the wrong Spanish word. Xander hired a tutor for her Spanish lessons. Instead of *grupo de amigos* (group of friends), she said *grupas de amigos* (horses asses of friends). But he thought she did it on purpose because she watched him laugh and smiled cunningly.

He related about the visit to an LA jeweler and her rejection of a sizable diamond engagement ring. "It's too ostentatious for a girl from Toledo." They decided on matching wide, gold bands with each other's names inside.

Their engagement was informal, no ring, just dinner for two at Tierra Encantado, where they had their first dinner date and then spent the weekend and made love the first time. Chef prepared a special dinner of sea bass under chunks of lobster in a buttery white wine sauce. The pastry chef made a small chocolate cake with thick marshmallow icing and two plastic rings held together with a white, satiny ribbon on top. Cat had said, "I want to take the leftover cake to Amelia."

Xander laughed. "I knew you would say that." And even though he had never taken home an uneaten portion of dinner from a restaurant, he loved that frugal part of her, or, he thought, *Maybe she just wants to share her happiness with friends.*

Nikolai put his glass down. "I want you and Cat to be married at my residence. With Cat's approval, my wife's dress designer will sketch several excellent wedding gowns. The designer can go to LA with you next week and return with the chosen design and fabrics."

"That's generous of you, Nikolai. I will check with Cat and get back to you. The decision will be hers."

"You are going to ask me to be Best Man, right?"

Zack snapped, "Not a chance. Just because you're the President, doesn't mean you get to lead this wedding."

Xander beamed. "I will have three Best Men of equal importance, my brother and my two best friends, exactly the way it was at your wedding, Nikolai."

The two men sat back, smiled at each other, both had won. Sometimes they were still those three boys, growing up together.

Beautiful women were available for the President's male guests when he entertained. After the first time Cat and Xander made love, he refused the company of other women. "I only make love with my Cat."

At one of his visits, Zack had chosen a lovely Russian girl, Nadia, and at each visit afterward she pushed other women away, promising him a splendid night. They had sex nightly each time he was in Russia and she began to plead with him to take her to Mexico.

Zack owned a condominium in a prestigious building in Mexico City and also a condominium in the same building as Xander in LA. He spent most of his time at The Compound in Sonora, where he had a house and separate office as Academy accountant, plus attending to his private investment company.

He wanted to be upfront and told her it was not possible for them to be together in Mexico or the U.S., meaning he had no intention of making her a permanent girlfriend or more.

Nadia, anticipating his refusal, was persistent and decided Zack would change his mind if she was pregnant with his child. She proceeded with her plan and moved out of her boyfriend's apartment to make sure the pregnancy would not accidentally be from her boyfriend's sperm.

Each meeting Zack questioned her about birth control and she promised the injection was never missed. In addition, he used condoms, which afterward he wadded in a tissue to flush down the toilet.

At Zack's last visit to Russia, a three-week stay, months before the birthday celebration, they spent many nights together. He never let her stay all night. After each time they had sex, she offered to flush the package while in the bathroom. Instead, she squeezed the contents of the condom into her vagina, flushed the empty condom down the toilet, and left.

The pregnancy took. She promised herself she would not have sex after Zack left or reveal the secret until verification of the pregnancy.

The next time Zack was at the President's residence, Nadia stayed away. She was afraid nightly sex might cause a miscarriage. Zack was relieved Nadia was not in attendance, not wanting to hurt her by refusing her advances. He felt that having sex would encourage her to think he might change his mind and take her home. There were other lovely women, happy Nadia didn't show up, giving them a chance for the President's handsome friend.

CHAPTER VIII

The Name Of A Rude Guest
Will Disappear From The Guest List

The Bodyguard Academy in northwest Mexico had been producing disciplined men for three years, experts in the art of protection, each an army of one.

The process of choosing the students was held in Moscow. Five officers of the Russian FSB (Federal Security Service) cut one hundred applicants to fifty. The commander in charge of security at the Kremlin took twenty-five of them. After poring over profiles and interviewing each prospect, Xander, with one or two members of The Team, selected twelve. The training took ten months and included appropriate behavior in different situations, such as guarding at social events, being on watch, but unnoticed. They attended classes for languages, martial arts, guns and knives training, and flying lessons in helicopters and airplanes. Body building was a daily routine. Strategy for finding and eliminating the enemy was a half-day class once each week. And only for those suited, handling of a trained dog was fitted into their schedule. Students also had sessions with the psychiatrist every week.

Xander sent Joe, The Academy psychiatrist and pilot instructor, to LA every Friday afternoon to bring Cat to The Compound for the weekend. He took a student with him to log flying time. Joe was an ex-Navy pilot who had been stationed on an aircraft carrier based in the South Pacific. Xander told Cat that while Joe was in the Navy, he also taught the men updated procedures of landing onto new on-deck equipment. "He was so precise, even in rough seas, Joe landed on-target on the carrier that looked like a postage stamp from the air. The other pilots teased Joe, saying he could fly a red Radio Flyer kids' wagon and land it in a sandbox."

On breaks from carrier duty, Joe counseled Navy men in the veterans hospital and taught a psychology class at University of California, San Diego.

Xander heard about the brilliant young psychiatrist/pilot, attended his class, and asked for private counseling. Xander was fresh out of university, taking a break before law school, Joe eight years older.

Joe was at the top of Xander's list for The Academy instructors. Xander called him and they met at the Officers' Club, Naval Base San Diego. Joe was sitting on a bar stool explaining to some airmen the secret of landing on an aircraft carrier.

They sat in a corner booth. "Are you ready to retire?" Xander asked. "I have a new job for you, much less dangerous."

"I doubt that."

"It's simple. At The Academy we will have twelve students for ten months, then two months are for the instructors' break. There will be six specialty instructors, I will be Manager, Zack will be accountant, a Team of eight. You will teach flying, planes and helicopters, and be the company psychiatrist, counseling the students and staff. And the instructors will be paid more money than they ever dreamed possible."

Joe opted out of the Navy, took his past-due retirement, and joined The Academy. "I'd like to know the other men you've persuaded to enter this perilous, uncertain adventure."

Xander laughed. "You wouldn't be happy in calm seas. You'll like The Team, they're as different as a box of crayons."

* * * *

During weekends at The Compound, their first night, Cat and Xander would join The Team for dinner in their private dining room, separate from the students. The next evening they dined alone in the main house. Chef would have a student deliver their dinner.

Xander made special effort to ensure that Cat had a friendly, easygoing relationship with The Team. After they got married, she would be living at The Compound. "We can't live together in The Compound until we're married," she said. "It would be embarrassing in front of all the people there."

"They know what we're doing when you spend the weekend with me."

She ignored his comment. "And I don't want to quit my job until I'm married."

The Team liked her unassuming, natural way and felt Xander was relaxed, laughed more when Cat was at The Compound. Joaquin commented and all agreed, "She puts a constant smile on his face."

For his relaxation, Oso had become a golf enthusiast, bringing a pro from LA two days each month for lessons. He invited Cat to hit golf balls with him at the driving range outside The Compound when Xander had a meeting. Oso, a student of psychiatry, was interested in her life, they shared their stories. She told Xander, "He's more than a friend, he's like a brother."

Joaquin took her for laps in the Lamborghini, not driving all-out, recklessly, like he drove when he was alone. An oval track had been laid out around the driving range. The car had been left in one of the garages at the main house by the previous Manager and somehow it became Joaquin's toy. Some of the men were curious, watched Joaquin speed around the track, tried it once or twice and lost interest in driving it regularly.

Zack played tennis during the week, but didn't join Cat and Xander on weekends when Xander gave her lessons, or offer to hit balls with her if Xander was busy.

After dinner Cat and Xander would sit in the library, have tea and talk about their life together in The Compound. Xander, sitting close to her on the soft suede-covered sofa said, "Next Monday is a holiday. You'll have a three-day weekend. Would you like to invite your girlfriends to come with you? I could take all of you in the helicopter for a day at the beach and stay for dinner. Oso and Joaquin might join us, they like the beach." He didn't add that Oso and Joaquin would be with them as bodyguards. "Back here, the Sunday Market in the village might hold their interest."

Cat interrupted, "And I want to show them the beautiful silver and turquoise jewelry and the colorful hand-embroidered blouses and introduce them to the women I've met."

Amelia and Mona were excited about the invitation and asked Cat if she had yet mentioned it to Geena. In LA it had been easy for Cat to avoid Geena since she was in Mexico every weekend. Communication for their girls' night out once a month was through Amelia, usually they would go to the local burger house, then to one of their apartments for wine and talk. Cat resented Geena's abrasive personality and felt she put a damper on their get-togethers. To

Amelia, Cat gently hinted she preferred just the three of them go to Mexico, but Amelia said it would be hurtful to Geena if she found out later they had left her out of a fabulous weekend. Cat agreed to invite her, thinking, *Amelia's right, I shouldn't allow her to annoy me. It's just her way, she can't help it.*

The weekend started well, Geena volunteering to pick up Cat, Amelia, and Mona from work and drive south to the small local airport where Joe would be waiting. The sleek airplane looked like an oversized toy, compared to the commercial carriers, yet it was large for a private jet with a capacity of eighteen.

Joe was walking around the airplane doing the routine outer inspection. He introduced the girls to his Russian student, whose knowledge of English had progressed quite well, but his accent still thick as he said, "Happy to meet friends of Cat."

Geena stepped toward Joe, turning her shoulder to the smiling, attractive man. "I thought pilots were required to speak English in order to get a license. I hope you're the one flying this miniature plane."

Before anyone could respond, she stepped up, into the luxurious interior of silver and gray leather-covered, contoured seats and plush carpet.

The girls were embarrassed and Cat was upset with herself for allowing them to talk her into inviting Geena. She put her hand on the student's arm. "She is a rude person, your English is very good."

Cat stopped at Geena's side. She already had her shoes off, the chair reclined, and her feet on the footrest. With a threat in her voice, Cat leaned over her. "Geena, if you ruin this weekend with your caustic sarcasm and harsh behavior, you will never be invited back."

In a sophisticated, soft voice, Geena purred, "Would you get a glass of Pinot Noir for me, please?"

Cat clamped her teeth together and sat next to Amelia, who whispered, "I'm so sorry."

By Monday afternoon everyone who had come into contact with Geena was angry, repulsed, had a deep aversion to her, and felt she conducted herself in a disgusting manner. At the market she sneered, "I wouldn't touch that jewelry without soaking it in lye."

In the main house where Xander lived, the small staff included Flora, a very attractive young woman from the nearby town. Her black shiny hair was plaited in one long, thick rope, from the top of her head extending down her back. Her lovely smile was contagious. Cat commented, "Every time Flora comes to our house, I want to hug her. That's the way I feel about my sister, May."

Flora was the same age as Cat and they had become close friends. Her husband, Franco, was in charge of the locals hired for additional security at The Compound. Cat was fond of their two small children, usually bringing them little gifts from LA. Xander or one of The Team often helicoptered Cat and the family to one of the beaches along the Sea of Cortez.

Flora liked to cook and helped prepare and serve the meals for Cat and her guests. Geena didn't miss the opportunity. "I can see who's in Xander's bed when you're in LA," and she laughed as though it was a joke. Cat bristled.

The next weekend when Cat arrived back at The Compound, she apologized to each person who had been assaulted by Geena's rudeness. Xander knew she was embarrassed. "Cat, you, Amelia, and Mona were very generous to include her, and all of you should be proud of yourselves. The people she comes in contact with realize she is an extremely unhappy person and has probably been miserable all her life. I suppose most people avoid her. Congratulations to the three of you for trying to put a little brightness in her life." He put his arms around her, gently, comforting. In his mind the anger was bubbling. He had learned at a young age to smile, agree, apologize and keep the eruption hidden inside until it could be eliminated.

I will not allow that ignorant woman to upset my love with her thoughtless and hurtful remarks.

CHAPTER IX

Mistaken Power Leads
To The Mistake Of Arrogance

Several times, El Torbellino, Drug Lord of his Mexican cartel, known for his tantrums, throwing and destroying objects at hand, sent one of his captains to The Bodyguard Academy to request a meeting with Xander and Zack. He had heard the rumor that they were childhood friends of the Russian President, Nikolai Ivanov. Then it all came back to him. In law school there were three arrogant friends: a Russian, an American, a Mexican, all from wealthy families with unforgettable names. They had gone to boarding school together since young boys. Out loud he told himself, "A direct line to a country with millions of drug users. I'll convince them to get me into Russia, show me the area where I can meet the dealers who buy drugs from Afghanistan. My men will scout out the buyers."

El Torbellino had sent captains with messages to The Compound previously, but they were never allowed inside the gate. He would try one more time; if he couldn't get a message to Xander and Zack, he would attack The Compound as he had done with the previous Manager, capture and force them to help him. He thought they were stupid for refusing to give him the opportunity to find the Russian contacts who buy big shipments of drugs. There were eight million drug users in Russia spending 1.5 trillion rubles ($37 billion) annually on various drugs. He drooled at the open market.

El Torbellino didn't believe anyone would turn their back on millions of dollars. Loudly he said to himself, "I have an offer the gods wouldn't refuse." He didn't know The Team.

A note was hand delivered to the guard at the front gate of The Compound. The messenger waited in his truck for a reply. In the note, El Torbellino did not ask, but informed them that his Captain would personally deliver his message in three days.

The Team was at their weekly meeting when the note was delivered. They scoffed at the impertinence.

Joaquin had brought his new long-blade knife to the meeting to show its glinting sharpness. The others knew that, like his other knives, barely a touch to skin brought blood. Joaquin wanted everyone to test it with their thumbs, but they saw the razor-thin edge, shook their heads. "No, thank you."

Joaquin laughed. That laugh with his head thrown back, loosening the thick, wavy, oil-shiny, blackberry hair. The laugh that drew you in, made you want to sit and have a beer with him, learn his secret for laughter.

Oso offered his opinion. "Let's return a message—'Send your Captain.' We know El Torbellino wants drug contacts in Russia. If we let the Captain know how we feel about his business, he will inform his leader and they will stop thinking we are going to help them."

Joaquin held up his knife. "Let me tell him how we feel about his business." The sly smile, slightly off to one side.

Oso told the messenger The Team would talk to the Captain.

The Captain who came to the gate was surrounded by ten bodyguards. Oso, Joaquin, and all twelve students searched and disarmed them, leaving many weapons in the gatehouse, then escorted the cartel group to the interrogation room. This was job training for the students.

The men stood, separating, to have guards at all four walls. They were trained soldiers, proud, even with no weapons they would fight for their leader's life.

The Captain sat up straight like a proper soldier, his chin jutting out, projecting leadership and ego, looking contemptuously at the men to whom he had been entrusted with official communication.

Five of The Team were sitting at the opposite side of the oblong table, also up straight, all at least a head taller than their guest. The overhead fan stirred the warm air, yet a heavy realization hung between them. The cartel group was outnumbered, had no weapons, and faced the home advantage—more men standing by.

Sarge, The Team's dog trainer, entered the interrogation room leading two black Doberman pinschers, strong, sleek bodies, looking at the men standing against the walls. They seemed to have instinctively picked out the opposing group. The short leashes were taut, connected to thick leather collars. Sarge said something to them, barely above a whisper, and they strained forward, sniffing the feet, legs, and chest of each cartel guard. As a dog came to each man, he stiffened and held his breathing still. Sarge looked at Oso, gave him a nod that meant, *No weapons you may have missed.* Sarge knew he wouldn't find missed weapons. He used the opportunity to test his dogs, then led them to the door where they stood like sentinels.

Zack spoke in Spanish, a simple question, loud, annoyed. "Why are you here?"

Oso stood at the end of the table, an intimidating bulk. Joaquin and the students stared at each cartel man, whose wide eyes showed they didn't have the confidence of their leader. They understood danger.

The Captain remembered he had been told to be courteous and gave a slight, phony smile, showing he was a leader, unafraid in enemy territory. He leaned forward slightly, cleared his throat, let a few seconds pass. He was too important to be rushed. "El Torbellino authorized me to give you his personal message." He felt satisfied to let them know he held significant information concealed in his mind. A smirk of importance came across his face.

"Don't waste our time. Speak up or get out." Zack had given up his patience.

Insulted, the Captain raised his chin. "El Torbellino would like to make an offer. With your contacts in The Russian Federation, you can get permission for our airplane to land and the names of the people who would like to do business with us. Of course, there would be millions of dollars for you." *How does that sound, you offensive bastards?*

Standing, leaning halfway across the table, Xander asked, "What kind of business?" *I dare you to say it.*

The Captain didn't catch the threatening dare. "The specialized business of happiness."

Before Zack or Xander could reach across the table, Oso clasped the Captain's neck and lifted him to his feet, strange noises coming from his throat.

Joaquin and the students moved closer to the cartel men, face to face, looking into frightened eyes.

"Put him down, Oso." Xander wanted him to take a message to El Torbellino. The grasp around the Captain's neck loosened and an iron hand pushed him down to the chair.

Xander sat back down, trying to calm himself enough to talk. "We are not interested in your filthy money. Millions of dollars connected to drugs would make a very large bonfire with your bodies in the middle. The President of Russia is cleaning up the drug problem in his country. The drugs coming across the border from Afghanistan are being stopped. He would kill you before you got off the plane. If you leave here alive, it will only be so you can deliver our answer to your leader. Tell him, the next messenger he sends will be killed at our gate."

The Captain had failed. *El Torbellino will be angry.* He tried one more time, with the mistake of arrogant anger. He sparked to Xander. "We will destroy your Compound, everyone in it." Then the pompous final blow, "And your house in Baja."

At the insolent threat, Joaquin turned and stared at the back of the Captain's head, seeing a stiff shirt collar around his neck. *Still room above the collar in the front.*

Xander's eyes flashed as he stood up. Amazingly composed, he asked, "You threaten us, Captain? Is your lieutenant with you today?"

A stocky man, older than the Captain, probably with more experience, but less grit, stepped forward. Xander addressed him in Spanish, "Señor, did you hear, and do you remember the message we are sending to El Torbellino?"

"*Sí, Señor*, I heard and remember." Unknowingly, with that answer he advanced to the Captain's position.

"Joaquin, show the Captain your new knife."

The blood brought color to the drab room, flowing across the table, spilling onto the chair, pooling on the floor. Oso shuffled the gasping, pale men out of the building, through the gate to their trucks, leaving weapons behind. Oso held up one hand, a motion telling them to wait until a body bag was thrown into the back of one of the trucks. When Oso lowered his hand, they quickly disappeared in a cloud of dust, taking with them their frightful experience, the message, and a bloody, zippered bag with a head barely attached to its body.

CHAPTER X
Can Killing Be Heroic?

It was 7:00 a.m. Xander was finishing his routine in the home gym, Cat was sleeping. His phone buzzed the *atención* (Attention!) code. Xander's workout tee was drenched, clinging to the brawny chest and back as he reached to turn on the speaker.

Oso was at the main gate. "There is a worn-out mule here, pleading to see you, says he has important information."

"Search him, put him in the interrogation room. I'll be there after my shower."

Workers from one of Mexico's drug cartels would sometimes make their way to The Bodyguard Academy, begging for asylum, promising insider information about the cartel, having dropped out of favor with their leader. Most of them were killed by cartel soldiers before getting to the main gate. The few who had serious intentions to abandon the drug world and made it to The Compound, Joe had given a ride to a small airport south of LA and left them to fend for themselves. Some were lucky enough to have relatives to call. Usually their information wasn't something The Team didn't already know, but if they had gotten themselves in trouble with the cartel, they needed to get out of Mexico and change their lives. The Team didn't want it known they had helped a few dissenters, the interference could cause war.

When Xander walked through the door of the interrogation room, the dusty, exhausted, ragged-looking man dropped to his knees in gratefulness, even if it was only to be heard. "*Señor, yo tengo información muy valioso para usted.*" (I have very valuable information for you.)

Oso had given him a bottle of water, empty now, and offered another.

Xander told him to sit in the chair across the table from him and wondered what this man, probably in his early twenties, could have done to be in life-threatening trouble.

The young man took gulps of water during the telling of his story. His job was to deliver a truck full of produce to the assigned Mexican port. His pickup was old, dented fenders, muddy, but new tires and a recently replaced engine. It looked overused and would not attract attention, but was in perfect running order for the driver to complete the important deliveries and pickups.

Special boxes of molded cartons for avocados were fitted into crates of thick cardboard. Under the shallow molds were packages of white powder, usually heroin. The merchandise went to a dock loader who filled a cargo carrier, which was then lifted onto a freighter headed for LA. The driver was ordered to stay in his truck during the unloading, so he could drive away at a moment's notice if dock police were headed toward them. When the unloading was complete, the tailgate was slammed shut, the passenger-side door was opened by a cartel worker, and large lime-green plastic bags printed with "*Juguetes de Juan*" (Juan's Toys) were thrown on the floor. Inside the toy-store bags were children's colorful backpacks portraying Spider-Man, T-Rex, ballerinas, Lots o' Hearts, and camouflage. Inside the backpacks were tightly stacked, vacuum-sealed packages of $100 bills.

In this deal there were three transactions. The buyer at the port was the middleman, paying for the drugs, taking on the responsibility of getting the cargo through the LA port. He doubled his money when the next buyer picked up the avocado shipment.

Hesitantly the cartel driver admitted to Xander that for six months he had been stealing a $100 bill from many packages, slitting the end of the wrap with a razor blade, and carefully removing one bill with tweezers. Secretly he sent his wife and two young daughters to LA with the pilfered money and costly, illegally obtained passports, thinking he would join them later and start a new life.

"*Señor, una información muy importante.*" (A bit of very important information.) He described an upcoming meeting at the warehouse district in LA. A new cartel, just getting started, and a U.S. drug syndicate were getting together to work on exclusive selling and buying drugs. His friend who talked about this dangerous mission would be part of the *conjunto de guardia* (group of guards).

"*Tambien, Señor Xander, hay más.*" (Also, Mr. Xander, there is more.) He began to shake as though he had been taken over by convulsions. Oso pulled up a chair for himself, gave the desperate man another bottle of water, and put a comforting big bear paw on his shoulder. Oso felt the DEA could use this information, interrupt the meeting, arrest the dealers, and terminate another surge of drugs into the U.S.

He told them of his harrowing twenty-four-hour escapade. After dropping off the shipment of avocados and receiving the backpacks of money, he drove to a motel, where he had paid for a room earlier and stashed empty suitcases with children's books inside. Then, filling the shallow bottom with stacks of $100 bills, he covered them with the backpacks full of children's books.

When he got to the airport with his new passport and luggage filled with cash, the parking lot and sidewalks were teaming with cartel soldiers in camouflage uniforms and berets. Machine guns were slung over both shoulders. He took a shortcut out of the area, drove north, toward The Academy. After burying the luggage, driving further and hiding the pickup in a thick mango grove, he walked to The Academy along animal paths. Begging for help, he told Xander he could keep the buried money if he would get him to LA to join his wife and children.

Xander looked at Oso, who gave him a slight smile and tilted head, sending the message, *Let's help him.*

"At this Compound, we do not associate with drug dealers, drug buyers, or drug users," lectured Xander. "The money is yours, you stole it. We will take your truck across the border into Chihuahua and leave it there. It's too close to our Compound, and we don't want them to know you came here or that we helped you. Hopefully, a local farmer will find it and make honest use of it to sell his crops. Joe will give you and your money a ride to the Arizona Air Force base where your luggage won't be checked. Be careful how you spend or show those $100 bills. Now I want to know the day, time, and location of the cartel and syndicate meeting."

The Team met in their administrative office. An ample, comfortable room, air conditioned, soft recessed lighting, an entire wall of built-in wood shelves filled with books of Mexican history, laws, products, maps, customs, and leaders, up to the current President.

In the middle of the room was an executive-style oval table of highly polished Sonoran wood inlaid with precisely cut turquoise in a swirling design. The table was surrounded by eight presidential-worthy, cushioned, glove-soft, leather-covered chairs.

Xander was standing to present the results of contacting the authorities, the DEA—California Branch, to let them know about the meeting in LA of the Mexican drug cartel and the U.S. drug syndicate, known as Dreamland. The news was disturbing and disappointing. Basically, the information was going through the political levels of authority, slowly being pushed up the ladder. Xander's friend in the California DEA office said he didn't have the authority to interrupt the meeting unless there was a large amount of drugs, and if there was a small amount of drugs, all the detainees would be back home in forty-eight hours. Then they would set up another meeting. It would only cause a delay of the inevitable negotiation and another stream would start running.

The Team thought there would not be any drugs, it was a business meeting. The results of the meeting were what they wanted to stop. Xander's DEA friend felt that by the time the information got to the decision-makers in Washington and they talked it over, the meeting and drug dealing-bargaining would be finished. Xander asked that his name not be connected to the supplied information. His friend let him know it had been tagged from an anonymous informant. However, he would take a large force to interrupt the next avocado shipment.

The joining of the cartel and the U.S. syndicate certainly meant a more abundant and steady flow of drugs throughout the United States. Could it be prevented?

Xander concluded, "Do we interfere in this meeting? We have our own problem with the cartel insisting we act as intermediaries between them and Russia, but we have the opportunity to disrupt this game, stop it at GO." Xander took a deep breath, looked at his brothers. "I respect the judgment of each of you and I will go with the majority."

At the weekly meetings, no matter the subject, every member was heard, each opinion considered, then voted on.

Joaquin stood and spoke first, responding to Xander's report. "I know the drug dealing on the streets of LA. Any kid, regardless of age, can buy. Many of them are recruited to sell, usually taking their business to playgrounds. I've seen the results of overdosing and the desperation of need from being hooked. As members of the human race, I believe it is our moral obligation to curtail this new surge of drugs, however we can. It is my suggestion to eliminate the members of both groups."

Hitch, a munitions expert, Academy instructor, and retired Army planner of schemes to ambush the enemy, unfolded his six-foot-five-inch body out of the comfortable chair that had contoured to his frame. He spoke, towering over the seated Team, in harsh guttural sounds. "I will do a thorough search of the premises and prepare plans to destroy the building and everyone in it, or—a specific scheme to eradicate the occupants without demolishing the building. We cannot let this drug plan go forward. It is our duty to stop it."

Sarge, The Team's dog breeder/trainer/instructor, gave his opinion, standing erect, as if he was still in uniform. "I have trained dogs to sniff out drugs and have found them in places of shocking discovery. Young mothers hide powerful drugs in their baby's stroller, ten-year-old children have stashes for themselves and to sell, owners of multi-million-dollar mansions share cocaine with their children. I volunteer for a mission to eradicate this intention of crime against humanity. I vote with Joaquin and Hitch."

Oso, cautiously humane, was concerned for the innocent. He shifted his bearish body weight from one foot to the other. His assessment would be opposing. "What about the guards? It's a job to them, a way to support their families. They are probably not aware of the depth of inhumane actions they are supporting. I want to defeat the captains, the lieutenants, the leaders, not the innocents." He quickly sat down, aware his viewpoint was not the same as his brothers, but proud he felt comfortable enough to oppose them and knew he was respected for standing up for his belief.

In his quiet psychiatrist voice, Joe stood to respond. "Unfortunately, every worker in the cartel has full knowledge of the drugs they transport and indisputable loyalty to their leader. They have been trained to kill for his protection the same as we train here at The Academy. I would like to believe as you do, Oso, but there are no innocents connected to drug dealing. We have the opportunity to win one small battle in the war on drugs."

Geoff, physical trainer and martial arts champion, his slim body enveloped into the cushioned chair, listened as though he was peering from tall grass like a cheetah. His eyes scanned the room. He stood slowly, the hard muscles visible in the trim frame as he moved. "I teach the powerful message of the destructive impacts of drug use on families and health. Drugs, our enemies, must be defeated and I want to be part of the army."

The methodical, mathematic mind of Zach had been evaluating the circumstances and opinions. Standing tall, he looked at each face as he talked. "We have received messengers from El Torbellino requesting that The Team join his drug cartel, then they threatened us for refusing their offer. We have direct information from a carrier concerning the success of their shipments. The U.S. government can't move fast enough on this incredible opportunity to curtail another flow of drugs into the U.S. We have the information, the manpower, the equipment, and the expertise. This transaction must be prevented. It is our mission, our moral obligation."

The conference between the two drug dealers was to take place at the LA commercial port in a large warehouse, for rent, no questions asked. It was used by companies to store containers taken off ships waiting to be picked up.

Hitch and Joaquin would go a day early to check the location and develop their plan. The ceiling was high with catwalks above the fluorescent lighting which could be disconnected and the light switch at the entrance connected to low dim lights, leaving the catwalks in darkness. Hitch drew a map of the locations from where the siege would take place, a specific site for each man on the catwalk.

Three of Joaquin's friends would be stationed as lookout, on the watch for interference, dock police, or rival drug dealers who may have heard of the competition. Any obstruction to the project would become part of the casualties.

CHAPTER XI

A Secret Told Is No Longer A Secret

Cat had stirred when Xander got out of bed, aware, but not fully awake. An hour later, her phone played chirping sounds of birds. *A real phone call, not a text,* she thought.

Her cell phone was one Xander had asked Hitch to make as a special safe-phone whose calls could not be intercepted. He wanted Cat to communicate with her sister and friends without worrying that an enemy would locate and put them in jeopardy. He stationed a guard in Cat's condo building to watch over her, following her to work, on runs, girlfriend lunches, shopping. The Team thought if the Mexican cartel was looking for ways to punish them for not cooperating, following Cat would be a good place to start, even if it was only a threat, a scare. They knew The Team would not help them if they hurt her and would probably retaliate.

Amelia's name came up on the ID screen.

"Good morning, my friend."

"Cat, something terrible has happened. Geena was killed after work last night, getting into her car." Amelia started to cry.

"Are you alone? Is Mona with you? Tell me what happened. I'm sorry for getting angry at her when she was here at The Compound. You were such a good friend to her, her best friend. This is shocking." *I want to comfort Amelia, but I feel guilty I don't have tears for Geena.*

Amelia took a deep breath. "The police called her parents. They are making arrangements for her to be cremated and sent back to Maine. I called them this morning to offer my help. They said there would be no service or celebration of life or 'whatever we called those meetings' and hung up."

Cat thought, *So that's where she got that icy personality.* "I'm sorry, Amelia. I'll be home tomorrow. Together we'll go to the police station, read the reports, and find what happened. Would you and Mona like to come to The Compound with me next weekend? We could have our own memorial for her and talk about our times together. Was it a robbery, a gun?"

"Her purse was taken. I was thinking she may have tried to fight back and wouldn't give it up. Remember, we always said, 'Give them whatever they want, it may save your life.' She was killed with a knife," Amelia sobbed, "in her neck."

Cat sat up, closed her eyes. *First Bradford Ayers, now Geena, people who were indecent and insulting to me. Is it a coincidence or am I being overly protected? Everyone in this Compound is capable of killing, teaches killing, or learns killing. This is my home, where I will live with the man I love, my husband. Do I want to know the truth, which may cause me to give up my comfortable nest, or shall I stay and snuggle into the warmth?*

* * * *

It was the weekend before Cat and Xander's wedding. Plans were all set to take place in The Russian Federation in the President's private dining room, used for entertaining his friends. The state dining room was reserved for entertaining dignitaries from other countries. Amelia, Mona, and May were at The Compound, sharing Cat's giddy happiness, holding her hand, reminding her to eat. They would leave for Russia the next day. Nikolai had sent a message to Cat that he assigned a guide to take the women touring Moscow and St. Petersburg. There were excited discussions concerning what to wear.

Cat hung an enlarged photo of her wedding gown in her dressing room, reassuring herself it was not a dream, she was going to marry the man she loved. Her extravagant dress made her feel like she was the princess at the ball. Cat had forbidden Xander to look at her gown and now he was not allowed to glimpse the picture. He laughed at her superstition, told her he wanted to wait and see it when they were standing together, being pronounced man and wife.

After the last fitting, the gown was taken back to Russia to have seed pearls sewn onto the flowery lace. The underlayer of heavy silk fabric formed a strapless bodice, fitted down to her hips, then flaring to the floor. The silk dress was covered with an embroidered lace coat, hugging her body, up to her neck, wrist-length narrow sleeves, and flaring over the long silk skirt.

The Russian designer had drawn a picture of her wedding-day hairdo and the three young women copied it, fussing, to show Cat how she would look. She had let her hair grow longer to accomplish the style. The hair was sleeked back, then wound into a French twist, the long ends circled like a rope on top of her head forming a tiara. A band, with tiny white roses, would be placed around the crown of twisted hair, a veil of two layers of silk tulle floating from her tiara, around her body and trailing behind as though she was enveloped in mist.

Cat didn't want May's husband, Marco, to attend her wedding, but Amelia convinced her it might cause problems for May if he wasn't invited. Cat agreed and decided to let May handle the invitation.

Since they married, it seemed to May and Cat that Marco had become increasingly self-serving, preoccupied with his own interests. Before May met him, she had proudly bought herself a fresh-off-the-boat white convertible BMW sports car. He had an old, faded black Jaguar, with a raggedy, torn convertible top. After he moved in, her car sat parked in the driveway while his leaked oil in her garage. He drove May's BMW, she drove an old Ford Explorer they bought from his brother-in-law. They had only been married two years when he traded in her BMW and his wreck-of-a-car and got himself an updated, used Jaguar. May didn't oppose him and Cat didn't want to criticize him, afraid to cause more problems in their relationship or worse, she was afraid Marco would hurt her sister. In two more years the Jaguar wasn't fancy enough for him and he found a slightly used red Ferrari online. He sold the Jaguar, barely paid off the loan, May made a down payment and financed the Ferrari, over $100,000. "This has always been my dream," he told her.

"What about your dreams?" Cat asked.

The next year he lost his job, something about a problem with his absences, and was unemployed for three years. May paid the bills. Marco had become fond of running, swimming, biking, having bought an expensive racing bike, and participated in mini-marathons. He had lots of spare time for his new hobby. He had no income, no savings, and used her credit card to support his new lifestyle, ordering Ferrari-red tee shirts, a fitted racing jacket, leather driving gloves, an alligator wallet, travel cups to keep his coffee hot while driving, all with the Ferrari logo.

Joe had flown to Toledo to pick up May, Marco, and their five-year-old daughter and bring them to The Compound for the three days before they would leave for Russia. May arrived at the small local airport alone. Marco had decided thirty minutes before the time to drive to the airport that he didn't like Russia and would stay home with their daughter. May called a taxi. The flower girl would wear her pink silk dress at home, dancing in her room, pretending to be a ballerina.

May cried all the way to Mexico. Joe asked her questions about Marco's behavior and she told him of incidents, the words rushing from her mouth as though she was happy to let them out.

"Last week Monica was invited to a birthday party. I was away and he was to take her to the party. My friend told me Monica was one hour late, got there after the children had eaten lunch and had started to play games. Monica ate lunch by herself, then joined the other children. He has no regard for time and has missed flights because he didn't get to the airport on time. He uses my airline miles to visit friends in Chicago, relatives in Miami. When he and Monica are supposed to meet me at a restaurant, I tell him a half hour earlier than I will be there and still, he is always late." She took a deep breath. "I could go on and on about his lateness problem. I'll just tell you one more thing and then I don't want to mention his name for this whole week. I never make a decision at home," she boldly went on. "When we needed new stools for the kitchen counter, he picked them out. A totally different style, they didn't go with the other furniture in my townhouse, but I didn't dare contradict him. Even our daughter has learned to talk carefully and smile in his presence."

Joe explained that Marco seemed to have characteristics of a narcissist who must always be in control. "I don't know enough about him to give a diagnosis. I'm just thinking about the incidents you've mentioned."

It was comforting to hear the opinion of a professional. She only shared her personal life with her sister, whose constant advice was to get a divorce. "You must get rid of him, I'm afraid for you."

Joe spoke softly. "Canceling his trip at the last minute and not allowing your daughter to go with you is simply a show of control. The same for having no respect for being on time. He sees himself above that requirement. Think about why you subject yourself and your child to his abuse."

"I travel with the lawyers in my office, taking notes for them at depositions, keeping track of appointments, etc. He takes care of our daughter and I don't have to leave her with a sitter." She was quiet for a few moments. "Truthfully, he won't allow me to hire a sitter."

"May, perhaps you should consider if he is a bad influence for her. Let's talk about this again." He wanted to get her mind out of the depressed mood. "All of us are excited about the big wedding, as I'm sure you are, and your sister happily wants you to be part of her special day. You will be treated royally in Moscow."

* * * *

The planned meeting of the Mexican drug cartel and the California drug syndicate was scheduled to take place the evening after Joe and Oso would take Cat, her sister, and friends to Russia in The Team's Gulfstream. The Team felt that Oso should not be part of the raid, taking into consideration his concern for guards he believed might be innocent. He would relieve Joe as co-pilot and serve as bodyguard for the ladies, though Nikolai would assign some for them, also.

Nikolai's unmarked private airplane would be parked at the Los Angeles International Airport to pick up the Russian Federation Ambassador and his wife who had flown from New York to LA to visit friends before going home for a family visit. The Team would occupy that plane. Though their names would not be included on the passenger list.

Records would show that The Academy's plane had left the day before the raid. The passenger list would include The Team, proving they were in Russia on the night two organizations of drug dealers were eliminated. Just a precaution, if rumors should connect The Team to that bloody night.

Xander explained to Cat they would not be on the Team plane with her, May, Amelia, and Mona to Moscow. "Please don't ask me to explain details about it now. We will be engaging the students in a secret, complicated objective. It's about stopping a Mexican cartel from joining a U.S. drug syndicate. I am telling you this because I want you to know The Team feels it is an important mission, an opportunity to curtail another flow of drugs into the United States. I must ask you to not discuss it with anyone."

Maybe Cat didn't want to know details. *There's only one way to stop a cartel. Can killing be heroic?* She looked at Xander, handsome, protective, her dream man. *I've chosen life with him, I don't want life without him.* "It sounds dangerous. Will you be safe?"

"I will be waiting for you, watching you walk toward me to be married, the happiest day of my life."

CHAPTER XII

I Am Your Pulsing Heartbeat, The Blood In Your Veins

The Compound had become home to Cat. She left her job only two weeks before the wedding, Mrs. G saying, "I won't find anyone who can take your place." She reached into her top desk drawer and presented Cat with a worn, Asian-design, silk-covered box. "This is a string of jade beads that belonged to my mother. I don't have a daughter to pass them on to. I would like you to have them." Teary-eyed, Cat held up the necklace of dark jade beads with a gold filigree clasp. Mrs. G put fleshy arms around Cat and she finally knew how it felt to receive a mother's warm hug.

Cat told Xander she wanted to keep her condominium as a rental. "My first investment, with income, so I can have my own money." He told her that was a good idea. "I like having an independent wife with her own bank account." Without mentioning it, he paid off the mortgage and Zack offered to help with the management, the rent going into Cat's personal savings, the expenses paid from Xander's account.

Three of The Team opted not to attend the wedding in Russia. Sarge refused to leave his dogs, including a pale brown German shepherd he was training as a surprise for Cat, a companion and guard dog. On weekends she stopped by the training grounds to ask Sarge if she could hold the puppies. He picked the medium-sized female who snuggled with Cat and ran to greet her when Sarge opened her gate.

Hitch decided to stay in Sonora, manage the security of The Compound and scheduling for the guards. He had been experimenting with new explosive devices, using the desolate desert as testing grounds, and wanted to include the information in his coming classes.

Geoff, language teacher, body trainer, dietician, had visited his mother in St. Petersburg during his last time off. He wanted to use the extra time alone, writing a new workout regimen for the next group of students. The regimens would be included in his book, *Nutrition and Exercise for the Healthy Body.*

In Russia, on the wedding day, preparation put everyone in celebration mode. Xander was up early, working out, then lunch with his friends who tried to make conversation, but his mind contained one thought. He would answer unrelated questions with the same phrase. "This is the happiest day of my life," not really hearing the questions.

Friends of Xander came from France, Mexico, and the United States, but his brother Wray apologized for his absence. He was ensconced in British history archives doing research for his new book on Alfred Lord Tennyson, the nineteenth-century Poet Laureate during the reign of Queen Victoria.

Cat was jittery, would stop talking and start crying. Amelia would smile and say, "A bride cannot meet her husband-to-be at the altar with mascara running down her cheeks. I want him to see you walking toward him emitting happiness, in your incredible wedding gown.

And every time you start crying, May cries. We can't have two faces with smeared mascara."

The Team, fitted for custom tuxedos, participated in the wedding. Zack and Nikolai, Best Men, Joaquin, Oso, and Joe escorting Cat's friends and her sister up a white-rose-petal-strewn aisle between eighty guests.

As Nikolai had suggested, guests were ushered to their seats as his harpist played Mozart's only concerto written for the harp, a lively composition to put wedding excitement in the air. The graceful, elegant instrument and formally dressed musician were at the front side of the oblong room on a circular platform. At the front center was an elevated stage for the ceremony. White and pale-pink roses, soft-blue hydrangeas, lilacs, and lavender covered a wide brass arch-trellis with the same flowers in the bride's and her attendants' bouquets, then duplicated in brass urns placed at each row.

Xander and his two best friends since childhood stood at the front, beaming at the guests, proud of the three beautiful couples walking slowly up the aisle toward them. May walked beside Joe, Amelia held Joaquin's arm, and Oso smiled at Mona, who blushed at the attention.

The "Bridal Chorus" from Richard Wagner's opera, *Lohengrin*, was played on an ornate organ. Cat had chosen the piece, known as "Here Comes the Bride," happy that it was about her. "I'm the bride," saying it as if she needed to convince herself. May, Matron of Honor, straightened her sister's veil, held back tears and whispered, "This is your day, Cinderella, you deserve it all."

Cat's bridal bouquet, heavy, needing both hands to carry, contained white roses in different stages of bloom, from buds to fully open, with a streamer of small roses spilling down the front. May's dress was of pale blush-pink silk, strapless, floor length with a lace coat dyed to match and a bouquet of matching roses and pink baby's breath. The attendants' dresses were the same design in different colors. Cat chose pastel blue for Amelia to match her eyes. Her bouquet of soft-blue hydrangeas was the same hue. Mona's ensemble was her favorite color, pale purple, and she carried a bouquet of lilacs and lavender. Before walking Mona to the front, Oso offered his arm and whispered, "This is my first tux and I've never worn purple flowers."

The bride walked halfway by herself, Xander met her, took her hands, kissed her fingers, and they walked together to the front to be married. Facing each other, sending messages of love with their eyes, they seemed to be enclosed in an aura of radiance, unaware of the surroundings, two people, in a place of their own.

The ceremony had been American, but the elaborate banquet was Russian. Dinner was served in courses on Wedgwood plates with gold trim: starting with the traditional Russian Olivier salad, chopped vegetables and boiled eggs with creamy dressing. Then stroganoff, a rich dish of creamed venison and mushrooms, pirozhki, baked salmon-filled pastries, dumplings of lamb and herbs. Between courses the guests sipped tea, sbitin, a berry juice flavored with wine and honey.

For the first dessert, blinis were buttery sweet with berries and cream. The four-tier wedding cake drew everyone's attention, a show of artistic decoration. Wrapped around the top layer and circling down three more layers were branches of cherry blossoms, scattered with butterflies, sculptured of tinted icing. Matching cupcakes, in boxes, were stacked on a table near the door for everyone to take as they left.

When Cat's friends had visited her on weekends at The Compound, Joaquin accompanied them to the beach, the Sunday Market, the shops in town. After dinner Joaquin and Amelia would walk the covered arbor path built inside the wall around The Compound, talking about their childhood, growing up, each other's families. He told her of meeting Xander, that he went to three years of continuous college, no break, then started the job as instructor at The Academy.

At the wedding Joaquin walked beside Amelia, enraptured by the red hair tightly pulled up and tied with a blue satin ribbon on top of her head, forming a mop of curls. At The Compound he could barely resist taking a curl with his fingers and playing with it. They sat together at dinner and he caught Xander quickly look at him and smile.

Guests were standing in groups, laughing, talking, each holding a snifter of French cognac. Joaquin came up behind Amelia and tapped her shoulder. "It was easy to find you. I looked around for a dress that matched my boutonniere." He avoided a comment about her unruly hair, which was starting to find its way out of the snare, breeding curls where it had been slick. He knew she was self-conscious about her unmanageable hair, but Joaquin was entranced by it. "It's a lovely evening. Would you like to walk in the garden?"

As they passed through the space that had been a wall of sliding glass doors, he said, "I'll carry your fancy lace coat."

May and Mona had removed their coats, feeling glamorous in strapless dresses, but Amelia needed encouragement. Joaquin held the ends of the sleeves as she slipped out, then removed his jacket and carried them over his arm. "Now I can enjoy the freckles on your shoulders. I like them almost as much as the ones on your face."

She knew he was seriously flirting. The attention made her feel pretty, she liked being with him. He had kissed her at The Compound under the arbor, not long desirous kisses, just light appreciative kisses, like *Thank you for the gift of being here with me.*

He led her off the path bordered with yellow, orange, and white lilies, past thick, peach-colored azalea bushes. When they stopped, she commented about the flowers scenting the warm air. She felt his hands rubbing her shoulders and wanted to be close, feel his lips.

"Amelia, may I have this curl?" He had picked it from the mass on top of her head. It sprang back into a wound-up corkscrew as he let go. "Did you say yes?"

Joaquin made her feel beautiful. She looked at his handsome face, softly murmured, "Yes," not knowing what she was agreeing to.

He retrieved a small knife, turned her away from him, cut the ringlet. Facing her, looking into her pure-blue eyes, tucking the ring of red hair in his pocket, he spoke softly. "Thank you. I must have some little memento to hold in my hand when we're not together." He kissed her, drawing her close, holding the nape of her neck with one hand, his arm around her back. His mouth close to her ear, he whispered, "Amelia, may I make love to you?"

Nikolai was upset when Xander told him that he and Cat would leave on their honeymoon the next day. "In Russia, we celebrate for a week after the ceremony with dancing, singing, toasting, banqueting." The visits with Xander and Zack were never long enough for Nikolai. He always tried to convince them they needed to extend their stay. He would say, "We'll go to my summer house and relax on the beach" or "Let's go to my chalet and ski for a few days" or "My pilot will take us to Istanbul, we'll watch the belly dancers." They laughed at the childhood memory, when they plotted to run away from home, meet in Istanbul, watch the belly dancers. Zack had found a magazine, in a tutor's briefcase, with pictures of the exotic dancers.

No one on his staff or in his family knew the sentimental Nikolai. His father taught him to project control, a serious face, steely eyes.

Xander wrapped his arms around his friend, thinking of their years of friendship since six years old. "Cat and I appreciate the extravagant wedding you gave us, but I want to be alone with my wife." Both smiled. "Zack will stay a few more days."

Joe, Oso, Joaquin, and three students, pilots and bodyguards, accompanied the bride and groom on their honeymoon to Bora-Bora in the Team's private Gulfstream with a custom-designed interior. If the cartel found out the honeymoon location, protection would be needed. The Team's enemies were multiplying.

Cat and Xander made love and slept, repeating the sequence, all the way to the South Pacific, not concerned about the time changes, the altitude, the slight turbulence, or the other people on the plane.

Oso would send a text, saying he was placing a bowl of iced shrimp and lobster outside their bedroom door. When the sun came up above the clouds, he texted of the scrambled eggs, croissants, and tea waiting on a cart, to be wheeled into their room.

Their over-the-water bungalow suite was at the end of the curved walkway on stilts, the bodyguards occupying the suites before it. The newlyweds spent sunny days on their lanai, watching the colorful, different species of fish in the crystal-clear, turquoise-tinted water, around and below them. They took pictures of themselves and the orange and pink sunsets. When they walked, holding hands, on the white-sand beaches, the guards spread out in front, toward the side and trailing, but never too close, to give them honeymoon privacy.

The students were left in Bora-Bora to guard the bungalows while Cat, Xander, Joe, Oso, and Joaquin explored Bali, enjoying the guide's history lesson. Another day they toured Tahiti, visiting the

Paul Gauguin Museum, and ending the day in a Tahitian pearl shop. Joaquin bought Amelia small stud earrings for her seashell ears and a pearl pendant on a fine gold chain.

Xander bought Cat a string of large, luminous, black pearls, which she wore back to Bora-Bora and every day, even with her conservative one-piece bathing suit on beach walks.

On the last evening of their honeymoon, dinner and champagne were delivered to their bungalow. Cat held her glass up to clink. "I'm reminded of our first night at Tierra Encantado. It was a wonderful night."

"Every night with you is wonderful. I love you more than all the stars in the sky. Tomorrow we go home to live our life as husband and wife."

CHAPTER XIII

If You Live With A Lie Long Enough, In Your Mind The Lie Will Become Truth

Zack and Nikolai reclined on thick cushioned lounge chairs on the rose garden terrace outside the President's residence. They spoke Spanish, to have more privacy. "If you weren't here, Zack, I would be depressed. The music, the laughter, the wedding, surrounded by friends, now my house is empty for me, I miss them."

"It was a perfect wedding for our old friend and his bride, both beautiful."

Nikolai looked at his friend. *Even if I hadn't seen him through all these years, I would recognize him. He has the same features as thirty-five years ago, the same dark eyes that draw you in, friendly, intellectual, hypnotic.* "Zack, I read the article in the *L.A. Times* about your successful disposal of the joint effort between the new U.S. drug syndicate and the Mexican cartel. The newspaper said a third drug syndicate killed their opponents to get rid of competition and there is no information as to whether they are from the U.S. or Mexico. The Team wasn't a suspect. Xander said his friend in the LA DEA wrote the tip as anonymous. Did Hitch plan the operation?"

"The U.S. Army lost a big asset when Hitch retired to The Academy. His scheme was perfect, our positioning and weapons, no damage to the building. Joaquin's old buddies kept watch for several days before the assault to make sure the syndicate didn't post backup protection. We were in place when the two groups entered. Mission accomplished. Then Joaquin's friends whisked us to the airport, your 787 waiting. They drove Hitch and Geoff to the border where our helicopter was parked and they flew back to The Compound."

They were quiet, each thinking about the daring, risky venture that The Team felt obligated to successfully conclude in order to prevent another large surge of drugs into the U.S. There was no one to give them praise, no talk of the good deed, just personal satisfaction of eliminating more drug sales. Zack changed direction, went on to talk about Cat and Xander.

"The Team is quite fond of Cat. Oso and Joaquin have become her personal guardians. Oso has hired a professional golf instructor, they are on The Compound practice range every open hour and he plans to take her to golf courses in Mexico to play the whole game, taking students for bodyguard practice. When Oso is teaching, Joaquin takes her in the Lamborghini around the track like they're practicing for the Indy 500. Joaquin doesn't drive his usual reckless style when she's in the car, but still, I'm surprised Xander doesn't red flag that. She tells him how much fun she's having, so he just threatens Joaquin, 'If you have an accident with her in the car . . .' An entourage takes her to the tourist market in town where she makes more friends. The possibility that El Torbellino may try to kidnap her, force us to cooperate with their plans to sell drugs in Russia, is always on our minds. Apparently he believes you will allow him to bring drugs to Russia and might be planning to offer you a substantial gift. Maybe he thinks you invited the Afghans in or that they bribed you like the President of Mexico was bribed. It's public knowledge now that the

Mexican cartels pooled money and came up with $500 million for his bribe. That gives them a lot of freedom to spread their drugs. The cartels are rich and powerful."

Nikolai sighed. "Why do people voluntarily put venom in their body? The drug problem in Russia is out of control. I asked several countries for help and the U.S. joined us in a raid on a heroin-processing plant in Afghanistan. There was just a little breathing space before they started up again. El Torbellino is a big threat for The Team. I don't want him in my country; on the other hand, maybe we can set a trap for him. Also, I was thinking we should move The Academy out of Mexico. Talk to Xander about it."

"Xander puts in a full day, checking each detail of The Academy schedule and helps me prepare invoices for my assistant accountant to write and send the checks. We audit the books ourselves every three months. Sometimes he's like that grouchy Headmaster we had at the prep school in Lausanne. Then he sees Cat and changes like Hyde into Jekyll. However, I see a problem on the horizon. Has he mentioned babies to you?"

Nikolai finished his red wine cooler and before he could set the cut-crystal goblet on the glass-covered wrought-iron table, a male attendant brought a silver pitcher and refilled both glasses. "I'm not sure he's told her about his vasectomy. It's been about ten years since he had that surgery. Remember, we argued, told him he might change his mind one day, tried to get him to wait. 'I don't ever want children.' He was so emphatic." Nikolai hesitated. "You know something. Tell me."

Zack related the story as Xander had told him. At The Compound, Cat had become friendly with Flora, who worked in the house and had two small children. He watched as Cat read, carried them, made cookies to have a tea party, and knew the subject would come up again soon. Before they were married, she asked him if they would have a baby. He answered, "Yes, we will have babies," because he knew that's what she wanted.

When Xander let Zack know what he had said to her, Zack didn't ask how he intended to accomplish it. He saw that Xander was upset, but thought adoption and in vitro were options.

Also, Xander had just gone through an anguishing experience. He told Zack, who had stored details and now repeated them to Nikolai—

Remembering a previous girlfriend who was a nurse in an abortion clinic, Xander contacted her, they met, his problem spilled out.

She rested her elbow on the coffee shop table, held her forehead with the palm of her hand, remembering he had helped her years ago when she had carelessly gotten herself in deep debt, her condominium threatened with foreclosure. She offered to pay back the money, but he had smiled and said, "It's a gift."

"I might be able to help you, Xander. I'm married to one of the doctors in the clinic. If he found out I told you this, he would be terribly angry. We never divulge names of patients. Last week a beautiful young girl came to the clinic with her boyfriend, two perfect specimens of the human race. He reminded me of you, a blond version."

They looked at each other, thinking of years past. Of all the women he had known, she was the one who stayed in the back of his mind, but he had felt something wasn't right or maybe it wasn't perfect enough, or maybe he wasn't ready. The relationship changed to friendship. *I helped her because she was an honorable, considerate person and I cared about her.*

She continued, "They waited too long to have the procedure at our clinic. The doctors are strict about late abortions. I'll get their names and how you can reach them. Perhaps she will give birth and give the child up for adoption."

Xander found the ten-year-old Camaro parked in front of the address written on a sheet from a memo pad with the heading "Your Body—Your Choice." A young couple were sitting in the front seat, she was crying. Xander tapped on the driver's-side window. The window slid down.

"I would like to talk to you about the pregnancy." The window quickly went up. Xander held an open stuffed envelope up to the closed glass and shuffled his thumb across $100 bills. The window glided down. A young handsome face, tousled blond hair, soft-blue eyes, looked up at Xander with a questioning expression.

"Come sit in my car, let's talk."

The beautiful couple sat in the back seat, Xander turned around from the front and spelled out the proposition. If she would give birth to the child, they could keep the $30,000 now, then he would bring $20,000 when he picked up the baby.

They wanted to talk about it, both went to his car, Xander waited. The young man walked back to Xander's car alone, got in the front seat. "We would like the $50,000 now. And I need proof that the money is real."

Xander smiled. He loved the bargainer, the skeptic, placed the heavy envelope in a hand big enough to encase a football. "Go to the gas station and fill up, pick a bill from the middle to pay. They know how to check for counterfeit money and always test $100 bills. $20,000 will be delivered to you this afternoon." He left his private cell number, instructions for the surrogate mother to eat properly, exercise, and no drugs. He wrote the football player's cell number on a small pad, would call them weekly.

The calls were brief. "Yes, she's feeling fine." "All is well, no problems." "I'm at work, talk later." "She's impatient, a little grouchy." Then an operator message saying that cell number had been disconnected. Xander told Joaquin the story. He and three old friends went to find them.

Xander quietly listened to Joaquin's report. "They had driven to Tijuana for the abortion. She transferred to Berkeley, bought new matching bicycles for herself and her new boyfriend, displays an enviable, tasteful wardrobe, looks good enough to be Campus Queen, according to sorority sisters. He's enrolled at UCLA, on a football scholarship, drives a new blue Camaro that matches his eyes, paid $15,000 down, works part time at a men's clothing store catering to rich college kids, in demand at sorority parties and, my god, he's a good-looking kid, cocky, too."

Disappointment, then anger, gripped Xander. He thought of how young people could be naive, single-minded, no thought of the consequences, especially when handed $50,000 cash. He held himself in check. "They're not bad, just young and stupid, but they must pay for a bold act of thievery against me." He didn't mention their deception, he was guilty of that himself. "They don't comprehend what they've done because I made it too easy for them. Joaquin, just teach them a lesson. Take them to the ATM and get the rest of their money, even if it takes a couple trips. Have your chop-shop friends pick up his car, take the bicycles, all the clothes from both apartments, shave their heads, and break his leg. No football this year."

"It will take a little blood to convince them to give up money, but I'm a good convincer."

"Remind them who and why and how lucky they are to be alive. Joaquin, it's not the money, it's the baby I wanted. I would have given them three times what I paid. Set them free, with their lesson learned. They will have a lot of explaining to do about why all that happened to them, why someone took revenge."

The story left Nikolai silent. He wasn't bothered by the revenge, but thought about how he could help their friend. He walked to a rose in full bloom, grabbed a handful of petals, and tossed them on Zack's chest. "Remember when you wanted us to leave our suite before you got back from a date because you were bringing a girl to your room? Xander and I picked roses and scattered the petals on your bed."

"She thought I had done that and deemed it quite romantic. Did I thank you for the help?" Their memories were alive for all three friends, their bond unfaltering. This was the other side of strong, domineering, controlling, overbearing, authoritative men. Only with each other, they felt comfortable showing their opposite side.

"Let's walk, I want to tell you something," Nikolai said. Clouds were gathering, a breeze swirling around the car-size, fragrant bushes of finished-blooming Moscow lilacs, covering the grass with white, pink, purple miniature petals. It would be a cool evening. The two friends, more like brothers, walked side by side on the rambling flagstone path, not needing to talk, grateful to be together. Nikolai was collecting information stored in his mind.

"Zack, let me present this idea to you, a supposition. As we finally learned last week, Nadia is almost eight months pregnant. She has kept this secret to spring out and pressure you into taking her to Mexico. I know you're doubtful, not convinced the child is yours, but let's think about this. It's simple to determine paternity: a blood draw from the female, a collection of buccal cells on the inside of the cheek, using a special swab, from the male. Also, there are two safe, scientific ways to determine genetic abnormalities: an amniocentesis, a small amount of fluid that surrounds the fetus is removed with a needle, and it will also give the sex of the fetus with one hundred percent accuracy, if anyone is interested. I would like to recommend these tests. First, if you are not the biological father, it's over. We won't think about it. But, if you are the biological father and the genetic test is normal, are you interested in raising the child?"

"I do not want a woman in my house, nor do I want children. If I had planned to have this child, I would take responsibility for it, be a father. However, I was duped, deceived, tricked. I am furious at her. If I am the biological father, I'll send money to support the child."

"Just suppose the tests are all in a positive way. The child has your genes, no abnormalities, and there is no mother or father. Would you consent to Xander claiming the child, assuming the responsibilities of father, taking the child home to Cat?"

"Nikolai, this is crazy!"

"Yes."

"First, there is a mother. She is going to keep this kid to hold over my head for the rest of my life."

"Nadia is very ill. Her problem is a respiratory system illness. She has never taken care of herself until now, but it's too late. As of yesterday I received a message that she has bacterial pneumonia. Antibiotics are not effective treatment and I won't allow them to give her other drugs that might go to the fetus, trying to keep it safe, healthy until we could have this discussion. I asked to be kept up to date on her condition, waiting to talk to you. To carry the child to full term, the doctors recommend total rest. I could have her hospitalized until the child is born, if she lives that long."

The two men looked at each other, absorbing the existing circumstance, then sat heavily on the ornate garden bench. "Nikolai, we all live together in a compound. A kid running around, mine, but not mine. I don't know if I could handle it. It would change my entire life."

"It would be a challenge, but a life change is always a good thing. We get stale. Look at me, mold is starting to grow on my feet. And think of the happiness you would give to Cat. Everyone loves her for a reason, she's a genuinely good person. It's simple: You would be Uncle Zack. I can see you in that role." He punched Zack in the arm, rubbed his hand. "You have steel in there?"

"And what about the truth?"

"My dear friend, I know this to be true. If you live with a lie long enough, to your mind, the lie will become truth."

CHAPTER XIV
To Help A Friend Is Your Reward

The day after arriving home from their honeymoon, Xander continued his morning schedule. By 6:00 a.m. he was in his private gym using equipment he had chosen for his unvarying one-hour routine, then shower and breakfast meeting with The Team at 7:30. Afterward, Xander went with Zack to his office and together they checked expenses, salaries, balancing the books with the income from Russia.

Lunch was with Cat. Malita, of the house staff, daily made a huge clay pot of stew for the in-house and garden workers. Sometimes, Cat would ask for a bowl, especially if Malita made green chili chicken stew. Usually, Xander picked up two plates, one in a warmer, from the kitchen where Chef prepared a rare sirloin with baked potato for him and a salad for Cat. Months ago he asked Chef to put salmon or sliced steak on her salad. She had pointed a finger at Xander. "Your body needs the big hunk of protein. My body is quite satisfied with veggies or stew for lunch. I will eat some fish for dinner. Don't be difficult about this."

He suppressed a smile, loving the feisty side of her.

Cat was given a Team Phone, a modified cell like her original safe-phone but with an earphone like The Team wore, connected to a small pocket battery pack, and special buttons to communicate with each Team member instantly and directly. She had been told by Hitch, who made it and taught her how to use it, "Never hesitate to call any of us, especially if you suspect even a small bit of danger."

Not surrounding like music from the intercom/music system, but inside her ear, Cat heard a short, sweet melody. Finding the pack in the pocket of her gathered, full, pale-pink-roses-embroidered skirt, the button next to Sarge's name lit up. She pressed Receive and heard barking in the background. "I showed her your picture, told her you are home, and she's standing at the gate barking, calling you, I think, watching for you."

"I'm on my way." Instead of taking her golf cart, she ran on the cart path to Sarge's kennel. The dog had been taught to not jump up. When she knelt, they pressed cheeks. The German shepherd puppy she had picked out of the litter, visited through the year, was a strong grown-up dog. Sarge started training her for guard duty at a young age, but never told Cat she was to be hers.

Now he said, "She is my wedding gift to you. She knows your name and understands she is your protector, your guard dog. What do you want to name her?"

"Her coat is lighter brown now, her eyes like caramel candy, she's grown so much and is so beautiful. I'll call her Bella. Can she go home with me?"

"Yes. Bella, go home with Cat." The dog walked to the gate, looking back, waiting for Cat to join her.

"She is the smartest dog I have ever instructed. I used your picture and she knew who I was talking about. Her vocabulary is about seventy-five words and she'll learn more from you."

Cat kneeled to hug Bella, tears spilling down her face, and felt a raspy tongue wiping them away. She rose to put her arms around Sarge. "Thank you. I never had a pet."

"Bella is more than a pet, she's your protector. If she feels you are threatened, she could break bones with her jaws, even kill if she saw a knife or gun pointed in your direction." Like a coyote, Bella knew to go for the jugular vein. A wild dog will attack and do damage, a coyote will kill. "Both of you come see me tomorrow. I'll tell you everything Bella understands, commands if you feel trouble around you. She may sense a problem before you. She is a loyal friend."

"So am I."

Joaquin and Oso drove Cat and Bella to the tourist market every week, ten minutes in one of The Compound Hummers, longer if they took a Compound golf cart. She bought silver earrings, beaded bracelets, embroidered stoles, for her sister and girlfriends. It wasn't the buying that Cat looked forward to, she liked the interaction with the women. They were merchants, selling goods from a factory or handmade by family members. She was fascinated with the method young mothers used to carry infants. Their *rebozo* (shawl) became a sling, crossed over one shoulder, ends meeting in the front, tied into a knot, creating a pouch, the baby's head at the other shoulder, leaving hands free to show their merchandise.

The tourists come on buses, a full-day tour, from the resorts along the Sea of Cortez. Sonora, known for producing the tender beef sought by the resort chefs, built the highway along the vast ranches, giving views of the vaqueros tending the bulky masses of herds. Though much of Sonora is desert, it is more humid than dry, with a four- to five-month rainy season. The orchards flourish with avocados, mangos, and far-reaching acres of many varieties of table grapes. The wheat fields, golden ripe, sway as one, like a surf moving in and out. Each ranch or farm is an oasis, incongruously thriving in the midst of the desert.

Flooding the town, tourists bargain for silver jewelry with turquoise known as the best in Mexico. The market consists of individual stands, a tarp stretched across the top of four posts with sides that can be rolled up and secured with rope. The town charges the vendors rent for the small patch of earth in a large park with trees and flowering shrubs. Their profit is very little, but it helps support the family.

"Oso, we should build a permanent market, rows of adobe structures containing separated stores and give them to the families. What do you think?"

"That would be a very ambitious project."

Cat drew diagrams of her planned adobe market. The roof would be elevated with vigas above the walls to let a hopeful breeze wander through, but every unit would have a ceiling fan. A double-wide screen door with scrolled wrought iron in the back for bringing in merchandise from a much-used pickup, a front wall of fold-open gates, permanent shelves and counters, and *bancos* for waiting husbands who are always looking for a place to sit while their wives shop. She smiled to herself.

"Xander, will you go to the Town Council and buy a few acres near town for the new tourist market? The place of the current market could become a lovely park, benches to sit under a tree and eat *elote* (corn on the cob coated with butter and chili powder, served on a stick). Oso, Joaquin, and I always get tacos of thin strips of pork and pineapple or tostadas, crispy fried tortillas piled with *frijoles refritos*"—(refried beans)—"cheese, and fried meat."

None of those foods would be on Xander's list that he would want her to eat, and from an outdoor market! But she was enjoying the experience.

"You should go with us and try these wonderful local foods. Even Chef visits the market to get ideas to make for the students."

"Maybe I'll do that." He smiled at his wife, knowing he would go with her, eat whatever she asked him to eat, he loved her too much to put a damper on her enthusiasm. And yes, he would go to the Town Council with an offer for some land to build a market for the women who had touched her heart.

He took Zack to City Hall to help negotiate for land and a permit to build. The Town Council was not friendly to the rich American, even if his friend was from Mexico. "Our land is not for sale. We will give each tenant a ninety-nine-year lease on their measured piece, payable each year."

Zack answered, angry at the insolence. "We will pay the ninety-nine years in advance. The families should have the right to pass their property on to relatives. Draw up the leases, we'll bring the money next week. And we also will need a building permit. You do realize we are doing this for the families in your town, not for ourselves."

They walked out of the office to the Hummer and to Oso anxiously waiting to hear the results. "Oso, where do you think they learned about ninety-nine-year leases?"

"The head honcho lived in California with relatives for several years, worked and went to school there."

Xander laughed. "We were outsmarted, but Cat will be happy with her project."

Zack was thinking of Cat's considerate, generous, thoughtful act for people less fortunate in this town. "I want to be part of this gift to the people, let me pay half of the lease money and half of the construction cost."

Oso looked at the men who were brothers to him. "I want to contribute, also. The Academy pays me too much money, stashed in the bank and invested with Zack's help. I support my mother and sister, but she tells me to put money away for my retirement."

"Keep your money, Oso. Zack and I inherited money and still, our friend Nikolai insists on paying us. We will need two good foremen to supervise the construction and supervise Cat, who will believe she is the foreman. Check with Joaquin, ask if he will be your partner. You won't have much spare time, juggling your classes and building this project, and I'm sure Cat will expect time on the practice range with her golf partner."

Cat, Xander, and Bella joined The Team two evenings each week for dinner in their dining room, separate from the students. Xander had asked their permission months ago, wanting them to know her and her to be comfortable with them. Now, she was relaxed and enjoyed the teasing and jokes.

One Team member joined the students each night to oversee proper manners, promote conversation in Spanish and English, and listen to their stories about growing up in Russia. When Xander and Zack would go to Mexico City, meet with the president of the bank who processed The Academy finances or to Zack's assistant accountant, Cat would join the students for dinner. They were polite and taught her words in Russian she hadn't yet learned from her tutor and corrected her pronunciation.

Bella never left Cat's side: at the golf range, in the dining rooms, or driving around the track with Joaquin, sharing the passenger seat in the Lamborghini. Fortunately, it was a convertible, which gave them a little more room. Bella's bed had been placed in a corner of Cat and Xander's bedroom, but she didn't approve of the location. With strong jaws, she grasped a mouthful of the cotton-stuffed rim and pulled her bed to the foot of Cat's side of the bed, putting herself between Cat and the bedroom door.

At the tourist market, Cat explained about the new market that would be built on land now being leveled by a huge Caterpillar bulldozer and owned by each family, no rent. The women put their hands on her arm, smiled, but doubted that the government would permit them ownership of their store and the land it was to be built on.

Cat felt their skepticism. They found it difficult to believe the town officials would help them. Never in their family history had they received assistance; on the contrary, the government took—taxes, fees, rent.

Not all the women at the market or in town liked Cat. Malita worked in Xander and Cat's house with other women including Flora, Cat's friend. Malita would admonish Flora with warnings. "You shouldn't trust her with your children. She wants a baby and is jealous of you because you have two. She may try to poison them." Or "She doesn't like you, only wants you to cook and clean." Or "All the dishes in the cabinets were here before she came. She doesn't know what or how much is here. We should take some home." Or "She buys beaded bracelets from my sister, not to wear, keeps them in little boxes. I'm going to take them back to my sister to sell again." Flora ignored her. *She just likes to hear herself talk. She's jealous of Cat who is so nice to her.*

After breakfast, Cat told Flora she and Bella were going out to run the arbored path around The Compound, inside the walls. Malita heard, and when Cat was out the door she headed for the master bedroom. Flora was cleaning the wooden parts of furniture with an oiled cloth.

Bella led Cat back inside the house. As they passed Flora, Cat said, "We didn't get very far, it's already too hot for these lightweight sweats. I'm going to change into shorts and a tee shirt."

Flora nodded, happy to be in the air-conditioned house. *My friend loves to exercise with her dog.*

Malita was standing at Cat's dresser, two drawers open. She closed the drawers and tried to pass Cat, who said, "Hold her, Bella." The large mouth bared teeth and gave a low warning growl. Malita backed against the wall.

The pockets of her apron were bulging. Cat put her hand in one pocket and it came up with a fist of little white boxes and silver hoop earrings clinging to her fingers.

Cat punched buttons on her Team Phone and sent a message. "Whoever has time, please come to the master bedroom. Bella is holding Malita against the wall." Sarge and Xander met, running, at the intersection of two cart paths coming from different directions, and ran the rest of the way to the house together. As they stepped into the bedroom, they were relieved to witness all under control. Sarge proudly looked at the animal he trained. "Good girl."

Bella knew her favorite treat always came after "Good girl." She would wait until relieved of duty. Familiar with Xander and Sarge, she still watched them out of the corner of her eye. Her allegiance was to Cat.

"What's the problem here?" Xander could barely contain himself.

Cat held her hand out, open, showing the loot from Malita's pocket, whose other pocket was protruding.

Joaquin stood in the doorway, quiet, watching, listening, a prowling cheetah. Instinctively knowing she had help, Bella relaxed, but kept watch on the woman.

Malita was sent home and told to never return to The Compound. Xander asked Flora to bring the house staff into the living room for a meeting. Joaquin, Oso, and Sarge joined them. They were told of Malita's attempted theft and asked if anyone could give information about her. It was not valuable merchandise, but it said something about her character. Xander wanted to dig deeper.

Flora volunteered a strange action that happened last month. She had entered the kitchen to get the requested bowl of stew for Cat's lunch and saw Malita sprinkling some yellow powder on top from a small unlabeled jar. She assumed it was a spice. Flora placed the bowl in front of Cat, who moved it between her and Xander and asked for another soup spoon so they could share the large serving. In the kitchen, as Flora retrieved the spoon, she casually mentioned both were going to have the stew. Malita quickly brushed by Flora, picked up the bowl and, in the kitchen, emptied it down the drain. She ladled stew into two smaller bowls without the added spice, and motioned Flora to serve.

Xander recalled the incident and now was upset with himself for not reading something into it.

Another housekeeper had seen a jar that contained several ugly centipedes. She thought someone had trapped them and was going to ask a gardener to kill them.

Cat and Xander remembered the night she saw a centipede run under her dresser. He sprayed insecticide under all the furniture in the bedroom. The next day he called pest control to spray the entire house and around the outside. Centipedes thrived in the Sonoran desert.

The male housekeeper, who managed the more difficult jobs of window cleaning, white-washing outside walls, roof repairs, spoke shyly. He had seen Malita and her husband talking to men in trucks he didn't recognize, near the construction area.

Cat sat quietly listening, rubbing Bella's head, ears, neck, hurt that Malita didn't like her. She would talk to Joe. Was this her failure, a staff member who didn't like her, or was she too trusting? Oso put his protective hand on her shoulder, letting her know she had a defense team, but also wanted her to stay aware.

Joaquin listened. Malita would not be adding yellow spice to Cat's bowl or collecting centipedes. Her husband would not be talking to strangers in unrecognizable trucks near Cat's new market, nor would they be returning to this house.

CHAPTER XV

You Can Try To Drown The Past, But It Always Floats To The Top

Zack was not at the 7:30 a.m. Team breakfast. Xander asked if anyone had seen him.

Joaquin was standing, holding his mug of coffee, a worried frown on his face. "Yesterday, when I told him I was going to take Amelia to Mexico City next weekend, he offered his condo to us and was to bring keys and remotes this morning. We are usually the first ones here by 7:00 to have our first coffee. He wasn't here at 7:15, I tapped on his office door and received a grumbling, 'Go away.'"

Xander pushed his chair back, quickly left the room. He opened Zack's office door and saw him staring out the window. Zack spoke without turning around. He knew who would come into his office without knocking. "How could we be so stupid? We go over our accounting pages, using half our brains. How did this get by us?"

"Sit down, Zack, what did you find?" He pulled the other office chair up to the oversized desk, next to the man his mind called brother, the one-third of the whole. Three men from three diverse countries, cultures, distinctly different yet distinctly alike. Strangely unusual, there was an external resemblance. From the back there was no difference in height, broad shoulders, stance. Internally they harbored a need for the companionship of one another from a young age, and it had grown stronger through the years.

Their eyes focused on the large screen. "I am sick about this, Xander, and I'm embarrassed to tell Nikolai I lost money he entrusted to us for The Academy expenses."

Zack's assistant accountant worked from his office in Mexico City in the same building as their bank. He received the spread sheets from Zack and sent the checks, paying the invoices. Unnoticed until now, items had been added to the invoices and paid, plus extra salaries.

"What kind of items? Salaries to people who don't work for us?" Xander queried.

"He direct-deposits an extra check every month for himself. His wife and two college kids are listed with our regular employees, names changed slightly, and each gets a monthly salary check. The gourmet grocer where Chef places an order every week, also makes a delivery to our accountant's house. The computer aerial view of the address shows the walled and gated house with Spanish-tiled roof, gardeners, and a four-car garage, in an upscale area outside Mexico City. I didn't think we paid him that well. We have many vehicles. The dealer obtained and finances them for us, a monthly payment. We regularly trade in vehicles, get new ones, the original list changing. Somewhere through the years, four expensive Mercedes got added to our invoice, included in our monthly payment, and those four cars are upgraded every two years. I don't know if the dealer is part of the scam or if the accountant convinced him it was okayed by us. Xander, I was too engrossed with my other job, handling our private investments. The Academy accounting didn't get proper attention."

Xander was not upset with Zack. He felt he was as much to blame for the oversight. "Both of us audited the books. We didn't examine the paid invoices closely enough. We hired an assistant accountant for you, paid him a very generous salary, thinking he would be grateful."

"*We* didn't hire him, I hired him, and I'm going to kill him."

"Zack, leave that to a professional, you'll hurt yourself. Get Joaquin in here, show him the thievery. He will be as distressed as we are and devise a plan to sell the house, cars, and take over the bank accounts. We'll get the money back."

The room was quiet. Zack glanced at Xander, put his hand on Xander's bare arm. "Fuck, this has triggered your spell. You're forcing yourself to talk calmly." He put his palm against Xander's forehead. "You are boiling and holding everything inside. I'm calling Oso to get your shot ready, put you under a cold shower, and get you to bed. Listen to me. Joaquin and I will take care of this."

Xander stood, dizzy, drums thumping at his temples. Oso received the call, rushed into the office, put a bear arm around the bundle of muscles, hurried him out the door before he was out of control. A golf cart was waiting, a student guard driver.

Inside the house, Xander held his head with both hands, keeping the volcanic eruption contained as Oso guided him toward the master bedroom, a cold shower to help the temperature recede and a potent, calming, chemical drug.

Cat and Bella watched. She recognized the symptoms and knew Xander was sinking into his sickness. *Why didn't he call me so I could get ready for his treatment?* She said, "Xander, go to the library." It was a calm but firm request like a teacher telling an unruly student to sit at his desk.

Xander stopped, stood still.

Oso's mind was processing the danger. Over the years he had seen Xander in this state: temperature rising to a dangerous degree, equilibrium threatening to fail, social disposition turning to anger, a wild-animal voice. The Team had seen him pick up chairs, smash them against walls. Joe could find no name for the illness, but had convinced Xander the temperature must be reduced with ice water, followed by a strong premixed tranquilizer injection and sleep. He counseled Xander after the outbreaks, Oso adding his well-read opinion. Digging deep, they realized something always triggered the outrage. They put him in a hypnotic state and learned the illness began when Xander was a child. The memories haunted him, he tried to bury them. An angry, unhappy, neurotic mother, swinging a belt, screaming at her children, him running to his room, burying his face in the pillow, hysterical, not understanding why. The Team carefully watched for his reaction when a problem was reported.

Oso was concerned for Cat's safety. The Team had witnessed this quick transformation and turned him over to Oso, who continued to study psychiatry with Joe, who sent him to classes, ordered home courses and books for him.

The struggle in Oso's mind lasted only a few seconds. The decision lasted less. *Is this the moment in my life when I must make a choice that will determine my future? Will I step aside and not interfere with his treatment of her? A blow to Bella's head with his powerful fist will knock her unconscious or kill her. Half that strength toward Cat—. No, I will not allow him to harm her. I will protect her with all my—*

Xander turned away from Oso's supporting arms, cut across the living room, Cat following, Oso hurrying to catch up, get between them. In the library she spread a sheet over a combination lounge-recliner while he undressed, tossed his clothes to a sofa. Before he leaned back, put his bare feet up, Cat brought two piles of different sized ice packs from a small built-in freezer to the side table. She slid a thermometer across his forehead, down the side of his face, announced quietly, "One-oh-four plus." She placed a small oblong contoured ice pack across his forehead down past his eyebrows, lifted his head to put an iced gel-pack under his neck, two large platter-sized packs across his chest and stomach. He raised his back and she slid another under his shoulders. Small packs were placed between his thighs, under his knees. She pulled on short socks with frozen gel soles. Holding bulky ice packs in her hands, she moved them slowly up and down his legs and arms. She pulled up a stool, sat at the back of his head, and began rubbing his temples in slow circular motions.

Bella lay in her bed, comfortable, but alert. Oso was standing a few feet away, taking in the scene. He noticed Xander's eyes were open slits under the forehead pack. He had been watching her, then closed his eyes again when she began the gentle massaging. *If we were in the office, this would be a different situation: growling, throwing chairs. I was afraid he would hurt her, but the sight of her affected him in a positive way. The anger probably still churns inside, but he is more relaxed. This ice pack treatment has been done many times, a routine she put together. But how did she know about his illness and how to treat it? Did he confide in her? Did she discover it accidentally?*

Near his ear she said something and the brawny chest swelled and released the air with deep breathing. Cat reached for the thermometer, ran it down the side of his face, told him "One-oh-two." He smiled, tilted his chin up, whispered, "Kiss," and she bent her head, kissed his lips upside down.

She smiled to herself, remembering the first time, when he sat with her at the highly polished Sonoran wood dining table, the thick rare steak on the ornate gold-decorated china plate in front of him. She had watched him: skin turning red, a pained expression, staring into space. She touched his face, it was frightfully hot. He said, "I need a cold shower." After his shower he was still hot. She remembered cold packs she had kept from ice cream shipments, saving them in the freezer. She placed them on his bare skin, got two huge capsules from his medicine cabinet he asked for. She slept next to him and awoke to see him on his elbow, looking at her. He told her about his illness and quietly came home to her when he felt it coming on. This time it happened too quickly, he didn't have time to call her and Oso was there to help him.

Cat retrieved another pile of ice packs from the freezer and replaced each around his body. She covered him with a thin cotton sheet, instructed him to sleep.

"Oso, give me a half dose. Order breakfast for yourself and my Cat." He took her hand from his shoulder, placed it over his heart. "Stay with me."

"I'll be here on the sofa next to you."

Oso's disease was different from Xander's, though Joe diagnosed them both under manic-depression, which, he said, was a broad diagnosis, it affected everyone differently. Oso would sink into himself, wanted no communication, unusually rude if disturbed, stayed in bed for days. Joaquin was the only one he allowed to bring him meals, no talking. Oso had discovered information about his depression in the medical books he read as a teenager. Sessions with Joe helped him understand more about it. He became Joe's student, reading, studying, discussing psychiatry.

With the loss of Zack's assistant accountant in Mexico City, he was overloaded with The Compound bookkeeping responsibilities and the investment decisions entrusted to him. At the Team meeting, Xander suggested Zack turn the entire Compound bookkeeping over to his accounting firm in LA.

Xander set up an appointment and Zack met the new accountant. Marshall, brilliant, young, single. He was unhappy at the previous firm he had worked with. It was small, a father and son business with no chance to move up, the salary raises limited. He applied to the Arthur Blake Accounting Firm, was hired, and impressed the company accountants. Xander called and asked that one accountant and an assistant be appointed to work exclusively for The Academy. Marshall was given the assignment .

When Cat left the firm, two weeks before she and Xander were married, she asked Mrs. Gilbert if she would be interested in interviewing her friend, Mona, for her job. Mona was hired, worked with Mrs. Gilbert, and kept her up to date about their favorite friend, Cat.

After his appointment with Marshall, Zack stopped at Mona's desk. He saw her often when she visited Cat. He asked if he could take her to lunch.

Eating a Cobb salad, Mona told him she was dating Marshall and was worried he might lose the assignment if the firm found out about her close relationship with Cat and Zander.

"What about your close relationship with me?"

It took her a minute to realize he was teasing.

Zack smiled at Cat's friend. The three girlfriends were so much alike, wanting to do the right thing. "No need to worry, Mona. The Team and your boss, Arthur Blake, are aware that you and Marshall are dating. Marshall is a very competent accountant, that's our only interest. I'm pleased to work with him. Both of you are welcome at The Compound anytime."

CHAPTER XVI
His Love Fills The Pores In Her Body

In the desert of Sonora, a cloudy sky suppressed the heat, a welcome rain promised. Cat, Bella, and Oso were at the driving range outside The Compound. Joaquin was speeding around the track in the Lamborghini, doing something to the engine to make it noisier when he passed in back of them, causing Cat to laugh. "Our Joaquin is such a bad boy."

Zack and Xander were having iced lattes in Cat's rose garden, admiring new species she had ordered from a catalog. They sat in two lovely, but uncomfortable, white iron garden chairs, shifting the cushions. "I need to order some chaise lounges. This would be the perfect place for a nap."

A wide arbor was covered with climbing white roses tinged with pink, up two sides and across the arched top. It was a pleasant shady spot when the sun had mean intent. Today the roses seemed to sigh with relief, looked toward the clouds, waiting.

Both men had received a call from Nikolai informing them the baby was three weeks old, healthy, beautiful, ready to travel.

Zack had agreed that Cat could raise the child as her own, Xander the father. He was still insisting he wanted to move back home to Mexico City and work from there. Like close brothers, they disagreed, argued, laughed, depended on each other, wallowed in their friendship.

"I want you to continue living here in The Compound with us, Zack," Xander said. "We need you. With time you will accept that the child is Cat's and mine. You won't be left out, Uncle Zack." Xander smiled, bumped his shoulder. "Don't feel guilty. You would have left the child in Russia to be put in an orphanage and adopted by someone who may have abused him. You will be making Cat a happy mother and the child will have a good home."

"How do you feel about it, Xander? Every time you look at him, will you be thinking he came from me?"

"I'm glad you brought that up. I'm going to tell you exactly how I feel. Because he is part of you, I will love him as I love you—no pretense, unconditional."

Both men were quiet, thinking of the bond that held them together for so many years.

"What did she say when you told her I was the biological father?"

"She was suspicious, she wanted to know if I was the father. That's my no-nonsense Cat, gets right to the core. I related the true story to her."

Xander had asked Cat to have an after-dinner Kahlúa in the library. He had wanted to surprise her, bring the baby from Russia and hand him to her. He loved buying her things, surprising her with them, but realized this was too serious, needed a discussion. He told her about Nadia and Zack, explained that it wasn't a love affair, only sex. Nadia wanted Zack to bring her to Mexico, he told her that was not possible, but she didn't give up. She had a plan to get pregnant. After sex, many times she would offer to flush the Kleenex-wrapped condom in the toilet. Instead, she squeezed the sperm into her vagina by rolling the condom down to make a small cup, inserted it into her vagina, and emptied the sperm by pushing it out with two fingers. Her scenario was successful. When she announced her pregnancy, five months into term, past time for an abortion, Zack was furious. The necessary paternity tests were performed, proving he was the biological father. He refused to have a girlfriend, a wife, or a child in his house. He said he would send support money to the mother. Further complicating the situation, Nadia was quite ill, a respiratory system illness, a fatal pulmonary condition, which left her weak with difficulty breathing and her system more strained with pregnancy. In her eighth month, Nikolai had her hospitalized to keep her alive, at least until Zack decided what to do with the child. She died the day after giving birth. Nikolai talked to him about allowing Cat and Xander to adopt the child if Cat agreed.

She asked, "Do you think I am not going to get pregnant with a baby of our own?"

Xander flinched. The secret he had kept from her was ready to burst out, an intense noise, swirling inside his head. He thought, *I must calmly explain the truth she deserves to know.* He stalled, held the face he loved with both hands, looked into her eyes, the secret was hidden so deep, but it was ready to come out. "I'm sorry I never told you. More than ten years ago I had a vasectomy." The words were rushing out. He gulped the Kahlúa, felt nervous. "I didn't want children then or to ever marry. When we were together I felt differently. I thought I could take care of it, vasectomies can be reversed. However, at the clinic the tests revealed I had low sperm count and a low percentage chance of producing enough sperm for you to become pregnant with our baby. Then this opportunity came up."

Cat began to cry. Xander put his arms around her, rocking her, talking softly, "Please forgive me for not being truthful. I love you, you keep me alive, I live for you."

She remembered assuming that pregnancy happens when it's planned, then the months passed and she was not pregnant. Her friends were encouraging, "Sometimes it takes a few months." She started to think about going to a fertility clinic. It had to be her fault, he was so masculine. Now she faced reality. He had lied to her, let her believe they would have children. *I must either accept his confession or end this relationship, which I know I will not do. Love is a strong bond. It even holds a broken heart together.* Maybe he was afraid he would lose her if she knew the truth. *I love him. It's a decision that will change our lives. I will not pass up this opportunity to become a mother.*

With quiet tears spilling out, she gave him a little smile. "Do you want to raise the child with me?"

"Yes, I do. I want him to be our boy. Can you accept him as ours?"

His love poured over her, filling the pores in her body. "Yes, I want him, Xander."

Zack and Xander decided the cushions on the white iron chairs were not padded enough to comfort their heavy bodies. They stood and started down the walking path.

"I know Cat. Believe me, Zack, she will bundle her child in a mother's love. Our only complaint will be that she overly spoils him."

"Someday, he will need to know the truth—about his biological parents." He stared out, seeing nothing, feeling numb. "Xander, I'm so angry about the deceit and my carelessness."

"Zack, whether he is here or in Russia, you still have to live with the knowledge that he exists. Be happy you are giving him a good life. And yes, we will tell him the truth when it's time. Joe and Oso will help us."

Xander usually didn't tell Cat he was going to Russia, meeting with Nikolai and his cabinet with reports concerning The Academy, until the day before. She worried about his safety, flying across the ocean, lectured him about calling her every day. She would put her arms around his neck. "I miss you too much."

This time he was going to Moscow for the business meeting and to bring their baby home. He told her he would be leaving in three days. They would have time to discuss more of their life-changing event. She told him she would stay home, order furniture, infant clothes, prepare for their baby. Also she wanted the time to talk to her friends and May, tell them how it came to be and get their thoughts.

After dinner, sitting outside under the arbor of climbing roses, sipping Kahlúa, Xander put his arm around Cat's shoulders. "Have you thought of a name for our boy?"

She smiled. "That's a happy thought. Do you have a name for him?"

"Yes, I would like to call him Alex, the other half of my name."

"That's perfect. I'm sure he will like it. I do."

She asked Joe if he would pick up Amelia and Mona to stay with her and help get ready for Alex's arrival. She called May to talk about this change in her life. May was working in Chicago with the lawyers from her office and wouldn't be able to join her sister yet.

Everyone knew Cat waited every month to announce she was pregnant. The Mexican women at the market looked at her with sadness, comforting her as she sat on the *banco* and held their babies. "When you least expect it, one day you wake up with morning sickness."

Xander, Joe, Oso, and four students flew to Russia, the students logging flight hours. They would have two days with family and a day with President Ivanov and some cabinet members, giving their opinion of learning at The Academy, their readiness for the job of bodyguarding. Some of the students had served in the Russian military or had been trainees in the FSB or SVR (Federal Security Service or External Intelligence Service) at the Kremlin.

Joaquin was in charge of entertaining the ladies: a day at the beach with a few students, who were bodyguards, golf lessons from the pro that Oso brought in every month, rides and driving the Lamborghini.

Even though building the new market was still in progress, the adobe walls were up, roofs overhead, the women moved into their claimed space, no rent to the city. The counters and showcases weren't yet installed, they used their folding tables from the old market. The women didn't want to charge Cat's friends, but she asked them to leave money on the table. She excitedly told her friends at the market her baby was arriving from Russia. They began crocheting light blankets, sweaters, booties, for cool evenings.

Chef prepared a four-course dinner for Cat and her friends to enjoy in the formal dining room of her home. They dressed in their new white peasant blouses and full gathered skirts, hand embroidered with birds and blue morning glories or vines of yellow roses or stocks of cerise hollyhocks. New silver hoops dangled from their ears.

The eight students remaining at The Academy asked Chef to let them be waiters for the ladies. He gave them a lesson on how to serve his preparations. There was much overacting, causing much laughter.

For the tortilla soup, each handmade, hand-painted bowl contained crisp-fried tortilla strips and julienne vegetables. Individual creamer-sized copper pitchers contained the soup, which was poured into the bowls with great flair. At each place setting, blue-corn muffins were placed on a side plate with a small ball of butter.

The salad, fresh spinach leaves, sliced strawberries, walnuts, in a hand-carved oversized wooden bowl, was wheeled to the table on a serving cart. The salad dressing, strawberry balsamic, was dramatically poured and tossed, the salad put on matching, hand-painted plates, and served with a handsome smile.

The main course was boned trout, on wild rice with honeyed carrots. One of the students poured wine, Louis Latour Chardonnay, a white napkin across his arm, and spoke French to them. "*Voulez vous encore dec vin, Mademoiselle?*" They responded, "*Oui,*" and laughed like schoolgirls.

Dessert was a scooped-out orange filled with orange gelato. The waiters invited them to sit in the living room where they were served ginger tea with a lemon cookie. The Academy students left them to enjoy their friendship.

Cat told them she wanted to share the details of her baby, arriving from Russia, and that she was a little scared.

They had always discussed anything that might be causing anxiety for one of the friends. Amelia assured her, "We specialize in mincing all worries and scattering them in the wind."

Cat was comfortable releasing troubling thoughts. They had gathered for sessions of helping each other ease their worries through five years of companionship. She repeated Xander's admission of his vasectomy and the discovery of his low sperm count when he tried to have it reversed. Then the pregnancy of Nadia, Zack's anger at the deceit, and Nikolai's suggestion for Xander and her to adopt the child.

The opinions went back and forth. They agreed: "Love is primary, takes priority, and Xander loves her totally, wants the baby for her."

They talked until their heads nodded and Cat announced, "It's bedtime. My friends, you are steel supports. Let's awake to a new day."

Hitch, in the communications room, received the message everyone had been waiting for. The Team's plane had landed on the Air Force strip in Arizona for some inside repairs and refueling. Xander, Oso, Joe, and the four students transferred to the helicopter, arriving in one hour, landing on the helipad inside The Compound. As they got closer, Xander's voice came through The Team's phones. "Bring Cat to meet us."

Sarge and Joaquin found the women laughing, talking, walking on the arbored path around the inside of The Compound wall. Bella saw them first, took a few steps ahead of Cat. Sarge was happy to see the dog he trained, seriously being Cat's protector. He gave the message to the ladies. "Come to the courtyard, watch the helicopter land."

Cat's Team Phone played her chosen tune from *Phantom of the Opera*. It was a text from Xander. "We love you more than all the stars in the night sky." She ran to the courtyard, wanting to get the first glimpse of the helicopter above her. Sarge walked with Mona, Joaquin put his arm around Amelia as they tried to catch up with Cat and Bella.

The roar of the helicopter put excitement in the air, drew everyone's attention upward. Amelia moved close to Cat, put an arm around her shoulders, feeling a little tremble.

Zach was in his office, five empty moving cartons stacked against the wall next to his favorite painting, a Jackson Pollock of sporadic swirls and lines, drips and splashes of black, gray, white, and yellow. He heard the muffled thunder of The Academy helicopter. *I should leave, what is keeping me from packing my office stuff in those boxes?*

The loud motor stopped. A wave of sadness rushed over him like a waterfall. *I wish I could run to my room and hide in the closet. My father always found me and made everything all right.*

The rotor stopped circling. Xander stepped down onto the helipad, a blue blanket package snug in one arm. Amelia put her arm around Cat's waist and ran with her to Xander. He opened the blanket flap and showed her the baby boy. "This is our son, Alex."

Tears streamed from her eyes and ran down her cheeks. Everyone was watching. Everyone except Zack.

Xander held the bundle out to her, she cradled him in one arm, moved the blanket ends aside to look at his face, head, body, arms, hands, and whispered to him, "You are my baby, Alex. I am your mommy."

Xander smiled. *And the possessiveness begins.*

She showed him to Mona, Amelia, and Joaquin. She bent over to let Bella meet him. "This is Alex, our baby. You must help me care for him. He will love you." She walked around the courtyard, introducing him to The Team, the students, who talked to him in Russian. He opened his eyes, perhaps recognizing the language and thinking he would answer them soon.

Cat looked around. "Where's Zack?"

Xander put his arm around her shoulders. "Let's go inside. Zack will see him later."

She hardly slept, afraid she wouldn't wake to feed him. Next to her side of the bed was a white wicker bassinet. She pulled it closer, held on to the side, as if it might roll away.

The next morning Joe, Joaquin, and three students flew Amelia and Mona to the small airport south of LAX. Joaquin drove them to their apartments in the Hummer that stayed at the airport. He remained with Amelia a couple hours to explain why he hadn't let her know about Alex. "I wanted to let Cat tell you the background as Xander had told her."

"We FaceTimed May to meet her nephew. Cat showed her sister the arms, legs, feet, toes of her boy. We're happy for Cat and she is elated with her baby."

Joaquin admitted he had been a little worried. "You never know how something this big is going to play out. The Team is proud of the way Xander handled it, letting Cat know the truth, from Alex's beginning."

Joaquin told Amelia when they could be together again. "I'm busy with the students the next two weeks—it's testing time. Then we can take a long weekend trip. I will call you every night, *mi amor*. Decide where you would like to go, someplace extravagant, like Quebec or New York. I'll get ballet tickets."

Cat had carefully considered the necessary baby furniture: bassinet, crib, changing table, chest of drawers, to be filled with onesies and diapers. Next to the master bedroom were two rooms, his and hers offices. Xander had taken over one and used the other for overflow files, boxes neatly labeled, filled with bank statements, investment accounts his father had kept. He brought them to The Compound, thinking he would have time to go through them, but he hadn't opened them yet. "I don't know why I keep those papers, all the information is accessible in the computer and I'm sure our accountant has copies. Throw them out. Make room for our boy."

An alcove in the master bedroom had an ornate French-style desk where Cat kept her laptop. "I don't need an office. I like this cozy space."

Sarge, Hitch, and Geoff placed the furniture in the emptied office next to the master bedroom. It seemed to Cat that everyone wanted to have a part in her baby's life. The men looked at the new nursery.

"A few pictures and I think Alex will like his room."

"Let's get some posters of Iron Man."

"Those aren't baby pictures."

Cat laughed.

Xander and Cat were in the library, she changed Alex, fed him a bottle of formula, Bella supervising. Xander smiled, gratified to see her so content. He told her he wanted to talk to her after she finished with Alex. Xander watched, waiting for him to burp and fall asleep. She held him, letting him sleep on her shoulder.

"I would like you to call Nikolai who will verify what I have told you and add his part. Also, I must tell you that Zack is quite conflicted about bringing Alex to The Compound. Nikolai helped me convince him Alex would have an excellent mother and be raised in a loving home. Still, he talks about moving back home to Mexico City."

She thought about Zack, feeling he had never been as friendly to her as the rest of The Team, but Xander explained, it's just his personality. "I understand why it will be difficult for Zack, seeing Alex grow up, wanting him to have stayed in Russia with his biological mother, feeling he was tricked with his conception. When she died he was probably angry he was left with the decision, what to do about his biological child, perhaps wanting his only responsibility to be financial support. I am Alex's mother now, he must accept that. He can't run away from us. The reality of one's past is permanent and inescapable."

The next morning was quiet in The Team's breakfast room. They weren't able to freely discuss the "Compound baby" yet, not wanting

Zack to be uncomfortable. He didn't meet their eyes, ate quickly, and returned to his office. He opened two of his computers, checking the stock exchange tape, the other on the page listing his investments. He was disturbed by a knock on his door, impatiently, with a grouchy voice, loudly asked, "Who is it?"

Cat opened the door, her baby nestled in a colorful *rebozo*, his head over her heart. She was edgy, not knowing how Zack would react—angry?—wondering if she was doing the right thing, yet determined in her mission. She shut the door behind her. "I brought Alex to meet you."

"Alex?"

"Yes, Xander wanted him to have the rest of his name, he says they are one." She easily scooped the baby out of the comfortable sling, wearing a new sky-blue onesie, held him to Zack's chest. He wanted to back away, but folded his arms, held the child with one hand under his infant shoulders, fingers supporting his head, the other hand under his butt and looked at the infant, seeing a reflection of himself.

Cat could feel his discomfort. "Isn't he the most beautiful baby in the whole world? Look at his perfect eyebrows and nose and lips from a baby magazine ad. I'm going to lecture every girlfriend, tell her she is not allowed to touch him, certainly no kissing." She looked up into Zack's eyes. "He's my boy, Zack."

"Yes, I see that."

She looked at the moving boxes, the bare wall. "I know this is difficult for you. Everyone knows the circumstances. I talked to Nikolai. He says you will be proud of your decision. Zack, you must not leave us, we need you. Promise you'll stay, help me, be here for us during the hard times, watch him grow up, see his first steps, first tooth." She looked at Zack's face, his lips were a match to Alex's. *He is the birth father of this child.* The tears she had been trying to hold back spilled out, running down her cheeks. He moved the baby to his bent arm, gently wiped her tears with his fingers. He felt a tear on his own face, she caught it with one finger. He looked into her eyes and experienced that feeling he always had for her, a feeling he wanted to escape from. Now, he would never find the strength to leave.

CHAPTER XVII
Stars Wink At Lovers Everywhere

When Alex arrived from Russia, Amelia had been coming to The Compound every weekend to be with Joaquin. She helped Cat care for the baby, insisting she nap and allow her to give Alex his bottle of formula. Monday mornings, Joaquin took her back to LA.

The Team teased him during the week, calling him "The Lovesick Guy."

The lovers talked every night. He sent flowers and wrote poetry that he showed to his brothers for approval. "Sounds like love to us," someone said.

To Amelia

I close my eyes,
stand in a fog, remembering
the sound of your voice,
gentle, sweet, like a caress,
reaching into my soul.

I dream of your heart
pressing against my heart,
the same rhythmic beat
singing to me,
becoming our song.

Without you
I'm a barren well, depleted,
a body with no breath,
a lamp gone dark,
my spirit has left me.

Come, put the rainbow
back in my life,
bring the lilt of music
to my morning,
put the million stars
in my night.

The florist delivered the poem with one long-stemmed perfect white rose, a white satin ribbon tied around the white box. She called him when it arrived. He told her he would come to LA to get her, asked if she would like to stay the night at Tierra Encantado before coming to The Compound.

Joaquin proposed marriage on the balcony of their suite, kneeling, eyes filled with tears. It was a warm California night, the moon a picturesque sliver, stars winking at lovers everywhere.

At The Compound, she showed her engagement ring, a two-carat oval diamond, small diamonds surrounding and halfway down the sides. She held a hand over her mouth to stifle the giggles.

Amelia, an only child, asked her friends to help select a wedding gown from a California designer's new line. They made some changes and arranged an appointment for a fitting. Cat, Matron of Honor, Mona and May, bridesmaids, selected fiesta dresses: strong colors of plum, raspberry, blueberry, a wide ruffle around the top, off the shoulder, the skirt of gathered tiers, ending at the calf with lace.

Joe and students picked up Mona, Amelia's parents, some aunts and cousins, Joaquin's mother, and some old friends Joaquin stayed in contact with. They flew to Toledo to get May and Marco, and their daughter. He refused to fly in the "too-small airplane" and would not allow their daughter to be "endangered," either. Once again, May was alone for an important occasion.

Cat, Mona, and May dressed the bride, taking over the master bedroom. They clipped a pearl tiara on top of a mass of red spirals and placed the wide neckline off her shoulders. Mona took pictures to send to the designer. "These photos should go to *Bride Magazine*." The friends held her arms and the trailing white silk gown, escorted her to the colorful courtyard, readied for the festival. Joaquin stood with The Team and three of his old friends from the streets of LA. He cried through the ceremony, they offered their handkerchiefs.

The wedding, at The Compound, was a fiesta. Three groups of mariachi bands played in turn, piñatas hung between lights strung across the courtyard. Chairs and tables covered with colorful serapes were set up under the expansive portal, trays of local food brought out continuously.

Joe looked for May and found her crying, off by herself, looking at the festive lights, drowning in the music and laughter. He put his arms around her, kissed her damp cheeks, drew her body close, kissed her softly, whispered, "You are too wonderful to cry, too beautiful to be alone, come home with me. I want you to know what it feels like to be appreciated."

The psychology talks with Joe helped May cope with her personal problems at home. When she came to The Compound to visit her sister, she and Joe would have therapy sessions in his office. Joe would ask a few questions about Marco, then let her vent frustrations.

She shared little with Cat, not wanting her to know of the unhappiness dwelling in her home. Her advice always ended the same: "Let's get rid of the narcissistic bum." Cat asked if she and Marco had sex. She answered, "Seldom. He told me I don't know how."

May was afraid Marco would take their daughter, Monica, and not allow May to see her. He had told May, "I will let the judge know you travel, you're never home, you're an unfit mother, I have raised her. The court will award her to me and you will pay me child support and palimony." She thought, *I want to support my child, how do I get rid of you?*

He had convinced her to buy a house in a nice area that needed some fixing up. He said he would do the renovation and then they could sell it for a big profit. She borrowed the down payment with a second mortgage on her townhouse. Within the week after the sale was final, his mother and two sisters moved into the investment house. May paid the mortgage, taxes, insurance, and the utilities were to be paid by the sisters. She received notice of unpaid electricity bills and it was going to be shut off. Cat said, "Don't pay. If the electricity gets shut off, they will pay the bill next month." May paid the back bills, not wanting to upset Marco.

In their eight years of marriage, Marco had worked a total of four years. His work was on a computer, he called himself an engineer. Between jobs he busied himself at the gym and participated in mini-marathons. One weekend, out of town for a race, May checked her credit card and noticed he was staying at an upscale hotel and there was a hefty charge for dinner at the hotel's restaurant. She called his hotel room, a female answered the phone, then hung up when May asked, "Who is this?"

When he came home, May calmly asked who had answered the phone in his room. He was prepared, angrily scoffed, "It was probably the maid."

May walked away. To her back he said, "I stay home to care for my daughter."

May thought, *You stay home because you can't hold a job.*

To Joe, she confided that she and her daughter always agreed with him, tried to be cheerful in his presence, not wanting to stir his rage. They were not allowed an opinion and were careful with their words.

Marco was having problems with his fancy dream car, the expensive red Ferrari, and hated having to use the old Ford Explorer that May drove to work. It was forgotten that before marrying May, he drove a torn, raggedy-top, oil-leaking, faded car and had traded in her new BMW she bought before she met him.

He decided to sell the Ferrari, told her she needed to borrow money from her IRA, and pay off the loan against it in order to have the title and be able to sell it. He said it was worth more now than when he bought it, so he would give her the money to put back into her IRA before having to pay the penalty and there would be a profit. After paying on the bank loan for three years, she still owed over $100,000. She withdrew the money to pay off the bank, taking a big chunk of her retirement account. He sold the car for $103,000, less than he had paid for it, and put all the money in his personal bank account.

May was devastated. *How could I have fallen for another of his schemes? We share no affection for each other and Joe is right, he is a terrible influence on our daughter. I keep thinking that our father left us when Cat and I were so young. It was traumatic. I can't abandon my daughter, and if we divorce, he will never allow me to see her, even if the court gives me visitation.*

Joe and May talked about their relationship. When he brought her to The Compound, she stayed at his house or they would go to one of the resorts along the Sonoran coast. They were passionate in their lovemaking, laughed, danced, drank champagne.

He carried a secret and it ate at him that he hadn't found the courage to tell her, perhaps because he was afraid she would choose to give up their relationship. He discussed the problem individually with The Team, his brothers. Each agreed it would be hurtful to keep it from her.

He reserved a suite at a luxurious seaside resort. They had made love, lounged in the swirling, perfumed bubbles of the hot water in their private Jacuzzi. Wrapped in fluffy white terry robes, they sat closely on the sofa, eyes closed, both wanting the moment to never end.

Joe interrupted the serene silence. *I must tell her. I love her too much to be untruthful, deceitful.* "May, I love you more than I ever thought was possible and that is why I want to confess something I have kept from you." He deeply inhaled, hesitated for a few seconds, talked to himself, *Okay, Joe, buck up. You love her, tell her the truth.* "I am bisexual, not capable of giving myself to only one woman or one man, but an uncontrollable desire to have both."

She felt a weight on her chest, like her heart was being crushed, might stop still. Silently she ran the current of a shocking announcement around her mind. *When you love someone, you either love them as they are or you walk away. Can I give up this man who loves me? Are any of us the perfect sitcom husband or wife of old television? No, I can handle this.* "Joe, I love you. I would rather have your love part of the time than not at all. Don't leave me out of your life. You are my happiness."

"What will you think, how will you feel, when I have left you to visit a man?"

May rested her head on his shoulder, her mind still racing. She tried to imagine the situation. *Would I be hurt, jealous, angry? I must either understand it as part of the person he is or let him go.*

He waited, allowing her to digest his confession, worried, anxious for her answer, thinking, *I can't help it, please bear this burden with me, I love you.*

She lifted her head, smiled at him. "I only want to be assured you will come back to me."

"I don't want to hurt you, but you must understand that I will go. If you want me, I'll always come back to you."

Alex and Oso formed a strong bond at an early age, Alex reaching out for Tío Oso, saying his name before "Mommy" or "Daddy," riding on the broad muscular shoulders.

Oso taught him the different ways to say words. Colors, numbers, objects in the house and outside were spoken in Russian, Spanish, and English. By eight years old he could communicate in all three languages. His friend, Amy, one year younger, Amelia and Joaquin's daughter, was also caught up in the different ways to talk. She joined Alex when Geoff set aside time from teaching the students to give them a daily language lesson.

Alex and Oso spoke Russian to each other, as though they wanted to communicate in secret. Mostly English was spoken at The Compound to help the students become fluent. When they had a break from their classes, Alex from his tutors, Oso from teaching, they visited the other uncles.

From Uncle Sarge, Alex learned about guard dogs, commands, and respect, and spoke in English.

Uncle Hitch gave him a Team Phone, taught him how to use it for serious times, not as a toy, and spoke in Russian.

Even though Uncle Zack didn't pay him the same attention as the other uncles, Alex was strangely drawn to him, seeming to study his face, lean against him, hold on to his arm. Zack spoke Spanish, gave him complicated multiplication and division problems, and laughed out loud at his concentration. They became comfortable together and sometimes Alex would say to Oso, "Let's visit Tío Zack."

Alex sat in the golf cart next to Tío Oso, who taught him to putt, then ordered a set of clubs for him. They hit golf balls on the driving range with his mother. Alex wanted to sleep at Oso's house, but his mother's rule prevailed. "Everyone sleeps in their own room." The rule, however, didn't apply to Bella, who split her nights between Alex's and the master bedroom.

CHAPTER XVIII
Time Passes And Life Changes

Alex Nickolas André Xavier celebrated his eighth birthday. It was an exciting party under the wide portal with his *tías* (aunts) May, Amelia, and Mona. Also, Flora and her two children, who pampered him as if he was their little brother, and six children of Cat's friends from the market, who attended classes with Alex at The Compound. Teachers were brought in from LA, rotating each month.

The verbal invitation specified, "No Gifts" to be brought to the birthday boy. Alex had always been told, "It's a celebration to be with friends and family." He would receive one gift from his parents. He received gifts through the year from his aunts and uncles.

Chef made crispy corn-tortilla tacos and chicken empanadas. The chocolate sheet-cake had "Happy Birthday, Alex!" in the three languages he spoke: English, Spanish, and Russian. A magician delighted the children with sleight-of-hand tricks, producing pesos from their ears and making them disappear. The Team and students took turns dropping in, picking up an empanada, sampling the cake, watching a trick or two.

A bicycle with a lustrous blue paint job leaned on its stand at the end of the portal. The outgrown one would be passed on to one of Cat's friends for her boy. Ten different-colored bicycles were lined up in the courtyard. Cat had asked him, "Shall we surprise your friends with a gift to thank them for celebrating your birthday?"

"I would like a new bicycle and to give one to each friend."

Two seven-year-olds, too full of energy to sit, played tag near the portal, a few younger children joining them. The girl's red curls bounced like dozens of tiny springs. She tripped, falling to the grainy cement, and started to cry. Her brother, with short-cut hair, thick and black, frowning dark eyes, ran to her side, lifted her to standing, then knelt to wipe her scraped knee with his shirttail and used it to blot her eyes. Slightly taller, he wrapped his arms around her. "Just a little scratch. Let's go to the kitchen, get a Band-Aid to make it better, and come back for chocolate cake." She brushed the gathered skirt of her pale-yellow party dress and they ran in the house, holding hands.

Their mother, Aunt Amelia to Alex, watched the scene with her friends. "He's like a miniature Joaquin, so protective of her."

Cat smiled. "He watches his daddy care for you like that."

May looked at the twins. "How can two babies, from the same stomach, from the same parents, have extreme opposite looks?"

Mona answered, "Because their parents have extreme opposite looks."

Amy and Emilio, both named by Joaquin after his wife, and Alex, brought an air of cheerfulness to The Compound. A family atmosphere gave the children feelings of belonging, a relationship where they were loved, safe, yet free to discover, learn, grow, care for one another as they were cared for.

* * * *

The previous year, Xander's friend Colonel Lawrence West, of the U.S. Air Force, in charge of the base located in the Arizona desert, called Xander and asked if they could meet, he had news to share.

The two friends were at The Scottsdale Golf Club, in the popular Restaurante Flamenco, sitting on the dining terrace enjoying frosty margaritas, looking out at perfectly groomed greens, golfers in pastel polo shirts, laughing, back patting.

"How do they grow all that grass in the middle of the desert, Larry?"

"This is America. Don't tell someone they can't do something or can't have something, they will show you they can."

Larry told Xander the latest military notice. "The U.S. Government has decided to close the Air Force base, either dismantle it or put it on the market. A private flying school has already submitted an offer."

Xander had passed the word around that the largest Mexican drug cartel was getting more and more aggressive toward The Team, wanting their help to get into Russia. The Team had been looking at land in Arizona and Nevada, a place to build a new Academy. As the cartel's business had grown by millions of dollars, so had their craving for more, an insatiable appetite.

"You've mentioned your intent to build a Bodyguard Academy in the U.S. As you know, Xander, it's a great facility, similar to your Mexico Compound, with officers' houses, a training building, housing for trainees, land for adding a kennel, and whatever else you need. The wall around is high with watchtowers, a walkway on top, though you won't need the security in Arizona that you need in Mexico. I know you are protective of your Russian students. If the word gets out—Bodyguard Academy for Russian students—I can see some righteous folks picketing or a 'crazy with a gun and lots of ammo.' We have three lighted landing strips, a huge hangar, and a helicopter area. There's a nine-hole golf course around the outside of the wall and a shooting range for target practice out in the desert. If you're interested, I'll find what the pending bid is and you can outbid them. Oh, one more thing. There's a monstrous helicopter in the back corner of the hangar. It's been on some dangerous missions. The government stored it there. I guess they were planning to restore it. Now they are placing a new order and told me to get rid of it. I think that means dismantle it. I know Joe would love to have this machine, I'm leaving it there for him. He will know people who can help him refit the exterior."

Xander smiled at his friend. "What a thoughtful gift. No one will appreciate it more. I won't tell him, I'll bring The Team to look at the facility, you can show the helicopter to Joe. The base sounds perfect to me, but after going through it, we will vote. I'll point out that we could remodel and not need to start from scratch. Thanks, Larry, Mexico is not friendly to us. I want a safer place for our children, our family. I can always depend on you to have my back."

"And I can always depend on getting your hand-me-down private jets."

The friends looked at each other, admiration coming from both sides.

The Team visited the Air Force base. Larry and Xander led them into the hangar, back where the bulky, almost scary flying machine was parked. Joe took one look and gave everyone a lecture. "This workhorse was developed for the Army. Modified versions were produced for the Navy, Air Force, and Coast Guard. The first flight was in 1974. This particular model is from the 2006 production with improved variants."

Larry put his arm around Joe's shoulders. "She's yours, Joe. There are a few problems, she's taken some ammunition. Fix her up and give her a paint job, so the Army won't recognize her. They cost $6 million each, but the Army has decided to replace her. They don't know there's a guy named Joe who will have her flying like a falcon."

Joe ran his hands over her body. "Tell me where you hurt, girl."

The Team discussed the possibilities of moving to the base, and sent an offer to the U.S. Government. After reaching an agreement, they hired an architect, worked on the remodeling plans, and reconstruction was started. They took turns checking the progress and a Team member was always available for the foreman's questions. Cat and Amelia excitedly checked on their houses and gave the foreman suggestions. Sarge supervised the building of his new kennel and training grounds for his dogs.

Joe contacted a mechanic he knew from his Navy days whom he still met for a drink and to get caught up. He loved and specialized in the many models of helicopters and helped Joe get the necessary parts. They had the powerful bird painted white, named her *The White Falcon*, wrote her name in script on the sides, under the windows.

* * * *

Cat and Xander sat in a cushioned, double lounge chair, under the climbing-rose-covered arbor. He had carried two glasses of iced tea; she, a plate of Mexican wedding cookies, covered with powdered sugar. Chef had made a double batch of her favorites, to keep in the freezer.

Xander could tell something was churning in her mind. She stared into space, looked at him, smiled, looked away, then into his eyes. He waited quietly, letting her get thoughts together, formed into words.

"I'm grateful for my boy. My heart thanks you, Zack, and Nikolai for making it possible for me to be his mother." She hesitated, said the words inside her mind, decided her husband would not be upset, most likely would help her. "I would like to be pregnant, carry a child in my body. In vitro is a proven and simple method. I don't want to get pregnant from a sperm bank, not knowing of possible background problems, health, mental illnesses. I guess you can never be sure of your own family." She was getting edgy, the words coming out faster, a little mumbly, quietly.

Xander watched her without moving, not wanting to interrupt her thoughts.

"What do you think about asking Zack to give us sperm for the procedure?" *Okay, I said it.* She took a deep breath.

Xander held her hand, placed her palm across his mouth, kissed, smiled, looked into her eyes. "I'm so sorry pregnancy isn't possible from me. I have asked Zack several times to help us. The last time was two months ago. He became quite angry, said it was complicated enough now, living in the same compound with his past. He yelled, telling me not to mention this to him again." He rubbed her back, kissed her cheeks, her nose, her lips. "Is there anyone else you would like me to ask? Everyone we know would do it for you. I'm sorry, Cat, you are my life, I love you."

Cat was upset that Zack wouldn't help her with the in vitro procedure, saying it was complicated with him and Alex both living at The Compound. *He should be happy Alex has a wonderful mother and father, who adore him.* She decided to ask him herself. She thought about what she would say, make it simple, and tapped on his office door.

Sitting at his desk, Zack turned to see who was disturbing him. Xander never knocked, just opened the door and entered, but Zack didn't consider him a disturbance. Cat didn't wait for an answer. She had tapped, opened the door, and walked in, shutting the door behind her.

As usual, Zack was upset with himself for being happy to see her. She sat in the chair next to his desk.

"Where's your guard dog?"

"When Alex and I are in two different places, Bella has to choose who to stay with. She watches me walk away, but doesn't follow me. It's interesting, she decides who needs her most."

Zack watched her talk, observed her eyes, mouth, the way she used her hands. He thought she seemed a little nervous. *Oh no, she's here to ask me to donate sperm. Xander probably told her I refused. Will I be able to refuse her? I don't want to do it.*

She smiled at him. "Zack, please help me. I love my boy, I'm so happy to be his mother. I would very much like to be pregnant, carry a child in my body, give birth. The in vitro procedure is a proven method. I need your sperm, Zack, you're the only one I would ask. Shall I explain about the process?"

He took a deep breath, let it out slowly. With an exasperated tone he answered. "No, I know the procedure." He couldn't look away from her face. "Cat, this isn't a favor you are asking of me that I'll do and it will be over tomorrow. This is something that will be on me the rest of my life." He could argue his point with her, but she might never forgive him, and that he could not live with. How would he feel, seeing her walking at The Compound, a pregnant stomach, laughing, happy, knowing she was carrying his child, but not for them? Her face was pleading, waiting for his answer. "Okay, I'll do it for you. Set up the appointment."

She jumped up, leaned over him, put her arms around him, kissed his face. "I relieve you of any responsibilities. If you prefer, I will never reveal to the child or anyone where the sperm came from. You will have no obligations."

He received her kisses, her hugs, sad that he felt disloyal to his friend for not pushing her away. *There will be repercussions, but she's so happy.*

Cat was oblivious to his feelings, overjoyed. "Stand up, Zack, so I can hug you."

He stood, allowed her arms around him, felt her closeness, kissed her forehead. *Obviously, I can't refuse her.*

"Thank you, Zack, I love you."

CHAPTER XIX
When The Enemy Strikes, Retaliation Follows

It was Thursday, 2:00 p.m. The Team, minus Xander, Zack, and Hitch, was seated in their conference room, Xander had called an emergency meeting. Everyone was on edge, leaning forward on their elbows, each with different thoughts: *Another accounting breach? Another threat from El Torbellino? An occurrence within our Compound?*

Xander, Zack, and Hitch, The Team munitions and communications expert, entered the room, all frowning, distress written across their faces. Hitch was holding printouts from voice messages. Standing, he said, "Let me explain this incident." He was calmer than Xander, who they kept an eye on, watching for a triggered spell. "All of us have taken advantage of Xander's generosity and vacationed at the house in Baja California, which he and his brother inherited from their parents. The staff includes a family Xander has known all his life, and who live in the home full time. As you know, Marta and Juan's older son, Ramón, is Chef at Tierra Encantado. Perhaps you met their twenty-one-year-old grandson, who may have been home from college while you were there. He sent this message to us one hour ago. The reception was sporadic with much static, deciphering was challenging. As we interpret the panicked call, the house has been invaded and taken over by armed soldiers. The grandson, Luís, and a friend from college were dolphin and whale watching, exploring the coast, saw trucks surround the house and watched the scene with binoculars. Apparently they had driven to a higher cliff north of the house. This call came as they were nervously driving toward Tijuana, wanting to get away from the frightening scene. Zack, tell them how you process the situation."

Zack was holding a paper pad. Like an efficient, organized accountant, he had made notes, detailing actions. "The boys, wearing only shorts and tee shirts, had left their passports and driver's licenses at home and have no IDs to cross into the U.S. We told them to stay in Tijuana, we will pick them up. I called a friend in the Department of Security and Civil Protection and asked for help reclaiming the house. As in the U.S., the request will go through the channels, up the ladder of government. There will be no quick action. We believe El Torbellino or one of his partners has moved into it as they have threatened."

The Team gave their opinion, all consistent. They would rescue the boys, Hitch would send a drone over the house to get some pictures and assess the situation. Hesitantly, their evaluation led to the same judgment. After years of intimidation, the cartel was now aggressively applying pressure.

They had received threats of invading both The Compound and the vacation house from the Mexican drug cartel. It was the same cartel that had failed at their attempt to take over The Compound when the Russian Manager had stolen their drugs and money and left the country. The Russian military had reclaimed The Compound. Rumor had been passed around that El Torbellino now wanted the Mexican-style mansion on the cliffs above the bay, looking out to the Pacific Ocean, for himself. It was majestic, suitable for a leader; after all, it had been the vacation house of America's Ambassador to Russia. Many dignitaries were invited guests, including the deceased President of Russia and his son, the current President. The house had a helipad, an airstrip, security housing around the walled-in mansion, and beautifully maintained grounds. Also, to claim Xander's home would punish him for refusing to furnish El Torbellino with help getting into Russia to negotiate drug trafficking. The Team surmised that the security Xander hired had either been killed or bought off.

Xander looked at each member of The Team he had personally recruited: intelligent, strong-natured men, competent, loyal to one another, a fraternity of brothers. "The house is not important. We'll get our staff family out, then destroy the house and whoever has decided to live in it. We will not be coerced by drug dealers who spread their poison."

Luís and his friend were furnished with duplicate IDs and passports, backpacks, clothes, and dropped off at their college in Southern California. A call from his grandmother, who spoke quickly and hushed, confirmed that the family—Marta; her husband, Juan; their son, Juanito, and his wife, Rosita, Luís's parents—had been kept on the staff. All the other employees were asked if they wanted to stay or go home. Choosing to go was a mistake. As they walked out the gate to their trucks, they were killed. El Torbellino wanted no information about his new acquisition going through the towns. Juan witnessed the murders from the portal, where he had begged friends to stay. "No, Juan, this is a drug cartel. We don't want to work for them." Marta and family had stayed, thinking Xander would surely defeat the invaders, who would leave and everything would return to normal.

Luís gave his grandmother the message from Xander. "Watch for a dark night, leave the house, drive north to the border, and contact me." Marta clicked off. She knew that was impossible thinking, they would never get past the soldiers. Xander didn't know their penned-in danger. She kept the cell phone Xander had given her turned off and knew it would be taken away if it was found, leaving her with no communication with the outside.

The market Cat had designed and built for her friends was successful. The number of food stands tripled and people sat on benches in the city-maintained park to try the tasty local food. The City Council charged the tour companies a fee to park buses in an area they paved and had recently enlarged to accommodate the growing number of buses. The vendors paid city tax on sales, but their income had quadrupled. The women were happy and grateful. Cat was pleased with her project, walked the market each week with Bella and Alex, who stopped often to give hugs to his *tías*. Usually Oso or Joaquin or a couple of students accompanied Cat. Today The Team was meeting. Oso planned to take some students and join her later. Flora walked beside her.

Cat visited each shop to verify there were no problems or complaints from her friends. She was a walking advertisement. Wearing the colorful embroidered blouses, skirts, shifts, jewelry of beads, turquoise, and silver, she talked to the tourists, telling them the number of the stores where the items could be purchased.

She walked into a store, the front expandable gate open wide, smiling, pleasantly asked the woman behind the counter if she had any questions or problems.

Dark eyes in an angry face emitted messages of hatred. "You don't know me. I am Malita's sister. You killed her. We found her and my brother-in-law's bodies in the arroyo behind the parking lot. You will pay."

Bella took a stance, growled at her. Cat quickly said, "No, it wasn't me, I would never do that." Flora led them out of the store. Cat was upset, frightened, the incidents with Malita came back to her: the soup she replaced when Xander thought there may have been poison or something dangerously similar, the centipedes he suspected she released in the house, the attempted jewelry theft, she and her husband talking to strangers in unrecognizable trucks. Cat wanted to call Xander and tell him of this startling confrontation, but she didn't want to frighten her boy. She would call Xander when they got to the shop of Flora's friend. While they distracted Alex, she would be able to step outside and talk about this woman.

Alex looked at his mother. Before he could ask, she explained. "Her sister worked for us, but she didn't like her job and never came back to work. I didn't know she was dead."

"She thinks you killed her."

"I guess when you lose a loved one, you need to place the blame somewhere."

Joaquin, Oso, and Geoff had previously visited the bars in town, talking to the local men, checking rumors reported by shop owners about an unrecognized pickup driving up and down the gravel road behind the tourist market and a helicopter landing in the corner of the bus parking lot. They made mental notes of the gossip, mostly opinions, to advise The Team. Perhaps some guards were needed— security for the shop owners. Xander thought the helicopter and its occupants needed to be checked, *probably tourists who felt they were too rich to ride the bus. Still, Cat needs to be aware of possible danger and kept informed.* Xander had told her their vacation house had been taken over by the cartel, El Torbellino probably involved. Both were concerned about the family Xander had known all his life.

Three long buildings in a U-shape made up the individually numbered stores. Each had a rear door that opened onto the back road. Shop owners could back up to their store, unload merchandise, then park in the blacktop lot labeled "Vendors Only."

The large courtyard formed by the U had benches, flagstone walkways, triangular tarps stretched between posts to form umbrella-like shade, patches of grass and flowering trees and shrubs. It gave tourists another park to relax in, stay longer and shop more.

Joaquin had called the unscheduled meeting after lunch. He confirmed the rumors, strange men in unknown trucks, an unfamiliar helicopter.

A warning signal flashed in Xander's head. Cat, Alex, Flora, and Bella were at the market on their usual Tourist Day visit. He told Joaquin and Geoff to call Cat, tell her that all should stay in one store where they would be picked up, brought home. He asked Oso to take some students, check the back road and parking lots, and ask if anyone had seen identification on the helicopter. The meeting broke up, Team members left on their assignment.

As The Team had been meeting, a sleek, black helicopter landed on open space in the bus parking lot. The rotary blade kept circling and five men in khaki work clothes jumped out, ran toward the back door of a shop where an accomplice was talking into an oversized communications device, giving location of the shop. The shop was where Cat, Alex, Flora, and Bella were talking, drinking iced watermelon agua fresca, barely able to hear each other with the noise outside. Alex was asking if he could go out to the back and look at the helicopter they had all heard. Cat was waiting for a moment to call Xander, tell him about the encounter with Malita's sister. Bella was alerted by a man at each door, taking a growling stance.

At the front door was another accomplice with oversized earbuds, wires attached to a control belted at his waist, blocking the entry with his huge intimidating body. He was armed with a short air rifle, a hypodermic needle filled with a dose of tranquilizer solution. He shot Bella in the shoulder. Alex saw her stumble, ran to her, hugging, calling her name as she slowly collapsed to the floor. Flora shielded both of them, leaning over, her arms stretched around them, watching the danger unfold with fear in her teared eyes.

Another man at the back door had a cylinder clipped to his belt and held a round mask-like object resembling a catcher's mitt connected to a tube that ran to the cylinder. Cat fumbled for her Team Phone, trying to find the pocket in her gathered skirt, as a muscular aide pinned her arms to her sides. Cat felt a mask cupped to her face, her hands couldn't grab it. She jerked her head side to side to shake it away, but the mask followed her actions. She heard her muffled voice, "Call Xander! Call Xander!" Cat wanted to calm her boy, who was trying to break away from Flora's protective arms. "Alex, Daddy will come get you." She wasn't sure if the words came out of the mask. Flora watched the big man carry Cat out the door, toward the parking lot.

Alex dug into his pocket for the Team Phone Tío Hitch had given him and pressed all the buttons sending his call to The Team. "Help! Men killed Bella and took Mommy away!"

Cat thought her legs were kicking, they felt heavy, difficult to move. She was being carried, told herself to keep her eyes open, look at their faces. "My boy, my boy . . ." Was she screaming? An answer in

Spanish, "*Su hijo está bien.*" (Your boy is fine) She felt a little relieved as she was transferred to other muscular arms into a truck, then to another truck, no, a helicopter, placed in a cushioned chair, everything blurry, she couldn't keep her eyes open any longer, tired, so tired.

Oso, Joaquin, Geoff, and some students were entering the market as Xander had directed. Cat was in the helicopter when they got to the market, so their call to her was not answered. She couldn't feel the slight vibration of her battery pack, her earbuds were hanging on to her ears. The panicked call from Alex sent an overpowering alarm to The Team. Xander, Hitch, Sarge, and his Dobermans took the Hummer closest to the gate. The cart would be too slow.

They heard the thunderous roar of a helicopter and looked up to see the black object shining, moving toward the cloudless, sea-blue sky. Joaquin had called Flora's cell, heard sobbing, begging for help in store number 37.

CHAPTER XX
Be Careful You Don't Fall Into Your Own Trap

Cat opened her eyes, slowly, only to slits. *If they see I'm awake, they might put me to sleep again.* A large window, wide wooden slats, slightly closed, showed an orange, pink, purple sky. *Sunset.* Without moving her head, she tried to shift her eyes around the room. *Where am I?* She closed her eyes to concentrate on the last she could remember, putting the pieces together. She saw Alex kneeling beside Bella, trying to hold her head up, then Flora's dark eyes, wide with fear, holding Alex to keep him from running to help his mother. Bruises on her arms reminded her of the strength she felt gripping her, unable to move, her own waning energy, not wanting to give in to the drug she breathed into her system. *Is my boy okay? Did they kill Bella?* She remembered being carried and yelling for Alex, a calm voice saying, "*Su hijo está bien.*" She recognized the room, the guest suite at their vacation house. May, Amelia, and Mona enjoyed staying in this room when she had invited them to visit. The pieces were coming together. She remembered Xander had told her their vacation house had been taken over by the cartel, El Torbellino probably involved.

Is that a man standing at the door? Suddenly she was more angry than afraid. She still had on her embroidered white gathered skirt,

179

twisted around her. Swinging her legs to the side of the bed, trying to sit up brought dizziness, a headache, nausea.

The man was big, like Oso, filling the doorway. "Don't get up too fast," he advised.

Her Mexican leather-strip sandals, huaraches, were on the floor next to the bed, ready to slip her feet into. On the dresser she saw her jewelry. "Where is my phone? I want to call my husband."

The guard was standing sideways in the open doorway, his back against the frame. She realized he was assigned to watch her. *Do they think I'll run away? The closest neighbor is two miles down the coast.*

He spoke English with a heavy Spanish accent. "Señor Ticiano has your phone. He will see you when you have recuperated."

Her headache had ebbed to a dull throb, nausea turned to hunger. It had been a long time since she had eaten the breakfast muffin with her tea. Her stomach felt empty.

She spoke to the guard in English, words in Spanish not coming as easily, pronouncing each word too clearly, in that annoying way people assume foreigners can't understand their language. "I'm worried about my son. Did you kill our dog?"

He smiled, knowing why she had spoken slowly, clearly, answered with the patience of a teacher. "No, Señora, your son was not harmed, your dog was tranquilized. Both are fine."

Her face showed a little relief, still leery, she wanted to talk to Señor Ticiano. "I have clothes in the master bedroom. I want to go there, take a shower and change."

"Señora, your clothes and bathroom items have been removed and put in the dressing room of this suite."

She stood slowly, still slightly dizzy, walked through the bathroom to the spacious closet. No clothes on the padded hangers, nothing in the drawers. Back to the bedroom, she reported to her guard. "The closet and drawers are empty."

He turned and talked quietly into his chest. Facing Cat, he said, "There was a misunderstanding. Your clothes are being brought to this room."

In the bathroom drawers were the usual amenities she kept refurnishing for guests. She heard a female voice, looked in the bedroom. Rosita had brought her clothes and a plastic bag of small jars and cosmetics, piled them on the bed. Cat happily stepped toward her, arms outstretched. "Rosita, wonderful to see you, are you all right? Is Marta here? Tell me what's happening with our house."

Rosita turned, walked toward the door. Over her shoulder, she scolded, "This is not your house now."

As Cat watched her walk out of the suite, chills ran through her body, now aware she was in the middle of danger. She would focus on finding her phone and calling The Team. First she would try to find out how many soldiers were outside, as Luís had described the takeover and who was the mastermind behind this seizure. She would get information to give to Xander.

Cat knew Rosita used the few clothes she left in the master bedroom after she and Xander would return to The Compound. She had been asked to put Cat's belongings in the guest suite, but had taken them to her room. Rosita would not be her ally. She hoped Marta and Juan were still in the house, safe.

From the pile on the bed, Cat picked out jeans and a tee, showered, dressed, put moisturizer on her face to help present a brave exterior, clipped her hair back with a barrette and asked the guard, "Is Marta here?"

"*Sí, Señora*, Marta, Juan, Juanito, and Rosita, all have jobs. The rest of your staff has been replaced."

He reminded Cat of Oso—bulky, tall, sinewy, with a contradictory tone of voice—quiet, patient. *He's one of the men who held the mask over my face, carried me to the truck, put me in the helicopter. I am a strong woman. I won't show fear or anger. I must stay in control.* "May I say hello to Marta before I talk to Señor Ticiano?"

He turned and talked quietly into his chest again, then to her. "We can stop in the kitchen for a few minutes."

Though she had been to the kitchen many times, Cat followed her guard to a chef-worthy kitchen of granite and stainless steel. Marta, a head shorter than Cat, fleshy, a worried face, started to cry. They wrapped arms around each other until Marta said, "I'm making chicken mole for dinner."

She was making Cat's favorite. *How did she know I'm here?* "I need some bread in my stomach before I put mole in there." She was eyeing the fresh-baked loaf, cooling on the wooden cutting board. Marta sliced a thick chunk, slathered it with butter, handed it to Cat as they talked in a hush.

"Did they hurt you? The news got to Juan from the soldiers outside."

"I'm fine, now I am going to see Señor Ticiano and learn why I'm here."

Marta whispered, "Be careful, he is El Torbellino."

Shocked, Cat asked, "Are you sure?"

"That's what the soldiers call him, and they have stories of his temper."

Cat's guard came in the kitchen. "Señor will see you now." As they walked down the hall, he instructed, "When you talk to Señor Ticiano, do not say, 'I want,' ask 'may I?'"

She nodded, hungrily took mouth-full bites, followed him to the library, appropriate for a mansion. Hundreds of books were listed on the computer with location numbers. The highly polished Mexican parota wood presidential desk was placed at an angle, so the occupant could look out at the Pacific Ocean or see someone enter. For casual meetings, comfortable sofas and chairs were arranged in conversation squares.

He rose from the cushiony black-leather chair and offered his hand. "I am Tomás Ticiano."

Cat didn't follow her own advice, put her hands behind her, took a step back. "You have kidnapped me, seriously traumatized my young boy, shot my guard dog with tranquilizers, stolen our vacation home—and now you want to shake my hand? Why have you done this?"

Tomás looked into her gemstone eyes, sparkling with barely controlled anger. He smiled inwardly, sat in his executive chair, leaned back and motioned with a hand toward the guest chair at the side of his desk. She sat, back straight, hands in her lap, glaring at his face.

Señor Tomás Ticiano wore a custom-tailored beige cotton suit, a crisp tan, fitted, dress shirt, the two top buttons open, all suggesting a body familiar with the gym. He was much taller than Cat, eyelashes too long and thick for a man, black wavy hair combed back and cut so perfectly, it looked like it had been painted on, using one bristle.

Cat surveyed the items on Xander's father's desk. "I notice you have my cell. I would like to call my husband."

"Yes, Cat, but let us talk for a few minutes. It's not a good time to call, you'll interrupt The Team's dinner. Let's wait until after 9:00 when Alex has gone to bed, so you won't upset him. He is spending the night at Joaquin and Amelia's house with the twins, a special night with friends while his mother is away. After dinner Oso, Joaquin, and Geoff are going into town, searching in the bars for information about the strange black helicopter that took you from the market. Oh, that reminds me—congratulations on the market planning and construction. It employs many people who are grateful to you, even though it cost your husband and Zack more money than it's worth."

Cat watched him talk, a bragging way, making her aware that he knew her life. *Someone has watched us, is watching inside The Compound now, giving him this current information. I must tell Xander, I'll say it quickly before he can stop me.*

Tomás continued, flaunting his information. "Xander hasn't let your sister know about the kidnapping, waiting until he has positive, or at least fairly good, news. Flora, Franco, and their children are at your house, keeping things running, so to speak." He spoke perfect English, some words had a slight British accent. She realized he had spent time there, perhaps studied in Great Britain.

He took a moment, looked out the window. The moon was on the rise, a glowing orange balloon. Cat imagined it reflecting on the foamy surf, rolling to shore in a rush, a favorite scene and sound she and Xander had shared many times.

"Cat, you are here because your husband has refused, for several years, to cooperate with me. I will hold you captive until we reach an agreement. I am the arbitrator. He will understand, we were in law school together."

"May I call my husband now?" She repeated her request as if she hadn't heard him.

"Of course. Tell him to give me the information I have asked of him and I will return his wife." He half smiled, a smirk of self-confidence, egotism. He slid her Team Phone across the desk.

Quickly she pressed all eight buttons. The entire Team would hear her. She spoke quickly. She had lots to say. "This is Cat, I am fine. I have seen Marta. She looks so tired, moves slowly. Xander, you promised you would let her and Juan go home, give them their well-deserved retirement. It's time." She wanted to help Xander bargain to get Marta and Juan released, also. He understood. "Our staff has been replaced and there are many soldiers outside. Now, I am talking to Señor Tomás Ticiano. He said both of you attended the same law school."

At The Compound, Xander, Zack, and Hitch were in the communications room, full of complicated murmuring machines, reviewing videos from the drone that Hitch had sent over the vacation house. Now, they were listening to Cat. When she said Tomás Ticiano, they didn't recognize the name, but as she went on—"you attended the same law school"—Xander and Zack looked at each other with questioning surprise and mouthed the words, *Tom the Bomb?*

They realized she was giving them information. Quickly, but clearly, she said, "There is a mole or bug inside The Compound, he knows details of our life."

Señor Ticiano sat up. *She is informing him instead of pleading for her return.* He scooted his chair toward her, roughly grabbed the phone from her hand, as she yelled, "He is El Torbellino."

The phone struck the wall with force that shattered the instrument and put a dent in the wall.

Another phone was ringing somewhere inside the executive desk. Tomás angrily opened drawers, slammed them shut, looked around the office.

Cat calmly watched him impatiently looking for the ringing device. Both knew it was Xander calling. Almost too quietly she said, "Remove the top right-hand drawer, it's on a shelf at the back."

He took the drawer out and threw it across the room. Reaching to the back, he felt a large, rectangular hand-receiver, brought it out, the ringing loud and constant. He pressed the Receive button. "Who is this?"

"Tomás, I'm ready to attend the meeting you requested. We need to talk. Do not harm my wife."

When Cat's Team Phone hit the wall, Hitch put The Compound on lock-down. Only Team members would be allowed to enter or leave until it was lifted. Sarge and three of his Doberman pinschers started walking the security stations, first the watchtower, then the main gate and around the wall. Oso, Joaquin, and Geoff returned to The Compound. They briefed the students and split into three groups. Inside the houses where help was finished for the day, they searched for bugs and questioned each employee.

Then a call came from security at the main gate. The housekeeper, who worked in Joaquin and Amelia's house, and her husband, a guard on the day shift, wanted to leave The Compound.

Joaquin and three students went to the detainee room where the couple were being held. Amelia liked the housekeeper, told Joaquin she was wonderful help with the children and did extra work in the house. Joaquin asked gently, "You always stay at our house until Friday, why do you want to go home two days early?"

The guard spoke. He was a little nervous. "I feel sick and I want her to come home with me, take care of me."

Through strong, loud objections, the students searched the couple, emptying pockets, removing shirts, shoes, pants, and placing the findings on the table. Joaquin reached for the cell, the guard tried to grab it from him, the students pinned his arms back as Joaquin flipped through texts. He looked at the man and woman he had foolishly trusted. "Who would be interested to know that Alex is staying the night with us?"

"My sister," the guard blurted out, fidgeting, starting to perspire.

Joaquin touched the listed phone number, it rang. An answer, the gruff voice of Señor Ticiano. "I told you not to call, just text. What do you have for me?"

"This is Joaquin. I have your mole for you."

Señor clicked off.

CHAPTER XXI

To Bait The Trap,
To Lure The Enemy

Nikolai, Xander, and the rest of The Team spent hours talking, researching, discussing the plan they would give to Tomás Ticiano. They had two goals: the release of Cat and the remaining staff, and giving enticing information that would draw the drug dealer into his seemingly most profitable scheme and unknowingly into a death trap. The Team would mix facts that could be verified by extensive online research with their ruse.

Russia's Federal Security Service, under Nikolai's orders, gave The Team valuable information with names and locations of the top drug buyers in Afghanistan who supplied the next tier of dealers. They moved the packages through Asia to the Russian border. Waiting for them were dozens of mules to take the heroin across the border. They were met by the many dealers/users who spread the heroin through the country. Each time the heroin was passed, profit was added on and the drug became more and more expensive by the time it finally arrived in Russia. The Team built their invented ruse on this collection of facts and now felt the script was polished. Xander called Tomás. "Let's get started. I want to have our reunion tomorrow morning."

Tomás had anticipated The Team's cooperation and started informing his agents who would go to Russia, investigate, and confirm the data. In Mexico, these agents kept the buying and selling running smoothly, in charge of removing problems and negotiating the bribes. Tomás took charge. "We will meet in Mexico City at Hotel Caliente. The top-floor restaurant has a private back room. You may bring two bodyguards."

"And you will bring an army?"

"Your life isn't in danger, Xander, unless my agents are met with a trap or your information is phony."

"I will be accompanied by four men." Xander ignored the two-guard limit and the threat. "We'll be in the private room at 10:00 a.m. Bring my wife."

"You know I can't do that yet."

Xander clicked off. All The Team members wanted to meet with El Torbellino, observe how the plan was received, protect Xander from evil danger. At The Compound each man sat quietly in his chair, mentally examining facets of the plan. With Nikolai's help, it could be possible to destroy Mexico's dominant drug cartel. To lure top partners into The Russian Federation where they could be eliminated would cut deeply into the cartel's management. Xander looked proudly at his brothers. "We must divide up for our advantage. Oso, Geoff, and Sarge will stay at The Compound, the dogs on watch. Joe will pilot our jet with five students, stay at the Mexico City airport to guard our plane. Joaquin, Hitch, Zack, and I will meet Tomás. We'll take our number one student, who has received rave reviews from all of you. Joaquin, he will be your partner. After graduation, Nikolai is putting him with the Federal Intelligence Service and wants us to include him in this meeting to observe. Joe, file the flight plan, let us know what time we'll leave, getting to the meeting at 10:00 a.m. We will return after the meeting."

In Baja, at the vacation house, Tomás was making his plans, selecting the right partner to accompany him to the meeting. On the top tier of the cartel, there were five partners. From their top-floor offices, in Mexico City, dressed in custom-made suits, they organized and ran a $100 billion business. Cartel-owned companies invested profits from selling drugs in legitimate businesses around the world. An important side-company employed lawyers for defense and to negotiate and pay bribes which easily ran into hundreds of thousands of dollars.

Señor Ticiano would take one partner to the meeting, but when Xander named Joaquin as one of The Team members with him, Tomás decided to bring five bodyguards and five soldiers. A distinct reputation preceded Joaquin and his lightning-precise knives.

Cat's guard told her Señor Ticiano wanted to see her in his office.

"Cat, I want you to pack an overnight bag. We will leave at 2:00 p.m. today and return after my meeting tomorrow." He did not tell her where they were going.

"If you are going to be gone only twenty-four hours, why am I going? Are you meeting Xander? I want to see him."

"My meetings with Xander are on the phone," he lied. "I have a business appointment and I don't want to leave you here without me to protect you."

"If I am in danger here without you, I want to bring Marta."

"Marta will stay." Cat annoyed him, but at the same time he was intrigued by her bold manner. Tomás never had a girlfriend who voiced an opinion or disagreed with him. His relationship with women was based on sex and money. He paid the bills and she performed. There was never talk of his occupation.

On the morning El Torbellino and his soldiers stormed the vacation house, he had walked slowly through the mansion admiring the furnishings and works of art from around the world. He had immediately claimed the library/office, sat in the presidential chair, and looked out where the ocean and sky merged, one absorbing the other. He decided this Ambassador's House suited him better than his penthouse apartment in the noisy, bustling city that never allowed one to relax.

Rosita, Marta's daughter-in-law, hated living in isolation with her husband's mother always asking her to help the house staff with cleaning. She craved excitement, adventure, dancing and drinking margaritas with handsome men. She felt stuck with a boring husband who worked on the grounds, smelled of sweat, and was too tired to give her the attention she needed. She resented the owner and his wife, their friends coming and going like birds passing through.

She liked her reflection in the mirror. Rosita was round and full in all the right places. Her shining black hair hung in dips and waves past bare shoulders. One thick mass of hair was tucked behind a sensitive ear supporting a silver, teacup-sized hoop. Rosita could move in a provocative way. It had been a long time, but she knew how to please a man, and this rich, handsome new owner could open the door to her escape.

She poured a tumbler of iced coffee, added cream, cinnamon, lots of sugar, put it on a tray with a plate of sliced Gruyère, freshly baked bread, and took it to the library.

"For Señor Ticiano." She smiled at two Olympic-sized guards at the doorway. One of them entered the imported-oak-paneled room, informed Señor, went back to the door, and admitted her.

She set the tray on the desk, bending at the waist, giving a view down the front of her peasant blouse. Señor leaned back against the cushioned chair and observed the whole voluptuous exhibit presented for him.

"Rosita, I'll be finished working at 8:00 p.m. Will you bring dessert and coffee to my room?"

"*Con mucho gusto, Señor.*" (With pleasure, sir.)

Cat was blindfolded as she stepped down from the plane's stairs, guided into the car's comfortable, cushy seat for the ride from the Mexico City airport to the luxurious condominium building in the elite downtown section of the city. She didn't see the modern beige granite and glass exterior or know the black Hummer had been driven into a private garage, separate from the expansive garage for the rest of the building occupants. The private elevator was overly spacious, a room, perhaps to take a group up to the penthouse for a party. Her guard guided her and said, "We will take the elevator," so she wouldn't be frightened when it moved. She slipped a finger up to try peeking from the blindfold, but the black cloth was too tight. "No, Señora, we're almost there." She liked him from the first day, maybe because he reminded her of her brother, Oso, a massive man who filled the doorway, yet a gentleness that showed in his voice.

Cat was El Torbellino's wild card. He could use her to make a winning hand. It was important to keep her safe and hidden. A partner, who opposed his plan to sell heroin in Russia, might want to remove her. Or her husband and his Team could find her and steal his bargaining tool. He trusted only his private bodyguards.

The guard removed Cat's blindfold as they entered the extravagant rooms. The furnishings were modern, heavy black iron, thick glass, with beige and black fabrics of stripes and abstract squares. There was nothing personal, no pictures of family or vacations, no souvenirs from travel, no cushions out of place.

"Is this a hotel?" she asked. No answer.

She was told the chef would have dinner ready for her in the dining room at 8:00 p.m., then led her to a spacious suite and stayed on guard outside the door. In the oversized bathroom was a spa tub for two with jets. She turned on the hot water, poured a large dose of bath oil, undressed, and slipped into steaming water.

Xander, Zack, Hitch, Joaquin, and his student walked into the top-floor restaurant, were led to the back room as hands on the two cartel partners' Rolexes peeked out from starched cuffs and ticked to 10:00 a.m. Five soldiers wearing khaki uniforms and five professional bodyguards in black had spread themselves around the room. Tomás was sitting at the head of a rectangular table, his partner to his right. Xander took the chair left of Tomás, Zack next to him. Joaquin sat at the opposite head, an elbow on the table, knuckles holding up a smirk. They had been searched for weapons outside the restaurant, none were found. The wires that followed the seams in Hitch's slacks were as fine as a strand of hair, but would send the conversation to recording equipment at The Compound, a recording to listen to later, and to Joe at the airport, keeping him informed of progress and when to expect them.

The two cartel men sitting at the beautifully grained, polished table looked like they were competing for the cover of *Gentlemen's Monthly Magazine*: custom-made sport jackets, pastel-colored silk ties, matching handkerchiefs casually tucked in their pockets. The Team wore no silk ties, no matching handkerchiefs, no competition for the cartel members.

Tomás spoke first, looking at Xander. "I would offer a handshake, but you would probably refuse, like your wife."

Xander laughed. "You met the stronger, more opinionated half of the family." He and Zack extended their hands toward Tomás. "I have memories of naive young men in law school."

Tomás answered, smiling slightly. "You three were never naive."

Zack and Xander thought, *Okay, now we know he remembers Nikolai and knows we have a connection. We were an obnoxious trio, I'm sure everyone remembers us.*

From his breast pocket, Zack took folded pages of copy paper, laid them flat on the table to use as notes, and spoke in Spanish, his native language. "You gentlemen probably know these statistics, but allow me to reiterate. The Russian Federation is the largest country in the world with a population just under 150 million. There are about 7 million people who use drugs regularly. The drugs come from Afghanistan, 375 tons of heroin produced from their opium fields. There are hundreds of refining labs turning poppy resin into heroin, conveying it by rail, air, and trucks through central Asia into Russia." Zack said the next sentence slowly, emphasizing the dollar amount. "Last year Russians bought *$17 billion* of street-traded heroin. Several Afghan labs have been raided by opposition countries, aided by the United States, destroying more than one ton of heroin." Here, a suggestion that the refining labs in Afghanistan were in danger of being eliminated and even more opportunity for the Mexican cartel. "Cocaine is coming from South America, Ecstasy from Europe, other channels bringing in synthetic drugs like fentanyl. Basically, this is your competition."

Zack paused, lifted the water glass to his mouth, drank half, his eyes alternately focused on Tomás and his partner. "We suggest entering Russia in the southeastern section. There is a modern city, Tolstoy, a major port on the Volga, connected by the Ural Highway and linked by rail to other major Russian cities. The heroin from Afghanistan comes in from the opposite border. The top police officers of the Politsia are underpaid and susceptible to bribery. We were able to get two names. You can check out these men, talk to others, set up your own operation. Bribes at this airport, or whichever you decide to use, will get you landings with no Politsia interference. Bribery is your key to every door. Once you get in the country, the word will spread like hot butter, especially if your product is cheaper than getting it from Afghanistan."

Tomás looked at his partner. "Squad five could check this information. One of those men speaks Russian, has a Russian mother."

The partner leaned back, squinted his eyes at Zack. "I don't believe you. You're laying a trap."

Zack didn't answer. They stared at each other, sending silent messages of distrust, loathing, repugnance, hostility.

Tomás took a deep breath, somewhere in his volatile personality he found calm, and responded, "We will send some men to investigate your information."

The partner scowled. "And if they don't come back, we'll kill our hostage."

Joaquin hit the table with both fists. Five rifles flashed and pointed at him. He leaned toward the opponents. Low, guttural words from deep in his stomach growled at the two men. "Tell them to put their rifles down. No one points a gun at me and lives to tell about it."

Tomás motioned with both hands, palms toward the soldiers, gesturing backward. Slowly, the rifles rested on the khaki shoulders.

The partner laughed loudly. "How would you kill five men with their guns aimed at your head? You wouldn't have a chance to blink. And you're unarmed."

As if a rattlesnake struck, the partner felt a tug on his shoulder. He turned his head, looked down and saw an arrowhead, thin as a razor blade, the end sticking from his shoulder pad.

"You crazy bastard, you knifed my shoulder."

"No, I aimed for your jacket pad and even with my right hand my aim was so good, I didn't even graze your skin. Think how easily I could have put that arrow in your throat. Your handsome jacket would be full of blood now. I'm a better shot with my left hand, but I was testing my right hand. I invented this weapon, perfectly weighted to reach its goal with a flick of my wrist." Joaquin was being Joaquin, goading, playing, displaying his talent, amusing himself. He turned his fist over, revealing another frightening arrow, cradled innocently in his palm, then opened his right hand and showed a third arrow, razor, knife, whatever it was. He changed his expression from smirk to serious, leaned toward the partner. "Do you know how many fractions of a second it would take me to reach five goals with these weapons? Quicker than a blink."

Tomás reached to his partner's raw-silk jacket, carefully pulled out the arrow, examined it, smiled slightly, and slid it down the table to Joaquin. His face was serious as he leaned toward his partner. "Go back to your office. You're hindering this meeting."

The partner gave Joaquin a hostile, threatening, quick stare. Joaquin smiled at him, tilting his head. "*Adios, Señor.*"

Xander spoke. "We have researched an area of Russia opposite the border that is saturated with drugs from Afghanistan. Our Team laid the groundwork for you. We have given you detailed information with contact names. We aren't going to go there and sell the stuff for you. We have our own business. What else do you want?"

Tomás stared at Xander's face, trying to detect a flicker of a lie, the hint of a trap being set. Xander returned his stare, unintimidated, confident. "If you will release Cat and what's left of our staff, one of our Team will accompany your men to Russia and help with plans for your first shipment."

There was a proposition in the works. The men were playing out the plans in their minds. *Have we thought of how we will handle problems that may arise?*

Tomás eased the tension that had filled the room. "And you will give me your vacation house? Your wife keeps reminding me I stole it."

Xander smiled. *Cat has not been the docile captive.* "Before you and your army invaded, I was thinking about selling that house and building a vacation house in the Caribbean for my family. Mexico is too crowded for us."

"How much do you want for it?"

"Twenty-five million U.S. dollars."

"I'll give you fifteen."

"I will take $20 million cash. The art is worth that." Xander was thinking about Cat. She enjoyed their "vacation house." *Even if I was able to get it back, it will never have the same meaning for us. I'll take the money and Cat can use it for her next project to help people. I'll build her another house. After this experience, I'm sure she won't want to return to Baja.*

"It's a beautiful house, I'm quite comfortable there. Something else. Tell me about our old classmate, who is now President of Russia. Is he going to have the Russian Army waiting for us?"

"He knows of the kidnapping, of your demands, of our research and information for setting up the receiving end of the shipments. He is aware of the number of people who buy drugs and the number of people who die from overdose or tainted drugs. He says, 'If people want to destroy their lives with drugs, that's up to them.'" Nikolai had told him what to say if asked about his involvement. Still, Xander felt a sense of betrayal. "He is occupied with serious problems of state, enemy countries." Xander held himself still, restraining the powerful urge to reach for the throat of this greedy, self-concerned, evil person, uncaring of the poison he distributed to people who used it as an escape and ruined their lives.

"Another question." Tomás sat straight, pleased with himself, a student who had done his homework. "I hear the government doesn't have any programs offering help to HIV-positive drug users."

Xander had enough. Nikolai was a childhood friend, they never talked politics. "Tomás, I have no comment about that. Read the newspapers."

The room was still and quiet as if each man was holding his breath. The soldiers watched Joaquin, perhaps not with as much thought to protect their leader as to protect themselves. The bodyguards felt undertrained. Martial arts were no match against a razor sent with precision to one's throat.

Tomás looked around the table. "Which Team member will accompany my men to Tolstoy? Someone who speaks Russian, can set the pins in place, get the ball rolling."

Each Team member present volunteered loudly. "I will go with your men. I speak Russian."

"How about you, Xander, will you go with my team?"

"I will go with your team if you come, also. I'll teach you how to drink vodka. First you must release my wife."

Tomás was well aware that this meeting and the business trip to Russia were possible because he had made the decision to kidnap Cat. He would not give her up until he was satisfied with the Russian contact. "Cat is safe, I will release her when we return."

Xander stared at Tomás, holding in the threats he was thinking. *If you harm my wife, you will die a slow and painful death.*

After the meeting in the Hotel Caliente, The Team went back to The Compound to await the cartel's answer. Tomás told them he would call after discussing their information with his partners. Zack had handed his notes to Tomás, for referral, to use at his meeting, making sure the statistics were passed on.

Xander was anxious for The Team to discuss the Mexico City meeting. *The quicker we wrap this up, the quicker I will have Cat back.* They didn't feel the doubting partner would be successful in convincing the other partners it was a trap. Hopefully they would be as awed by the numbers as Tomás. He had asked more about the Afghan refining labs and The Team suspected he intended to eliminate the competition.

Nikolai was streamed into The Compound meeting. "If he destroys the Afghan labs, I will personally thank him."

The cartel partners voted four to one in favor of sending a small shipment of heroin to Russia as a test. Two partners plus bodyguards would go with Tomás. A cartel squad would leave today, spreading the news of heroin coming from Mexico, landing on the east coast at Tolstoy.

CHAPTER XXII
The President Entertains, Entices Them Back

Nikolai cleared the landing of the Mexican cartel jet at Tolstoy, Russia. He sent a team of his top undercover men from Federal Security Service to allow the bribes and ensure the smooth transfer of the first shipment of heroin.

Xander, Zack, Joaquin, Hitch, and five students accompanied Tomás, two partners, and ten bodyguards. Ten cartel men, on tourist visas, a squad who specialized in setting up cells of buyers, had landed the day before. Gossip of the new drug source traveled through the country like a whirlwind, reaching buyers who bought bundles of drugs directly from the Afghan labs. They would be able to obtain the drugs in Russia without the expense of passing through East Asia, cutting out the middlemen and the risk of losing the shipments at the borders. Also, included in the rumor was the opinion the Mexican heroin was strong and pure.

The cartel squad bribed the manager of a shipping warehouse to temporarily store the bundles after the jet from Mexico arrived.

The Team and cartel members checked into the best hotel in town, which caused much frowning from Tomás and his partners. Looking at the stark lobby, they proclaimed, "So ordinary." All met in the restaurant for dinner, more frowning. "This is the best Russia has to offer?" The Team's student bodyguards, the Mexican specialty squad, and the cartel's ten bodyguards sat separately at their own tables. The Team, Tomás, and his partners sat together in the back corner. Xander ordered the food: Russian salad, venison stroganoff, and salmon-filled pastry. The restaurant had a wine cellar and stored a wine he liked, Château Le Grand Vostok, from a new winery near the Black Sea, a Russian-French venture. It was very good French wine and for the time being, not expensive, until people learned about it. The cartel partners frowned again. "Cheap wine? I haven't had cheap wine since I was a teenager."

Joaquin had enough. He was glad the partner he met at Hotel Caliente in Mexico City had chosen not to accompany Tomás on this trip, but it seemed these partners also enjoyed self-admiration. He addressed one partner who particularly aggravated him. "The price tag doesn't determine the quality or the beauty or the good taste of the product, which is evident in your expensive, neon ugly shirt, and the bad taste of your heavy, gold bracelet, your name in raised gold letters. You remind me of the pimps on the streets of LA."

The insulted partner sat up, bristled, responded, "I could have you killed with the motion of my hand."

Joaquin smirked. "Only if you could lift your hand. I wear no gold to impress you because I have no need to impress you. I could kill you and your bodyguards with the flick of my wrist."

The table of men was quiet, no one wanted to interfere. Hitch excused himself to go to the men's room. On his way back to the table, passing through the bar area, a man sitting on a bar stool, asked in Spanish, "You have something to sell, Señor?"

It was basic Spanish with a Russian accent. Hitch stopped, stared with a serious face, waited a few minutes, in Russian said, "It's possible."

Smiling, changing to his own language, pointing with his chin to a table of five men, he said, "My comrades might want to buy."

Hitch glanced at The Team table, Joaquin was on his way to the bar, greeted the Russian. "*Buenas noches, Señor.*"

"This man and his friends might want to buy, Joaquin. Do you think they look rich enough?"

The Russian and his comrades were dressed in the current casual fashion of jeans, button-down shirts, bulky, lined, leather jackets, and ankle boots.

Joaquin showed his Joaquin smile, a little off to the side, with mischievous eyes. "Would you and your friends like to join us?" He and Hitch turned, walked back to their table, informed the group of their conversation, looked up to see six beefy men walking toward them. Joaquin noticed at least three had guns in the inside pockets of their heavy casual jackets. From his days on the streets of LA, he learned to observe the slightly off balance way the jacket hung and maybe pooched out on one side. The carrier's hand was held differently than his other, up closer to his belly, open, as if ready to grab something.

At The Team's table, everyone scooted their chairs together, the students fitted in six more chairs, checked their weapons with pats to their bodies, and stood nearby.

Tomás spoke in Spanish, several men had blank expressions. Joaquin translated to Russian. The price was for kilos, ready to be picked up, ten minutes from the airport. Tomás retrieved a small plastic bag he kept in his shearling-lined suede jacket and had transferred to his slacks pocket, anticipating the need for a sampler. He placed it in front of the guest who had the smuggest expression. "A gift," Tomás said. Zack translated.

The smug looker opened the zip bag, wet his little finger with his tongue, stuck it in the white powder, shook off the excess, and tasted it. "Strong."

Tomás grinned. "Strong enough to be cut with something else for a bigger profit or perfect for the purist."

The Russian tried to haggle the cost. Tomás leaned toward him. "The price is the price, in U.S. dollars."

Still he argued, "The shipment is not enough for us. We will sell it in one day. You have a big airplane, fill it up, bring that for us, my comrades will take all of it. That will be enough for three-four weeks, same quality. I will test each bundle. When can you have the next shipment here?"

"We will leave Russia after you pay for what we brought and return in one week. Will your comrades have enough dollars to buy a planeload?"

The smug face became insulted. "We will give you $50,000 earnest money. If you don't return, we will find you in Mexico."

Tomás almost showed his full volatile personality. With a low, steady growl, with as much calm as he could manage, he answered, "Don't threaten—$50,000 is nothing to me." He held a hand out to his personal bodyguard, who seemed like a mind reader, laid a Montblanc pen and small pad of paper in the open palm. Tomás wrote his guard's cell number, handed the paper to Mister Smug. "Call me when you have the money for the too-small shipment. This meeting is finished."

The Russians knew they had been dismissed by the arrogant Mexican. All at the same time stood, walked out of the restaurant without a word, not even "See you later." Now it was a waiting game.

Xander quietly said, "We have an invitation from our friend, Nick. He would like all of us to be guests at his seaside residence."

Tomás was staring at the backs of the Russians, scowling. He turned to Xander, "Are you talking about our classmate?"

"Yes, I told him we were here, he remembers you, Tomás. Zack and I visit him often. He gave Cat and me a fabulous wedding in his private residence in Moscow. If you and your partners decide not to visit him, Zack and I will go for a couple days before heading home."

"Would he allow us to bring our guards?"

"You can take your army. One more thing—no talk of business. The visit is a reunion, purely social. He loves to entertain, rolls out the red carpet for guests."

Tomás looked at his partners, who gave a slight nod, a slight smile, both thinking, *The summer residence of the President of Russia.*

Xander got his Team Phone from his slacks pocket, touched the Nikolai and speaker buttons. Nikolai answered. "Tell Zack the chef is making octopus for him." A mischievous laugh.

Zack grinned at the joke. "Thank you, I'm bringing an old friend who will eat my share."

"It sounds like you're in a tunnel, is the speaker on?"

Xander set the phone in the middle of the table. "Say hello to our old law school classmate, Tomás Ticiano."

"Tom, The Bomb? I want to see you. Remember the professor who criticized your answer and you threw a textbook at him? You caused lots of gasps." Everyone at the table laughed. "Can you come see me for a few days? Bring your entourage, I'm sure you have one."

Suppressed elation showed in the tone of Tomás's voice. It would be unsophisticated to show excitement. "When do you want us?"

Xander knew the answer.

"Now. Come tonight, the vodka's chilling." Even though these were preprogrammed words, it was with the charm Nikolai always showed when a party was planned, eager for a friend's arrival, like a kid anticipating his birthday celebration.

Xander was in control. "We'll be there tomorrow morning." It would be more sensible, not seem preplanned.

"Breakfast will be waiting and so will I." Nikolai was the perfect host, making everyone feel special. "Is Hitch there?"

The husky voice spoke up. "I'm coming for Russian breakfast."

"Glad you're here." A serious moment from the President. "I was going to call you. We need your advice. I'm being summoned, call me when you arrive. Some cars will be at the local airport to pick you up." Nikolai clicked off.

Zack, Joaquin, Hitch, and Xander were worried about the buyer. *Has he heard the rumor of a seller from Mexico, come to check it out for his boss, or is it someone playing the big shot, not really able to afford the small shipment? Or perhaps the Afghan lab owners have heard of the possible new competition and are sending blocking forces.*

Nikolai had a backup plan. He would buy the small, test shipment through his undercover Federal Security Service. That might get the cartel back to Russia with a planeload, and hopefully first- and second-layer cartel men on the plane with the personal desire to be entertained by the President of Russia.

The Team and Nikolai's goal was to eliminate as many top cartel partners as possible, destroy a large shipment of heroin and the multi-million-dollar airplane they used to deliver drugs to other countries. At the same time, Nikolai and Hitch were discussing the destruction of Afghan labs. It would look like a drug war; the Mexican cartel pushing into Russian territory, which was already claimed by Afghanistan.

There would still be lower-levels in the Mexican drug business, but it would put a major kink in the world distribution, at least buy some time for world leaders to plan their own raid.

The next morning as The Team and cartel members were deplaning, the cell phone of Tomás's guard rang. It was the smug buyer, confirming he had the money. Tomás showed his usual confidence. "We will meet you at the hotel tomorrow afternoon. We're at the coast, visiting a friend."

The President's beach house was built above the sea in the side of the mountain as though it was growing out of the rocky cliffs. The funicular, a car raised and lowered by a cable system, was available to take guests down to the rough sandy beach and cold water. Pilots were informed it was forbidden airspace above the entire area. Guards, in camouflaged stakeout huts, were armed with shoulder-carried missiles and ordered to shoot any flying object, including planes, helicopters, and drones.

Brunch was served on the covered terrace. The view showed the shallow aqua water change into deep sea-glass blue, bringing a cooling breeze. They played shuffleboard, commenting they had joined the senior category. At the basketball shoot, Joaquin took ribbing, was called "Eagle Eye," never missed a shot. He thought, *I should tell them my LA gang was called Eagle Men.*

The men dressed casually for dinner, still they were elegant in sport jackets, starched button-down shirts. The partner didn't wear his showy gold bracelet. The Kobe beef filets were flown in from Japan every week, delivered wherever Nikolai decided to be. Dinner was served on an inlaid marble table with twenty-four high-back, padded chairs. An intimate place for a small dinner party. For dessert, the chef presented blinis with a cream filling, covered with slivers of sugared orange peel and Grand Marnier.

The group adjourned to the extravagant library, books in many languages. A lodge-like fireplace, ablaze for the cool evening, oversized chairs upholstered in glove-soft leather, sat facing each other for conversations. Cut-crystal glasses containing the President's private-label vodka were being passed, Nikolai teaching them Russian toasts. Beautiful women mingled, suggestively bumping arms, shoulders.

Tomás joined Joaquin and Xander, talking off to the side. "Which ones suit your preference?"

Xander smiled. "None. I only make love with my Cat."

"This isn't love, it's sex." Tomás grinned.

"I don't want another woman to touch me." Xander showed a serious face.

Joaquin interjected his view. "I can barely keep up with my redhead, I save myself for her. I've never seen a woman who can compare."

The cartel partner brought a box of premium Cuban cigars, handed it to Nikolai, who passed them around. The Team took the offer, put them in a breast pocket, making polite comments, "I'll enjoy this later," "I'm saving this for a good friend." The Compound was a No Smoking facility.

The mixed collection of men slept late, met for breakfast, and Nikolai made them promise to return. "You made me laugh. I don't laugh much in my job. Bring your friends, next time I'll give you a dinner party at my private residence in Moscow, but don't tell my wife we had a good time here."

Xander announced that the Mexican group would probably return next week and bring all their relatives because Nikolai exceeded the host role. He told Tomás that Zack would stay to help with translation in their business negotiations, and Hitch was staying to assist the

Russian military munitions commander on a project for the President. Both would be there when Tomás returned. "I will stay home with my wife and son," he concluded.

The buyers were waiting at the Tolstoy hotel. The manager of the shipping service warehouse delivered the bundles to the hotel, the cartel guards loaded them into a covered truck for the Russians. Packages of $100 bills were sporadically opened and checked to be authentic with an ultraviolet counterfeit currency detector. Twenty million dollars was put into four large Gucci suitcases, tagged with Cat's name, for the purchase of her family vacation house in Baja California.

Buyers and sellers agreed on a return date of seven days, the number of kilos in the next shipment, and concurred on the price.

On the cartel jet back to Mexico, Xander and Tomás sat together. Xander was anxious to know that Cat would be released on their arrival. "Nikolai enjoyed our reunion. He loves to be the center of attention when he entertains, and your group was enthralled. Now for the serious part. Where is my wife?"

"She is staying in my apartment in Mexico City. My chef prepares her meals and two of my trusted guards protect her. I'm impressed with Cat. You're a lucky man."

"Yes, good fortune stopped at my table the night I met her. Tomás, I've done more for you than I intended, you certainly must be satisfied with the results. Now I want you to bring my wife to meet me. And will you do a personal favor? Before you leave for Russia next week, please take Marta and her family to San Pedro, a small town below the border in Sud Baja."

"Aren't you going back to Russia with me?"

"Hitch and Zack will still be there to help you. Everything is in place, including an invitation from the President. I will be in Hawaii with my wife." Xander smiled at him.

Tomás nodded, looked at Xander and for the first time felt envy. He dismissed the feeling. "Actually, Zack and Nikolai are more fun than you." He hesitated, perhaps regretting that he must give up his hostage. "I've arranged for Cat to be at the Mexico City airport when we land."

Cat was sitting in the black Hummer with her guards, ten more were in a double-cab truck, parked on the side of the cartel-owned hangar. She had been told that Xander and Joaquin were in the cartel jet in the landing pattern now. They pointed at the plane taxiing toward them. She recognized The Academy jet. Joe brought the plane close to the Hummer, turned it around, the nose facing out, as though preparing for a quick getaway. The door opened, metal stairs locked into place.

She alternately laughed and cried, happiness running through her body, circling her heart. On signal, the security squad from the truck double-timed to the Hummer. Cat, with a black scarf tied under her chin like a babushka, surrounded by soldiers, walked quickly with the mass to the set of stairs, up and into the familiar arms of her brother, the bear. He calmed her sobs with gentle talk, quietly he whispered, "There's a boy at home waiting for you."

The cartel jet landed, taxied toward the hangar, turned, facing into the huge open space, ready to disappear safely inside. The door opened, a tall, muscular figure framed in the opening. Before the stairs were locked in place and the cartel security could give the signal to disembark and be escorted to the other plane, Xander jumped on the narrow platform, down the stairs two at a time, ran to the outstretched arms of his wife, waiting in the doorway of The Academy jet. Two guards carried Gucci suitcases as Joaquin followed. The steps folded up into the plane, the door closed and locked. Joe started the engines.

Joaquin sat next to Oso, who looked at a face and body of exhaustion. "Are you okay, *mi hermano*?"

"I have a story to tell you that will make your mind loco. We accomplished part of our project, a dangerous conclusion coming up. And we have rescued our Cat."

Oso smiled. "The face that launched a thousand ships."

Sarge, three Dobermans, Alex, Bella, and a welcome-home group waited at The Compound landing strip. One of the Dobermans, Thor, whom Alex had named, decided he would take over Bella's job as Alex's bodyguard/protector. Bella was ten years old, slower, heavier. Thor didn't growl at her, just pushed her shoulder with the side of his head toward Amy or Emilio. Bella understood, seemed happy to have her old job back, now waiting for her friend and their conversations. Sarge knew Bella would attack if she felt Cat was threatened. Thor would be her backup.

Joe touched down the big jet with just a chirp from the tires, not even a small bounce. The students looked at one another, thinking, *That's the way I will land airplanes.*

The door opened, steps folded out the plane, Xander and Cat appeared in the doorway, Joaquin behind them. It was like someone opened the corral gate. Adults, children, dogs ran to the plane. Cat had only to bend slightly to wrap her arms around Alex. "Mom, Mom I missed you so much!"

"Not as much as I missed you."

They played the game many times—"I love you." "I love you more than the whole world." "I love you more than all the stars in the sky."

CHAPTER XXIII
The Light Has Left My Life,
I Will Live In Darkness Forever

The Team, minus Zack and Hitch who were in Russia, met in their Compound conference room to discuss the intended scheme. The good news was that Tomás scheduled a shipment of heroin to arrive in Tolstoy in seven days. The cartel's squad, sent in advance, did a great job of getting the word out, a buyer paid for the test shipment and was waiting for the next planeload. As presumed, the price was less than the Afghans', which included the cost of transporting the drugs through East Asia and across the Russian border.

Nikolai played a huge part, enticing the cartel members back to Russia. He was an extravagant host, invited Tomás and "friends" to his personal residence in Moscow when they returned, an invitation which hopefully would attract more top partners. The Team understood that the more partners and management on that next plane and the bigger the shipment of heroin, the more successful their mission.

Zack stayed in Moscow, told Tomás he would be there to help with translation. Actually he would be helping Hitch, The Team's aerial image specialist (among many other talents and accomplishments), calculate the distance and release the Hellfire Missiles from the

Predator Drones, exploding the cartel jet over the Pacific before it got to Russia. According to plan, the planeload of heroin, with the sellers would drop into the ocean.

Nikolai would send his Federal Security Service to Tolstoy to confiscate the buyer's money and get rid of the buyers, who had been the top purchasers in Afghanistan for many years, responsible for bringing much of the heroin into Russia.

At the same time, Hitch devised a plan to destroy the largest of the processing plants, again using the Predator Drones.

Xander sat, made notes of more information while Joaquin stood to give his opinion. "It's a risky, complicated plot, but with the Russian government behind us, we have powerful help. Our unknown is the cartel's exact departure time and route. Zack and Hitch need that in order to calculate the plane's location. Tomás only said he would return in seven days."

Xander now had a relationship with Tomás where it would be possible to make a friendly phone call. An offhand question about departure could come from that. If Tomás and "friends" were planning to take Nikolai up on his invitation, the arrival time might be told to Zack. They would wait for the opportunity to get the information.

If the plot proceeded as planned, The Team would have the next seven days to complete The Compound evacuation. They had been packing, moving furniture to the new Compound over the last two months when returning to check the progress on the individual homes. The renovation was not complete and they had thought there was plenty of time. But if the cartel heard that their jet exploded over the Pacific Ocean off the coast of Russia, the first act of revenge would be to destroy The Compound.

Anticipating success with their plan to rid the world of some of the top drug producers, sellers, and traffickers, The Team also wanted to protect their families and students. The new Compound in Arizona, named The Desert Oasis, had been put on double-time to finish up. The students began to disassemble, pack, and load the equipment from The Academy into covered trucks and Hummers.

Oso, Geoff, and two students dismantled, padded, packed the guns and targets for teaching, plus exercise equipment, and loaded them into a covered truck. They fitted Hitch's communication equipment into another truck and started driving north to Arizona. The Compound used four-passenger golf carts with open carrying space in the back, the model used at resorts to take guests to their suites. One was put in each truck, boxes stashed in them. A few that didn't fit would be left at The Compound to be taken by Cat's market friends.

Xander, Joaquin, and two students wrapped Zack's computers, office equipment, and his favorite painting, the large black, white, yellow, gray Jackson Pollock, in bubble wrap. All was tightly compressed together for the least moving, rubbing, rattling. The students drove, following Oso and Geoff.

Joaquin wrapped his teaching knives and private cache in soft sheets of foam, placed them in boxes to fit in the trunk of his Lamborghini, and asked his star student to ride with him. They would have private time to talk knives: personalized inventions, targets, the skill of accuracy, and—importantly—the timing, which included surprise.

Joe, in *White Falcon*, took Sarge and his dogs to their extreme kennel and training facility which Sarge had designed. Joe made two more trips for Flora, Franco, their children, and Cat's boxes. The students flew back and forth with Joe, helped everyone load and unload the plane, helicopters, trucks, and Hummers.

Xander flew one of the helicopters with Cat, Alex, Bella, and Thor. "We'll return once more tomorrow morning, do a walk-through, a check to make sure we have taken everything we want."

Zack received a call from Tomás. "Are you still in Russia?"

"Of course. I'm waiting for you. What's happening in Mexico?"

"Three of my partners and the five associates under us are going with me to Russia, but they request that Joaquin not join us."

Zack smiled. *Joaquin's reputation is well deserved.*

Tomás continued. "The partner you met at Hotel Caliente, who had the conflict with Joaquin, lectured us about our bad judgment concerning the new business deal. I have replaced the money I used to buy the vacation house, from my personal account. He kept bringing that up. He wants to use our army to take over your Compound, live in Xander's house, and says it won't cost him $20 million. To calm him down, I invited him to stay at the house in Baja while I'm in Russia. He's jealous that I own that house. I'm still in Mexico City and he is already there, probably having coffee and dessert in my suite with Rosita. Anyway, he was outvoted. Do we still have an invitation from Nikolai?"

Zack had put the call on conference, The Team was quietly listening. "Nikolai is under so much pressure, he is looking forward to laughter, music, vodka, and diversion. He keeps asking me if you have called with an arrival date. He loves to entertain and show off. Your associates will have a memorable time. Plan to stay a few days."

Tomás gave Zack his estimated arrival time. They would avoid flying over Europe and Asia, instead head toward Japan, over the

Pacific Ocean coming into East Russia as before. The Team had suggested landing in Tolstoy, a much shorter flight time and not all the varied control towers to check in with.

Xander and Cat were at their new home in The Desert Oasis, planning their last trip to The Compound, a quick walk-through. They would also look in Zack's office for iPads, cells, small items that may have been overlooked and the same in Hitch's communications room.

A call came in from Tomás. Xander put the call on conference to include The Team, wherever they were, and answered the call. "Are you in Russia?" a casual question. He knew the cartel hadn't left Mexico.

"Not yet, are you in Hawaii?"

Xander imitated a laugh. "Not yet."

"My heli-pilot took Marta, Juan, and Juanito home to San Pedro. Rosita refused to go with them. I have enough women, I'll introduce her to some friends. Did Cat get the money for the vacation house? I don't want her to tell me I stole it." He talked as if they would be socializing, like friends going out to dinner, talking, laughing.

Xander was carefully polite. "Thank you. I'm sure she'll find another project and I won't have to finance it." Both laughed. Then, as though it was an afterthought, but to confirm, he asked, "When are you leaving?"

"Tomorrow morning, about 6:00 a.m."

Xander took two deep breaths. "I'm sure everything will go as planned for you, with Hitch and Zack there to help. Your group will be impressed by Nikolai's residence in Moscow. He'll go all out for you, and will be doing it for himself, also. He enjoys entertaining, takes his mind off problems. And he thought it was a kick to see you after all these years."

Xander piloted the helicopter, taking Cat and Franco, The Team's Security Supervisor, Sarge's right-hand man at The Compound, now supervisor at The Desert Oasis, to the vacated Compound.

They would only be gone a few hours. Geoff scheduled a language class for the children, helping them settle into their new home, continue classes. Flora gave Franco some bags of gifts to deliver to her friends. The helicopter set down easily in the courtyard.

"Cat, you get started checking through the house." Xander saw a stepladder on the portal. "I'm going to use that ladder to look at the nose, see if there is any damage from that flock of birds that flew across our path. We hit a few."

Franco offered to help, but Xander told him to do his errands and return quickly.

Standing on the ladder, examining the wide nose for dents, Xander heard the roar of a military helicopter. *Larry must need to use our helipad. I told him it may not be safe after today.* As he looked toward the oncoming helicopter, he was aware that it did not angle its course to the landing strip area, but seemed headed to The Compound. *Why would he want to land in the courtyard?*

Franco had gone through the front gate, using an abandoned cart, and was on the asphalt path leading to town. He turned at the now deafening racket, saw the giant machine flying defensive zigzag over The Compound as if they were expecting to be fired at. He shouted, "Xander, get down!"

Four automatic weapons targeted the helicopter on the ground. Two lines of fire struck across the body standing on the top step of the ladder.

Inside the house Cat put her back against the wall, frightened by the roll of thunder, steady booms it produced. An eerie calm made her run back outside, see the horrifying scene. She knelt, put Xander's head in her lap, murmured, "The light has left my life, I will live in darkness forever."

A steady voice next to her interrupted her falling into an abyss. "Cat, get up. You must help me put him in this cart. We will make a plan. You need to get back to Alex."

From somewhere came strength. She put her arms around the lifeless, bloody man who carried her heart and had taken it with him. She helped lift him into the cart. *I am numb. My body has no feeling. I want to lie beside him in the cart, go wherever he goes.*

"Cat, listen to me." Franco shook her shoulders. "Go in the house, get a backpack, fill it with bottles of water. Put on running shoes, dark-colored jeans, a black shawl and scarf for your head. Go quickly, we must leave, they will be back."

I am a mechanical being. No—I must get back to my boy. She ran into the house. On a shelf in his room, she found an old black backpack with the white Nike swoosh. The blood-soaked tee and shorts lay on the floor as she pulled on dark denim jeans, slipped her replacement Team Phone in a back pocket, a black tee, a black hooded sweatshirt, and old running shoes. She entered the kitchen, filled the pack with small bottles of water, took one out, replaced it with a loaf of banana bread from the freezer, got a black marker to color the white swoosh on the pack and hurried outside. Franco had covered the body with a tarp, had just driven the cart close to the portal steps, she sat next to him. He released the brake and stepped on the pedal.

"Cat, you must walk to a place where Joe can pick you up. Find a hiding place where I drop you off. Listen to my directions. Walk at night, hide during the day. They will come back, look for us. They will be asking if anyone has seen us, even pay for the right answer. The dirt path has been used for many years to get from one village to another. It follows the base of the mountain for a few miles, then it leads you over three short hills. At the bottom of the third hill is a fork, go left, stay on that trail, winding around the mountain edge. That's where you will get cell reception. Keep walking, the trail leads to a meadow. Joe will be waiting for you. I am taking my hero to be cremated as he instructed all of us many years ago. Take this pistol. You can do this, *mi hermana*. Go, hide until dark. Make no noise. Then start the journey to your boy."

It was the gun Oso taught her to shoot. It felt familiar in her hand, small, not too heavy. She sucked in her stomach, stuck it in her waistband. She breathed out, the gun was secure. She thought of Oso's words: *If you're going to carry a gun, it's because you need it, keep it handy.*

I should have carried a gun the day I was kidnapped.

Franco let her off near a small well-watered mango grove, turned around and drove the cart toward town. She watched the tarp in the back of the cart until a bend in the path took them out of her sight. *I am a strong woman. I must get back to my boy and make a good life for him. Together we will survive.*

Bushes of thick foliage were growing around the bottom of a lush mango tree. She edged herself into the center, scratching her face, feeling cocooned by leaves. She sat on the ground, leaned back against her pack, supported by the thick tree trunk. The painful thoughts that were dammed up in the back of her mind now flooded forward. She hung her head and silently cried, tears gushing, the picture of his smile soothing the agony in her soul. Pulling her knees up to hold her crossed arms, she rested her forehead and the memories came back to life. The vacation house in Baja was built on a cliff above a small bay with a natural beach. There was no road down to the water. Xander's parents had a walkway built for any hearty person willing to walk the hundred wooden steps. Every twenty steps or so, there was a platform for viewing and deciding if one wanted to go further down. It was a playground for Xander, Zack, and Nikolai, racing, jumping, running around the beach, being fish in the shoal surf, picnicking in a shallow cave carved out of the rock at high tide.

He told her of the childhood games and she understood his memories of friends, still so meaningful to him.

He took her to the secret cave. They huddled together, removed each other's clothes, caressing with hands, fingers, mouths. With the heat of passion they made love and she knew this would forever be their special place. They had made love many times since that first night, but there was something special about the cave, the beach, the surf. It was as though he gave himself to her in a different way, told her his secrets with abandon. She remembered telling him there was sand on her body where there shouldn't be sand. He had laughed, carried her to the water, stood her in the surf, cupped his hands, scooping water to wash her body. He found a large, broken shell, wrote their names in the wet sand, stood back and said, "Everyone will know we were here, loving each other."

Then, coming back to reality, she thought, *That is where I will take your ashes and let it be known my ashes should join yours.*

The sun set behind the mountains and it was like someone closed the drapes. No street lamps, no porch lights, only dull glows from small squares in the matchbox houses of the outskirts village. The half-moon barely outlined the path. She could feel the cold water from the backpack cooling her warm body. At first, she walked carefully, feeling the uneven dirt path, some ruts where something had been dragged or maybe a bicycle rider taking a bag of big purple onions to sell at a market. As she became accustomed to the trodden path that made the world a little bigger for the village people, she started to run, sometimes stumbling, catching herself, thinking, *I'm on my way, Alex.*

Cat noticed the trail had changed to rocky and led her up a slope, not too steep, but she kept tripping. There would be no running, especially in the dark with no help from the moon.

Going down the slope was slower and more difficult, the rocks sliding under her feet. She fell backward, scraping elbows, bruising her hands, side of her hip.

Up and down the second hill she felt the rocks through her worn shoes. Her legs were achy and tired. *I will not cry, I am a strong woman.* Above her the light was changing, the sun ready to come up over the mountain. The rocky hills had no foliage. Cat looked for a hiding place off the trail, going up, then back and forth, finally three short bushes growing close together. She nudged, crawling into the center, making room for herself and her pack. Hungry, she sat numbly, breaking off bites of banana bread, sipping water. She closed her eyes and saw Alex, a baby. It was deep into the night, she brought him to bed, sitting up to give him his midnight feeding. Xander was awake, sat up close to them, kissed the baby's head, her shoulder, neck, chin. When she put Alex in the bassinet next to her bed, Xander was at his desk. He had written a note and handed it to her. "Read it to me," she had asked. He took the note, read.

I am the soaring hawk,

watching your every move,

the warbler singing his song for you,
the child walking in your footsteps.

I am the pulsing heartbeat,
the blood in your veins.
I am the man whispering
of love and promise.

She didn't know if she had slept and dreamed of Xander or daydreamed, awake with closed eyes. The memories were so real, she would open her eyes and look for him.

Just at darkness, she emerged, did some stretches, looked around for the trail. She remembered walking further off the trail, looking for bushes or a boulder. From her bush hide-out, she walked in one direction, returned, walked in another. *I am not lost, I will find that rocky path. Stop, breathe, think. The sun was rising behind me, so I will walk toward the sunset. The trail will be on my right, keep walking, you will find it.*

Cat stepped onto the trail and followed it, facing the hills where the sun had disappeared. She felt bruises on the bottoms of her feet, her left hip sent messages of pain as she walked, her hands were scraped from catching herself when she fell, and scratched from pushing into the dry bushes. *One more hill, then a path to the meadow where Joe will be waiting. Eat some banana bread, drink water, stay hydrated, I'm strong, I'm coming, Joe.*

She walked as though in a trance, staring at the path ahead of her, thinking of her goal. *Are those voices?* She looked ahead, she was near the bottom of the third hill. *A fork, go left.* The voices and flashlights were coming toward her from the fork on the right. *Step off the trail, hide.* A few yards away, she knelt on hands and knees, pulled her black shawl out of her pack, covered herself, hoping to look like a rock in the darkness. The voices were male, slurred words, laughter, erratic light beams. She waited until long after they had passed, the laughter seeming far behind her, shook off the dirt, left the stole hanging around her neck, stepped on the trail, taking the left fork. *Franco said I will get reception when I get around this hill.* She put her Team Phone in the pocket of the hooded sweatshirt, waiting for it to vibrate.

The trail was the same as when she began, a rutted dirt path, not the rocky trail. *Maybe I can run. No, I'll walk fast.* As Cat came around the mountain edge, she felt a vibration in her sweatshirt pocket. *Is that my cell?* She pressed Receive and heard Joe's voice.

"Cat, can you hear me?"

A quiet whisper, "Yes." *Is it really Joe, am I dreaming?*

"Are you on the path at the base of the mountain?"

"Yes."

"Keep walking. Three students are coming to meet you. Oso and I are waiting for you in the helicopter. Do you hear me?"

"Yes." *I can't cry yet, I have to wait until I see Oso.*

The students knew the trail, they had run it many times from The Compound, part of Geoff's training program. They exchanged thoughts. *The trail is difficult in the day, at night, impossible. And we wear sturdy hiking boots.*

Two made a chair for her, clasping each other's upper arms. The third lifted her up on their forearms, put her hands across their shoulders, walked behind her, his hand flat against her back to keep her from falling.

Oso was in the doorway of the big helicopter. He reached under her arms, pulled her inside, she collapsed onto his wide chest. He whispered, "You're safe now, *mi hermana.*"

He felt the gun, gently removed it, handed it to a student. Finally she had the luxury of crying out loud. The sound came out of her body like a wounded animal, the release of pain, moaning, sobbing, wailing, a low, steady groan. Oso sobbed with her, mournful sounds of suffering.

The students removed her shoes to rub her feet, found the tops of her socks embedded with small insects, her feet had blue-black bruises and puffy blisters. Another student picked the live bugs out of her tangled hair.

As a student closed the door, Joe, at the controls, murmured, "Okay, *White Falcon*, take us home, girl."

CHAPTER XXIV
Proceed With The Intended Scheme, Surrounded By His Spirit

The cartel jet had left Mexico, was in the air, headed for Russia. On board was Tomás, three of his partners, plus the five associates below them in the order of command, all looking forward to being entertained by the President of the Russian Federation. They were checking the invoices that detailed the number of bundles, the kilos of heroin in each, the dollar amount for separate packages in case there was more than one buyer.

The fifth cartel partner had voted against taking the large shipment to Russia, even though it was pointed out that the test shipment had been sold. They argued that more buyers, by now, had heard about the heroin that would already be in Russia, the convenience of not buying in Afghanistan and planeloads coming in regularly.

He also didn't trust Zack or Xander and despised Joaquin, who had thrown a knife at him and put a small slice in his coveted raw-silk sport jacket. He had a plan and decided he would implement it on his own. *I could run this cartel by myself.*

He remembered that Tomás had told the cartel partners of his scheme to occupy the Baja house, didn't ask their opinion or for their help. In this partner's mind, with his superior judgment, there was no need to inform others of his plan. He would take over The Academy Compound, make it his headquarters. *The other managers and associates will meet there, in my center of operations, I will be leading the conferences. Tomás only has this vacation house. I will have a fabulous house and office for myself, houses for my generals, training facility for my army, and a private runway for my airplane and helipad for my helicopter.* To further boost his ego, he brought the cartel men under the associates in order of authority. Ambitious, eager to move up, all five diligently accompanied the top-rung figure, aspiring to be his protégé, be chosen as an associate. He was sure the main house at The Compound was as luxurious as this one, where he had been ensconced for several days. *I'll take Rosita with me, she prefers me. I'm better with women than Tomás.*

From his spies in the town near The Compound, he heard that The Team had moved to the United States. He decided to take control of The Compound as soon as the cartel plane left for Russia, to avoid arguments with the other partners. By the time they were back in Mexico, in his view, the cartel business would be controlled from his center of operations and he would be in charge: *First, the helicopter equipped with machine guns will fly over, eliminate any life. Some local people might be looting my compound or maybe another cartel will be trying to take my compound for themselves. My army will go in and finish the job, secure my command post.*

The general leading the army was told to check each building and kill anyone occupying his compound.

In Russia, Zack and Hitch were inspecting the monitor and equipment, getting ready to send the Predator Drones on their missions. They had received Franco's call along with the rest of The

Team and Nikolai. The room was quiet, voices lost in grief as they concentrated, determination centered on retaliation.

In the town near The Compound, Franco parked the cart, straightened the tarp in the back, went inside to ask for help from an old friend he had known all his life. The mortuary was a three-generation family business. Franco's friend knew there was trouble at The Compound, the gossip of The Team's move had gone through the town, started when Cat visited her friends to say good-bye. He told Franco to stay with him until he finished the cremation and would drive him to the airport near the resorts on the Sea of Cortez.

"I don't have my passport to take a commercial flight, but Joe will pick me up. I must call The Team now."

No one in the new Desert Oasis conference room wanted to talk. Backs were bent forward, heads hanging over hands and elbows spread on the table.

Nikolai, streamed into the meeting, understood the scene, sharing their feelings. His voice circled around the room, competent, firm with authority. "The news is devastating, our hearts are broken. We must console each other, regain our courage, our strength. The Team has lost its core in the middle of a risky undertaking. We cannot disappoint him, his spirit surrounds us, boosts us to complete our venture. Help Cat and Alex, give them warm support. Bring in her sister and Mona to be with her, console her with soothing reassurance, and tell Amelia to not leave her alone. Oso, watch over Alex, your godson. He needs you."

As Nikolai was speaking, Hitch and Zack were busy at the Predator Ground Control station in the Russian Federal Security Building in Tolstoy. The drones were now in the air, over the five targets. At the station they received images sent from the drones, which were equipped with two Hellfire Missiles each. At a military base near Russia's west border, the Predator Drones had been prepared for the demolition of the two largest drug labs in Afghanistan. At another military base on the east coast of Russia, two Predator Drones were readied for the destruction of the jet en route from Mexico City. Colonel Lawrence West, at his new command near San Diego, California, supervised the preparation of four Predator Drones, now loaded with Hellfire Missiles and flying over The Compound in Sonora and the house on the cliff in Baja California. There would be no record of the drones' mission from San Diego, no questions to answer from the U.S. Government.

All locations were shown on screens at the Ground Control station in Tolstoy with Hitch and Zack directing the operation. Nikolai sent ten munitions experts to assist, putting two special-skilled technicians at each screen. As the explosions went off, images would be returned from the drones to the Ground Control station to check for completion.

On one screen in Tolstoy, the technicians watched as an army entered The Compound in Mexico. Trucks stirred the dust, loaded with soldiers carrying machine guns. The heavy iron gates were open, no opposing guards. A helicopter, riddled with holes from machine guns, sat collapsed in the middle of the courtyard. The general ordered it dismantled and removed. The rotor blades were taken off, a heavy, thick-link chain hooked to the helicopter, pulled it through the open gates, pushed it down a hillside to lie in wreckage. In only two hours the general called the cartel partner to proclaim, "The Compound secure."

The partner wanted the moment of walking into his new headquarters surrounded by his army to be his own accomplishment. The young cartel men would be left at the house in Baja to hear the story later and admire his power, success, wealth, intelligence, then brought to The New Headquarters to praise their idol, admire his conquest.

He was flown to The Compound landing strip, driven inside on a golf cart to start inspecting his headquarters. His army stood at attention, he straightened his back, pulled his shoulders up, lifted his chin, trying to look down on his servants. He was too short.

At the control center in Tolstoy, Zack surmised out loud to Hitch, "If four of the five partners are on their way to Russia, this has to be the fifth partner. He walks like the pompous guy who attended the meeting in Mexico City. Taking over The Compound is his way of outdoing Tomás."

Hitch agreed. When they had tested the drones several days ago, by flying one over the house in Baja, they saw the partner arrive with five men in suits. "They are probably the tier under the associates, watching for their chance to impress, get noticed, but they didn't come to The Compound with him. We couldn't be luckier, so many hot-shot cartel managers, associates and gofers exactly where we want them."

Hitch took over the seat at Ground Control. He pointed two Predator Drones coming from opposite directions at The Compound and released four Hellfire Missiles. The explosion was a violent bursting, like a volcano erupting. The drones sent pictures of utter ruin to the Ground Control station. The outer walls and all the buildings inside were reduced to fragments. Hitch and Zack's emotions were a mixture of elation and sadness. It had been their home with a family they loved, yet destroying it was part of their plans to eradicate this cartel. "The Compound is now part of our past."

Zack watched over Hitch's shoulder. "My turn." He sat at the screen with images of the vacation house in Baja. "Hope you ambitious drug dealers are appreciating the art. You're going to be buried with it." He hesitated, inhaled deeply, thought of three young boys kicking a soccer ball in the walled courtyard, running down wooden steps to their private beach. *Years pass, life changes.* He directed the Hellfire Missiles at angles heading from different directions. It was intense annihilation. They would later see the house, surrounding buildings, even the encircling wall, all lay in rubble. Quietly he murmured, "Sorry, Ambassador. Your beautiful house fell into corrupt and evil hands."

The cartel jet was almost within the area planned for its destruction. Hitch asked the two Russian techs, sitting at the screen with blinking red dots pinpointing the oncoming plane, to give up their chairs for him and Zack. The techs understood: These men had planned the scheme and taken the responsibility of eliminating the managers, leaders of a top drug cartel who were bringing a planeload of heroin to be spread in Russia.

"Hitch, you developed this plan of action. The honor of firing the missiles goes to you."

"I feel Xander's presence. This is for you, my brother. It's the highlight of my career, no, the highlight of my life."

The screen showed an explosion lighting up the sky, a grim fireworks display. The intense rupture would leave remnants to drop into the Pacific Ocean, just outside the Sea of Okhotsk. The Russian techs couldn't restrain themselves. Fists punched the air, reserved shouts praised the success, tears from their leader, who felt he must explain. "My son died from heroin."

Hitch called the tech leader to the next two screens. "These are two of the largest labs in Afghanistan, the source of much of the heroin going into Russia. Sit here, we will destroy both at the same time."

The tech team stood behind their leader, who concentrated on the picture in front of him showing the drones, which carried the Hellfire Missiles. His hands were steady at the controls, positioning the drones, tears running down his cheeks. "This is for you, my son. I have dreamed of this moment. I'm ready."

At the screen next to him, Hitch responded. "On three: One—two—THREE."

The processing labs were in the countryside, no houses, a narrow, rutted dirt road, a high wall, an armed guard at the gate. There were many opium production labs in back rooms and small factories spread around Afghanistan, but these two labs were huge factories. The country has the optimum conditions for growing fields of poppies. The opium syrup is harvested from poppies and processed into heroin.

The explosions were eerie, violent bursting with clouds of fire, smoke, yet no sound from the screen. After the initial eruptions, more smaller bursts, perhaps from the chemicals needed for processing.

The five explosions were the culmination of their achievement, the success of the strategy, scheme, purpose.

It was quiet in the Ground Control room, only their eyes congratulated each other. Hitch sent the message to his Team and Nikolai. "Mission complete. We're coming home."

CHAPTER XXV
Set Out For The World,
Take Him With You In Your Heart

The Team, students, families, had settled into life at The Desert Oasis. The Academy was in full session, the instructors engrossed in teaching, giving their complete attention to the twelve Russian students.

At The Team meetings, Zack sat staring at his brothers, not hearing the discussions, not responding when asked his opinion. He was moody, grouchy, had dinner alone, delivered to his house. He didn't respond to taps on his locked office door. Oso called Nikolai, asked for his help, but he said he called Zack every day, without an answer.

At dinner, Cat explained to Alex that Zack was still deeply depressed and she was going to his office to talk to him.

"He may not talk to you, Mom. Oso is worried about him, says Zack tells people, 'Go away.'"

Alex had dropped the Tío from his uncles' names and his mother was now Mom. He explained to Oso, "I think it's babyish to call you Tío and I'm too old to say Mommy. It's okay with Mom."

Oso gave him a bear hug. "You can call me anything you want, just remember I'm your number one Tío, *numero uno*."

Alex answered, "*Numero uno*," and hugged back.

Oso thought, *How fast my boy has grown up. Is he twelve years old already? Where have the years gone?*

Cat knocked on Zack's office door. "It's Cat, open the door, I want to talk to you." She spoke loudly, but with kindness in her voice.

"Go away, I'm busy."

"You're being selfish. Are you aware of people in this compound who need you?" Cat knew how to get his attention. The Team was his family, he would do anything for them. He explained he wasn't capable right now.

She tapped again. "Open the door, Zack."

The door clicked and opened. Zack stood in the doorway to block her passage. Cat put her arms around him, her head on his shoulder near his neck, her hair touching the side of his face. Slowly he lifted his arms around her.

"Cat, I'm having a difficult time." He removed her arms, sat at his desk, his back to her.

"We understand. All of us are having the same difficult time, but we are helping each other, Zack."

"I can't help anyone."

"Nikolai calls me and Alex every day. He told us he leaves messages for you. Zack, take your computers, go to Moscow. It will be helpful for you and Nikolai to be together. The Team supports me and Alex and I also have my sister and my girlfriends."

He asked her to please leave him, and said he would talk to Nikolai and consider going to Russia. He was suffering, Cat saw it on his face, the way his head slumped, the drag in his voice.

The Team wanted Cat to know about the destruction of the two heroin labs in Afghanistan, the cartel plane loaded with heroin and top management that had been blown up in air, the vacation house in Baja and The Compound, both taken over by the cartel, destroyed, in total ruin with the occupants buried in the rubble. Xander had told her that Marta, Juan, and Juanito had been taken home and retirement money put in place for them. They let her know Xander had been part of the planning and they completed the scheme in his name.

Her body felt numb. "He would have told me all this, but he didn't get the chance. He was waiting until it was finished." She looked at each face. "Thank you for telling me, I love you."

Cat and Alex had long talks about losing someone you love, moving on with life and keeping memories. They found it helpful to share thoughts with Oso or Joaquin, Amelia, the twins, or May and Mona when Joe flew them to The Oasis. They all noticed that Cat had not finished furnishing her new home. They talked about their feelings for the present, the people who were family to them, and the future.

Alex, Emilio, and Amy attended a private school, one-hour drive from The Oasis. Cat and Amelia took them in the morning and picked them up in the afternoon. The first week Alex met a student, Mikhail, a Mexican boy on scholarship, who became frustrated with being teased and murmured some words in Russian. Alex smiled, and when they sat near each other in class, Alex asked in Russian, "Is your mother from Russia?"

Surprised, Mikhail smiled cautiously, "Yes, and my aunt."

Oso had told Alex about the Russian girls who came to Mexico as au pair workers, like his mother, and taught their children to speak their language.

The father of one of the teasing boys was on the school board and mentioned to his son there would be a classmate, very smart, who had been awarded free tuition. He meant for his son to be friendly to the boy, who might be lonely, missing his parents who were in Mexico. However, to the spoiled boys of wealthy parents, a freebie was good fodder for mockery.

Mikhail's mother and father were waiting for legal papers to enter the U.S. His mother's sister and brother-in-law had received their papers, sponsored by other relatives. Mikhail's mother asked them to take him as their own child, in order to attend U.S. schools. The teachers in Mexico told them he was capable of better education. He quickly became fluent in English, excelled in the advanced classes, and was recommended for a scholarship to the private school. His aunt drove her own three children to local school, Mikhail to his new school, before going to her job as a hairdresser.

During the year of living in The Compound of quiet grieving, Cat received comfort and support from her sister, girlfriends, and brothers. Finally, she told them she could no longer live at The Oasis.

Zack had been living in Moscow since their conversation earlier in the year and had started communicating with his brothers. They happily noticed a change, sometimes a smile, an interest in the new class of students.

Cat addressed The Team at their regular meeting. "I have obligations, and in order to go on with my life, I must take care of loose ends." She reminded them of the $20 million sitting in luggage next to Xander's desk. "I would like the money used to build a drug rehabilitation clinic in Mexico." Also, she explained she needed their help to take Xander's ashes to the beach on the bay, down the cliff from the vacation house.

"It was our place, holds memories of our love, devotion, admiration. We will rendezvous there someday." She told them she wanted to go to Xander's apartment in LA. "I want to lounge among his things, wear his jacket, sit in his reading chair, sleep in our bed. Also, I would like to go to the house at the end of the boardwalk where we met." Cat was standing, looking at each of her brothers who had become her family. She thanked them for their support, their love.

The Team watched her, straight, strong, crying inside, only one tear escaped, she quickly caught it. Joaquin volunteered to manage the construction of the clinic, planning to hire an architect and builder. He asked for The Team's help and their opinion of building near the U.S./Mexico border. It would be easier for the people of Mexico to get help in a facility in their country and convenient for The Team to check on the building progress.

"When school is finished this year, Alex and I and Mikhail will go to Moscow. As you know, I have two boys now." She smiled and it brought smiles from each man. "Nikolai will help us find a home of our own. Joaquin, I would like very much for you, Amelia, and the children to move into my house. It has guest rooms and we will stay with you when we come back to visit. We are not going to live here, it will be too difficult for me. All of you must promise to come see us wherever we're living."

The Team was fond of Alex's friend, who spent most of his time after school and on weekends at The Oasis. The boys told each other their life stories, thoughts, feelings, hurts, angers. Joe said it was better than talking to a psychiatrist. They shared an understanding, listened without judgment.

From their French Art History class, the boys had become interested in learning French and Geoff set aside time on weekends for lessons. Amy joined them, Geoff called them the language sponges. Emilio was interested in the human body and spent time with Tío Oso and his medical books, studying bone structure, the heart, muscular and vascular systems, body organs.

Joe flew *White Falcon* down the Pacific coast of Baja California, then out further to come low inside the bay to Cat and Xander's beach. It was a tricky maneuver, but the expert pilot hovered over the sand. Oso was holding to his chest the plain cardboard box containing Xander's ashes. Cat had invited Xander's brother, Wray, but he had an appointment with his editor in New York. Zack had returned for a few days to attend the solemn scattering of Xander's ashes and would leave for Moscow when they returned to The Oasis. Cat sat in the co-pilot's seat, Joe reached over her, unlocked, slid her window open. Oso placed the box in her hands, she held it out the window, turned it upside down. The ashes scattered in the wind, falling on the sand, in the surf, flying up on the cliff, perhaps even to where the house had been that held many of his childhood memories. Each person murmured a personal good-bye, thinking of their first meeting, that he had adopted them, generously selected them as his family.

Joe talked to his big flying machine. "Good job, girl, let's go home."

Sarge had been working with Thor and Bella, acquainting them with wearing leashes, which many cities required. Thor was overprotective, now had another boy to watch over, plus Cat and Bella. He made himself protector of all. Sarge taught all of them hand signals and reinforced the command words, mostly to ease Thor's suspicious, aggressive personality.

During the sessions, Sarge noticed that Bella seemed sluggish, walked slowly, had difficulty rising from a sitting position and coughed. He called the vet he had met while building his kennel and lined him up for help after moving to The Oasis. He asked Cat when she first noticed the cough.

"The cough started a few weeks ago. I thought she was just getting old, didn't feel like eating as much. She choked a little on food."

The vet tried to lift her to an examining table in Sarge's kennel office, she winced and cried out. Both men gently put their arms around her body and lifted her up. "I would like to take her to my clinic, run some tests, take some X-rays."

Cat rubbed Bella's head. "I'll go with you, hold her in your van."

Oso was standing in the doorway. "I'll carry her to the van, then follow you in the Hummer."

Thor reached up, put his nose to Bella's cheek. Sarge fingered her ears. "Thor and I will stay here, wait for news."

After looking at the X-rays, a gentle examination, reading the blood test results, the vet asked Cat and Oso to join him in his office. He told them Bella had congestive heart failure. She had difficulty breathing because fluid had built up around her heart and the heart couldn't deliver enough blood throughout her body. He said there was an herbal extract she could take three times a day, but he wasn't sure it would help her pain. "Her stomach is quite swollen. She might live three more months, but it would be difficult and painful. I recommend you tell her you have loved her all these years and say good-bye."

Cat began to sob, Oso put his arm around her. She looked at the vet, tears streaming, holding her chin up. "I can't let her suffer, I will let her go. Let me say good-bye."

Joe, Sarge, and Oso flew with Cat, the boys, and Thor to LA. Thor would be tested on his leash. They settled into Xander's spacious apartment with views over the city, still maintained and lived in by Decker, his wife, and daughter. Then they drove to the boardwalk.

Cat pointed to the house she remembered, a numbness took hold of her body, she wasn't sure of going any further. The breeze off the ocean reminded her to breathe. She told them about the strings of lights on the board fence and around the pool, mannequin-beautiful women in colorful sundresses and model-beautiful men with toothpaste-ad smiles. They followed her as she stepped off the boardwalk to the sand, walked around the fence and stopped when she almost bumped into a body-builder-type man in pale green scrubs. At the end of the cement driveway, where it met the sand, a man was looking toward the ocean, sitting in a wheelchair. He turned, smiled at her, she recognized him.

"Rodney?"

"Yes, and you are?"

"Cat. I met Xander Xavier at your house, fourteen years ago."

"Xander called me when you were going to be married, invited me to your wedding in Russia. I know he has passed away. My deepest condolences. Cat, he was an incredible man. Zack came to see me about a year ago, stayed a few days, caught me up to date. He was on his way to Russia."

Thank you for not making it necessary to tell you he is gone. She introduced him to her boys, her brothers, her dog. He invited them into his house. She wanted to see the pool area, the spa where she met Reny, the lounge chair where Xander was sitting when she first saw him, the dark corner where he covered her with a towel.

"This is my nurse, Dean. I have muscular dystrophy, a gradual wasting of the muscles." The way he said it, the simple stating of facts, advised them he had acknowledged his fate, come face to face with it.

They accepted flavored iced water from Dean, who put down a bowl of water for Thor.

Cat brought up an image of Rodney at that pool party: a blond Adonis, dressed in white slacks, a white cardigan lying across muscular shoulders bulging under a white polo shirt. He was surrounded by cover girls, flinging their trendy long, straight hair. She walked to the spa near the shallow end of the pool, remembered Reny, Rodney's girlfriend, sitting on the top step, her pretty yellow dress shrinking, clinging, makeup smeared, tear-stained face. He had picked her up, tossed her in the pool for his partygoers' entertainment.

It was a new lounge chair in the place where Xander sat. He had turned to look at her, watched her boost herself out of the pool, covered her with a towel, driven her to the unpretentious apartment building.

Rodney had been talking to Joe, Oso, and Sarge. He told the boys they could come anytime, swim in the pool, go to the beach in front of his house. His voice was just above a whisper, another punishment from the muscle disorder.

"I'm so happy Cat brought all of you to see me. I no longer have parties for her to crash. May I take you to dinner, Cat? I know lots of stories about Xander, between his schools and world travel."

He was trying a little bribery, but Cat didn't mind. She studied him. *He's lonely, has a fatal disorder, thinks about death. I've heard lots of stories of growing up with Xander, I'd like to hear Rodney's.* "Yes, thank you, I would like to meet you for dinner."

Joe, Oso, and Sarge drove Cat to the elegant French restaurant, La Tour, located in a boutique hotel down the LA coast. They would wait for her call to be picked up. The boys had been promised cheeseburgers and chocolate shakes.

Rodney's wheelchair took the place of the luxuriously upholstered chair. His alpaca, caramel-colored sport coat was almost the color of his hair, his plain sky-blue silk tie matched his eyes, a caramel and blue shirt, all so perfect, seemed new, just from the box. He looked into her eyes, smiled, and the rascal that was Rodney was sitting across from her.

Cat wore her new dress, a fitted black sheath, a strip of heavy black lace across the top, running off the shoulders, in-out diamond hoops Xander had insisted on buying.

Rodney had placed a dime-sized speaker on the table, a wire hidden somewhere, connected to a tiny microphone. It allowed him to speak without straining and easier to hear him. "Allow me to order for you, Cat. I've been here many times, I know what the chef has perfected. I'm at the stage in my problem where I can't swallow regular food. Dean purees everything for me, a liquid diet, which I had earlier. I will enjoy watching you eat while I talk."

He gave her his memories of Xander. Their parents lived in the same town, a suburb of LA, lots of impressive mansions. He recently had bequeathed the house, with money to support it, to the state, to be used as a library. It contained thousands of books, cataloged in library order. It was also to be used for writing retreats, lectures, readings. He had gotten the idea from Xander, who had done the same shortly after his parents passed away.

"Xander took me to that elegant house, gave me a tour, showed me his room, now a comfortable parlor with seating for small group readings. We walked the manicured grounds, inspected the hundreds of species of trees, shrubs, flowers."

Rodney smiled at her. "Growing up, it didn't occur to us that we lived in mansions, it was just our house. We belonged to the same club, the overindulged rich-boy's club. We never had a job, never worked. With a few friends we went to school, lots of schools—universities, law, medicine, culinary, flying, until we were much older than the other students. We fell into different lives. Zack always had his computers and fascination with investing. Everywhere Xander went, people he met became his friends. They wanted him to stay. During his travels he was looking for something that would complete his life. That's when he met you, the treasure at the end of the quest. 'Rewarded,' he said, 'at last.'"

Cat ate slowly, relishing the rich sauce on perfectly cooked salmon, watching him, listening. He coughed a few times and she heard a rattle in his throat. His face, though still handsome, was thin, drawn.

She was curious about her onetime friend, who sat in the spa as they talked that night she met Xander. "Do you still see Reny?"

"Reny was much too good for a bastard like me. I introduced her to a friend, my personal trainer, a sincere, honest, upstanding guy, not a Rodney type. They married, have two boys, come visit me, take the children to the beach in front of my house. I'm leaving a trust fund for the boys' education."

"And you, Rodney? Is there anyone I can call for you, anyone you would like to see?"

"Thank you. Dean is my secretary, also. I live under my own shadow, Cat, it's cold and dark, requires patience, but I'm trying to right some of the wrong. I'm grateful to have had Xander as a friend. He never gave up on me, called regularly and dropped in to check on me. And all of us were happy for him when he met you. He called himself 'fortunate.' The happiness was not only on his face, it was in his voice, in his walk, it surrounded him."

CHAPTER XXVI

Keep The Memories, Push The Pain In Your Heart Aside, Make Space For The Future

Zack was comfortable in Moscow, spending the days on his computers, his mind focused on the responsibility of investments. Evenings, he and Nikolai reminisced about their young years together, laughing at the memories of three young boys, their pledge of eternal friendship. They talked about The Academy. Xander had never worked, never had a job, yet he collected the expert instructors, set up the training program and managed the school, for which he had no specific knowledge or training.

Nikolai stared at something on the wall, not seeing it, his mind seeing the young Xander. "He loved a challenge, had a drive to prove his intelligence, his capability. When I asked him to take over The Academy, I knew he would figure it out."

"Do you believe in fate, Nikolai?"

"I don't want to believe our life is predestined, that we are not in control. I know Xander believed Cat came to Rodney's that night because they were meant to meet, written in the stars, all that."

Zack was quiet, thinking, *What is in my future?* He looked at Nikolai, "I'm still waiting for my destiny."

Nikolai felt sadness coming from him. "Zack, if you want something, go get it. Don't wait for it to show up. Not everyone is as lucky as Xander."

"I believe it eases the pain to talk about Xander, just to say his name."

"We'll never forget him, but I encourage you, Zack, move ahead. You're young, handsome, intelligent, get out in the world, drink wine, talk to women. As I remember, you know how to do all that."

Some old friends of Zack and Xander's from Paris heard the news and invited him to visit. "You need to visit friends, be with people who will make you laugh." He was invited to parties, only stayed a half hour. The friends planned to go to their house in Nice, cruise the Mediterranean on another friend's yacht. Zack declined, booked a suite at the George V, and set up his computers.

He and Nikolai had streamed into The Team meetings, he continued from Paris, apologized again for his behavior at The Oasis.

He must be getting back to being Zack, The Team thought.

He went to Amsterdam, opened an account in a bank with the $20 million The Team had asked him to get out of the U.S. The bank would send money to Joaquin as needed for construction of Cat's clinic. Zack transferred The Compound expense account from the Mexico City bank and the investment accounts to another bank in Amsterdam. He called a real estate broker in Mexico City and listed his condominium for sale, using his second passport name, André Zackery instead of Zack Andrez. Each Team member had two passports and alternate IDs. These helped avoid questions from Immigration if their name had been tagged by the U.S. government or the cartel. *We must not leave a trace of The Team in Mexico. I'm sure, to some people, we are the bombing suspects. We don't know if anyone from the cartel we destroyed was left behind and might seek revenge. Although, the other cartels may decide we gave them a gift, eliminating competition.*

Zack called Marshall, with Xander's accounting firm in LA, who had been assigned to handle The Academy bookkeeping. Zack gave him the information about the accounts he had transferred to Amsterdam.

It's said, "Paris is a place one can be alone and not feel lonely." Zack was up early, walked along the Seine on the Left Bank, talked to the book stall vendors, stopped at a café for fresh croissants and coffee, listened to the waiter's story.

Before meeting friends for dinner, he usually stopped in the George V bar for a glass of Burgundy. He and the bartender had a running conversation about Cat, the death of her husband, his friend, the guilt he felt because he loved her. The bartender asked personal questions, like, "Does the sight of her make you brisk?" and gave his advice, making Zack laugh.

Nikolai sent his private jet to LA for Cat, Alex, Mikhail, and Thor. She packed all her clothes, feeling she was leaving The Oasis behind, not knowing where she would be living. She bought the boys new blazers, khakis, jeans, tee shirts, and polos. *It seems I replace these clothes every two months. How fast my boys are growing.* The outgrown apparel was handed down to Emilio or Mikhail's cousins. His parents had given their permission, blessings, and a grateful thank-you to Señora Xavier for their son's opportunities.

To keep the boys from being bored, Nikolai arranged French and Russian tutoring. "Your accents are slightly off." He requested a Russian history scholar to accompany the boys with an escort and bodyguards to the historic sites of Moscow. When they excitedly showed their journals with notes and hand-drawn sketches, Nikolai arranged a trip to St. Petersburg for them. Cat remembered she and May, Amelia, and Mona had received the same wonderful trip a few days before her wedding.

Cat rode in the security-escorted, chauffeured car with them to the airport. As she hugged each boy, Mikhail asked, "Mrs. Xavier, do you think it would be okay if I called you Mom? In Mexico I have *Mamá*, in Arizona I have Tía Angelica. You are like a mother to me."

"It would make me very happy if you called me Mom." She choked a little on the last word and hugged him again.

Nikolai was busy with meetings during the day, saved dinner in his private residence with Cat every possible night, sometimes leaving the table to take calls. After dinner they took their goblets of Cabernet Sauvignon to the living room. She put her bare feet up on the sofa and leaned back against him, he massaged her neck and shoulders. "Whatever you need or want, just tell me. I'm here for you."

She asked him to help her find a place where she and the boys could live. "I have lots of requirements. We need good schools, sports activities for them, museums, art galleries, and ballet for me."

"I know the place. I'll get more information for you. Meanwhile, you need to take more French lessons."

"Nikolai, would you put your arms around me, hold me?" She closed her eyes, her thoughts went to Xander. *I miss the feel of his body, his strong arms, the warmth, the whispering of love. I'm so lucky that his best friend is my best friend.*

Nikolai kissed her forehead. They were quiet, each with their own thoughts, they drifted into light sleep.

The next evening the boys were back from touring and had joined Nikolai and their mom for dinner. With unconfined enthusiasm, they detailed their St. Petersburg history trip, speaking in English for their mom, then slipping into Russian as they recounted the lectures from the history professor.

When the blinis, filled with cream, topped with sliced strawberries, were served, the boys finally stopped talking.

"I was waiting for a break in the history trip." Nikolai and Cat laughed. "I have a suggestion for the next step in your lives. School starts in four weeks. Lausanne, Switzerland, has everything to choose from to make a life complete. If it was possible, that's where I would be living now. The city is known for its world-class education. Children come from all over the world to attend the boarding schools. Zack, Xander, and I spent our youth in one of them and there are excellent day schools. We learned interesting sports: rowing, fencing, archery, rugby, to name a few. The city is friendly, music festivals, museums, art galleries, ballet"—he smiled at Cat—"and the enchanting Old City with medieval shop-lined streets and a twelfth-century Gothic cathedral."

Cat was watching the boys, who were attentive, wide eyed, waiting for more.

Nikolai went on, "A couple more things. The nearby lake and mountains, with more activities, are beautiful, no, enchanting in the four seasons. I have a picture of a newly built chalet for rent outside the city."

He handed the listing to Alex, which had a picture and description of the chalet. Alex read to Mikhail and his mother. "Three levels, balconies, views of the lake, mountains, and the city, six bedrooms with en suite bathrooms, plus a master suite, a game room with a ping-pong table, a media room for showing movies, and an outdoor spa. Wow." He looked at his mother, then Mikhail, who was smiling broadly. "There's more, Mom, designer furniture throughout."

She was remembering that the new living room at The Oasis was never furnished and she wondered if he had noticed that.

Alex looked at his mother. "How do you feel about living in Switzerland, Mom, in a chalet?"

"It certainly sounds like an ideal place. Let's go visit, spend time in the city, walk by the lake, investigate the opportunities, visit some schools."

Cat called The Team from the hotel in Lausanne, told them of the schools she and the boys had visited, and about the one they chose. She called Mikhail's mother for permission, enrolled the boys, paid tuition, and rented a chalet. "Promise you'll come visit, we have lots of room."

The Team was proud of her. They knew she was strong, but she had risen to independence, taking control of her life. Geoff called a bicycle and sport shop in Lausanne, opened a charge account, and sent a message to Cat. *Three bicycles, three pairs of hiking boots, three pairs of walking/running shoes, all accessories, waiting for your choice at the sport shop in the city. If you're going to live in Switzerland, this is necessary equipment.*

The next day she leased a BMW SUV. "We need a four-wheel drive for winter." She practiced driving on the dirt roads in the countryside. The boys laughed as she slowed to a crawl when another car was coming. She defended herself, "I'm driving in a foreign country."

Each boy could have had his own room, but together they chose a huge room with four built-in bunk beds, four large desks, four cushioned reading chairs. The extra bunks were for friends they hadn't met yet and would invite to stay overnight.

Attached around Cat's waist was a fanny pack with a hoop securing a water bottle. The boys' backpacks bounced from energetic running ahead, then back to Cat. "Mom, there's a man in our parking area."

They had left the walking path that ran in back of the chalet, were coming down an incline toward home and afternoon snack of apples and cheese.

"Madame Xavier?"

He's tall, maybe taller than Xander, no, about the same, older, lots of gray hair, handsome smile, pleasant-looking. "Yes."

"I'm Antoine Bisset, owner of this chalet." He stepped toward her, held out his hand. Thor pulled on his leash, Alex whispered, "Friend."

"I recognize your name from the rental documents. It's a beautiful house, we're almost settled in." *I hope he hasn't changed his mind about renting.*

"I stopped by to answer any questions about the chalet and to give you and your sons some maps of walking and biking paths. I see you have been exploring on your own."

She had told the rental agency, "Only three of us for this big house, but we plan to have lots of guests." Nikolai was sending a married domestic couple, who were looking forward to living in Switzerland. The man would also be bodyguard, a backup for Thor.

Monsieur Bisset was standing next to his G-Class Mercedes, which looked like a Jeep Wrangler with a Mercedes emblem on the grill. He had parked in the large graveled area next to his chalet.

She liked the sound of his voice, the lilting accent, almost like singing. "Please come in. I do have a couple questions."

They walked around to the back door. Three new bicycles stood secured by their front tires in a rack. Inside was a long bench to sit and remove hiking boots, muddy running shoes, and shelves for hats, gloves, wooden pegs for sweaters, coats. Half of the room was set up for exercise: a treadmill, a rowing machine, a stationary bicycle. Some thick mats for stretching, yoga, meditating, were leaning against the wall.

She stepped into slippers and led them to the gourmet kitchen. He watched her cut up apples and cheese, spread slices of both on a glass plate, and pile four baggies full, talking, telling him she liked the details of the chalet. She handed the plastic bags to the boys with two bottles of berry juice. "Be back in one hour." She shook a finger at them. "And keep Thor on his leash."

"*Oui, Madame,*" they chimed out the door. "*Adieu, Monsieur.*"

Cat smiled. They were showing off.

"Would you like a glass of berry juice?"

"Yes, I like the color, similar to claret."

On a whim, she stood on tiptoes to reach two stemmed wine goblets, poured two bottles of juice into them, smiled and held the glasses out to him. She picked up the plate of cheese and he followed her to the balcony. There were two woven bamboo chairs like scoops, cushioned, hanging from chains attached to beams. She put the plate on a low table, sat in the swing chair as he handed her the goblet of pretend-wine.

They looked across to the high mountains and below, a few sailboats, toy-sized, in the huge lake.

She was wondering how this chalet came to be, her only connection to him. "Tell me about your house. I haven't seen many new chalets."

"The idea started three years ago. My wife and I and our daughters were skiing in Chamonix, where there are many beautiful new chalets.

My wife took pictures, showed them to an architect, and he designed this modern version. We were eight months into construction, furniture ordered, and she became ill, died six months after we moved in. That was two years ago."

He was staring beyond the mountains, which were still snowcapped, seeing the smear of clouds above them. Cat was enjoying the hush, not wanting to interfere with his thoughts, she understood the needed quiet time, then the strength to move on. He turned to her. "Let me answer your questions."

They took the empty wine goblets and plate to the kitchen. She stood in front of a machine that could be found in a café. Gesturing with both hands toward it, she said, "This must be a coffee maker, which I have no idea how to use, I don't drink coffee, but what I want to know is—does it make tea?"

He laughed. "I've never known anyone who didn't drink coffee. It makes latte, cappuccino, espresso, café mocha, and over here on the end is plain hot water for tea."

"The hot water is all I need for myself, but maybe I should learn how to make those coffees for guests. You won't believe this, a sip of coffee has never touched my lips." She put a finger to her mouth.

He looked at her lips, into her eyes, gave her that Swiss-French smile that made him even more handsome. "No, I don't believe that."

She looked away. *Am I blushing?*

He showed her how to grind coffee beans, make the frothy milk, and the difference between the coffees.

"I should be taking notes. Oh, I also want to ask you about the heated wires on the roof. Do they go on automatically when it snows, like a windshield wiper, or do I turn them on?"

He took a moment, thinking about the naive question. *I don't think she is really naive. Perhaps everything was always done for her. Is she newly on her own?* "You must turn on the electricity when there is an inch or two of snow. Let's go to the electrical cabinet, I'll point out some switches."

The boys came in, sat on the bench, took off their new running shoes. "What are you looking at in that cabinet?"

Monsieur Bisset explained. "These are the electrical switches. Come and learn about them so you can help your mother."

Cat listened to him being a father, patient with their questions, like Xander would have been.

She walked with him to his car. "I'm enjoying the lovely flowers planted around the chalet. The rose bushes and the blooming flower boxes on the balconies greet me every morning."

He opened the door, turned to her. "Would you have dinner with me, Madame Xavier?"

She laughed. "Yes, I'd like that. Please call me Cat." He made a U-turn in the parking area, waved as he drove onto the paved road.

Her shoulders slumped a little, a wave of sadness passing through. *Xander, my husband, it's taking lots of time, but I'm moving forward.*

CHAPTER XXVII

I Am Never Going To See His Beautiful Face, Or Hear Him Call My Name, But That Doesn't Keep Me From Wanting To

May was standing on the curb in front of the Swiss Air Lines terminal, watching every car pass, looking for a silver BMW SUV, her sister driving. She had come on an overnight flight, arriving 8:30 a.m.

Cat saw her sister and that feeling from so many years ago flooded her being. *There she is, now I'll be okay.* She parked, pushed the button to open the tailgate, and met May with open arms. "I'm so happy you're here, I have so much to tell you." Then the tears spilled out.

May held the top of her arms, talked like an older sister. "Don't cry, we can handle anything."

Cat thought, *Sometimes when I see May, I fall back into the role of little sister. I still want her comforting hugs like all those years she cared for me.*

The sisters took mugs of hot tea out to the balcony, to sit in the swing chairs. Cat put a glass plate of flaky pastries filled with raspberry cream on the table in front of them. "This is a midmorning snack." Then to justify the sweet she said, "It's full of sugar for energy. We'll have a healthy lunch. Switzerland is a country of pastries, cheese, chocolate, and wine. The chocolate is exported all over the world, but the wine stays in this country. 'There's only enough for us Swiss,' they say."

Cat's Team Phone chimed. Hitch had updated it for transmitting and receiving international communication to easily stay in touch with her. She looked at the ID screen and smiled. "It's Nikolai." She handed the phone to May.

"This is May."

"May, come visit me, bring your sister and the boys. The President of France is coming this week. I'll introduce you. Tomorrow I will send my plane for you. I want to walk around the reception with my two sisters, one on each arm."

"Nikolai, you are my favorite host and my best friend, but I only have one week off work, I want to spend it with Cat, walking and talking."

"I'm so disappointed, call me if you change your mind. Remember—The President of France." He clicked off.

They laughed, both thinking, *The President of Russia takes the time to call us, invite us to his house. That's what happens when you know Xander Xavier.*

May looked at her little sister, seeing the doll's face from the storybooks she had read to her every night, remembering the little girl who lifted the covers, got in bed with her, snuggled, quickly fell asleep. "Cat, I'm inspired by your strength. You have stepped forward with a positive attitude, moving ahead for yourself and your boys."

"I still cry, but not as often. I'm aware that I am never going to see his beautiful face or hear him say my name, but that realization doesn't keep me from wanting to."

"Joe said that Xander would come to the morning meetings with a bounce in his step and a wide smile. They knew a little incident about Cat was coming. 'Sorry, I'm late, I was teaching my wife how to spit.' He would laugh, thinking about it. 'If she spits, she washes her tongue.' Then a big laugh, 'Isn't that great!' The guys would tease him, 'Thanks for giving us that report, Xander.' Joe said he loved every solitary thing about you."

"I miss him most at night when I have too much time to think. The memory of that day I ran outside, saw him on the ground, so much blood. I remember helping lift him into the cart like I was a robot, someone, something controlling me. When I stood back I wanted to get in beside him, hold him. For a long time, my body ached as though I had been crushed by rocks, caught in a landslide. I felt like my heart was going to stop beating."

They sipped tea, took bites of the cream-filled pastries, looked at each other's faces, a childhood passing through their minds.

"I want to hear about Monsieur Bisset, the new boyfriend."

Cat took a deep breath, gave her sister a serious face. "It is the strangest situation. I have put myself in the middle of a family drama."

Antoine and Cat went to dinner, the first time, several months ago. He came to the chalet, she offered him a glass of wine, he said they would have wine at the restaurant. He asked the boys if they felt comfortable staying at home with the household couple.

In his young confident way, Alex answered, "Sure, they're great, from the Ukraine, speak Russian to us."

Antoine raised his eyebrows. "You and Mikhail know Russian?"

"Sure, and Mom, too, but she thinks her pronunciation is not good. All of us are working on our French now. We have a tutor who comes to our home, also Mikhail and I have a French class at school."

Cat was glad he didn't mention he had spent time with his uncle, the President of Russia. That would be difficult to explain. *I must remember to tell the boys we'll keep that to ourselves for now.*

The Café Poétesse, set back off a side street in the Old City, was the epitome of romantic dining. The maître d' greeted Antoine by his name, showed them to a table in a back corner, almost hidden in a bay. Through the café, talk was a whisper, candlelight emitted an aura of mystery, burgundy-colored wine was sipped slowly, rich-sauced food savored.

Cat and Antoine had finished dinner, he was holding her hand, her fingers to his lips. A woman's loud voice disturbed the sereneness as she argued with the maître d' at his station.

"He is not here, Madame. I must call the police if you disturb our patrons."

Loudly, in his face, she countered, "You fool, I received a phone call, reported to me that he is here with a woman."

He tried to block her, she shouldered past him, inspecting the diners at each table. She saw Antoine, with a scowl on her face, she leaned close to him. "Father, how shameful of you."

He pushed back, directed the maître d', who was standing next to her, shushing, "Monsieur, please call the police."

She screamed at her father, "You have no respect for my mother, and how dare you spend my inheritance on this American woman in this overpriced restaurant!"

The police seemed to have been waiting for the call. Three neatly uniformed, brawny policemen walked toward her as she folded her arms, defiantly tucking her hands underneath. Easily, they pulled her arms down, cuffed her wrists, shuffled her through the café, past the maître d', who was shaking his head, and out the door.

To Cat, it obviously was a replay. The woman had tried to keep the police from getting to her wrists, knowing it was the next step.

Antoine inhaled deeply, took a big swallow of red wine. It seemed the other diners did the same, averting their eyes to save him the embarrassment of people staring.

Cat put her elbows on the table, leaned closer to him. "Antoine, I'm okay. Tell me what just happened."

"I can't apologize enough. I wanted to tell you about her before tonight and regret that I didn't. I foolishly thought she wouldn't know where we are and I'd have more time. Let me fill our glasses, I'll start at the beginning."

She saw waves of heartache pass across his handsome face as he began to explain. She reached for his hand, looked in his eyes, smiled encouragement.

"I have three daughters. The youngest lives in Zurich, has a serious boyfriend. They work with determination, saving for their future, still make time for laughter and calls to her father. She continually asks me to move to Zurich, away from her sister, who she believes needs psychiatric help. My middle daughter is just that, in the center, alternately agreeing with each of us. That means I can never depend on her support at times of disagreements because she has no opinion of her own. Tonight, you met my oldest daughter: brash, disrespectful, mean, selfish, insulting."

Cat felt his discomfort. "You can tell me the rest another time."

"No, I want you to know everything, so we won't have to talk about it again." The waiter set a small plate of creamy chocolate truffles on their table. Antoine placed one in her mouth and continued the tale of his oldest daughter.

"From the day she opened her mouth to talk, she was shamefully rude, and disagreeable. She and her mother had shouting matches daily, which they seemed to thrive on. Our other two daughters and I escaped to our own space, trying to shut them out. The three of us breathed with relief when she left for college, but her mother tried to continue the arguments with us. It was a difficult time. After college, the two younger girls never returned home. They did join us for a few ski vacations."

He put another truffle in Cat's mouth, both sipped wine. *Red wine and silky dark chocolate, our compensation for making it through the painful times.* She remembered the idea of the chalet came from a ski trip. "Did the girls ever live in the chalet?"

"They brought their boyfriends to look at it, stayed a couple days. Our oldest daughter told her mother she had wasted the money. Since her mother passed away, she has demanded that I give her half of my money and investments now, since she is the oldest, then a third of the rest when I die. I am not to 'vacation, spend money, and certainly not to socialize with women.'"

"Does she live in Lausanne?"

"She lives in Geneva. The police believe she has hired a detective to spy on me. He calls her and she drives the hour to Lausanne. The maître d's at my favorite restaurants try to help me by telling her I am not there, but as you witnessed, she knew. The police take her to jail for disturbance, it doesn't deter her, she threatens to sue them."

Cat had absorbed the humiliating story, thinking, *What would I do if I was the subject in a situation like this? Other than call Joaquin for help.* She asked him if his daughter had ever talked to a psychiatrist.

"When she was a teen, seemingly at her worst, I took her to see a psychiatrist, against her mother's wishes. It caused a heated controversy in our house, her mother accusing me of destroying our daughter's intelligent character. Since her mother's death, she has become overwhelming."

"Antoine, perhaps you need a bodyguard. If she gets angrier, she might be dangerous."

"I need a Thor." They laughed.

"Everyone needs a Thor." *Especially you.*

They finished the bottle of Pinot Noir Suisse, both feeling safe, his daughter detained in jail. An arm around each other, they walked the old streets, looking in the shop windows. They were relaxed with each other, contentment coming from their need. Cat was unsure about a continuing relationship and she wondered why she felt like that. It's unfortunate for a parent to have a child with mental problems, but that shouldn't influence her feelings for Antoine. Perhaps she enjoyed his company, but didn't have a stronger connection like love. She would talk to Joe, get his advice.

May listened to her sister's account of Antoine and his seemingly psychotic daughter. Now she would worry about her safety. "The girl has a serious problem, Cat, her behavior is not normal."

Cat was afraid she might come to the chalet, frighten Alex and Mikhail. She had Antoine's daughter presented with a restraining order to keep her from approaching her and the boys. Also, Cat knew Thor would not be as patient with her as the police.

She and Antoine had gone to dinner many times since that first episode, tried to evade being followed, sometimes taking a taxi, but his daughter found them two more times, made the embarrassing scene, police taking her away. Even when they successfully eluded her, it seemed they still watched the entrance of the restaurant.

Cat thought it would be less stressful and more enjoyable to stay home. She asked the Ukrainian housekeeper if she would include Antoine on Saturday nights when she prepared dinner for her and the boys. He hid his car in the garage.

The last time Cat saw him, he had joined them for dinner at the chalet. Afterward, the boys were in their room, she and Antoine were on the sofa. The evenings were getting cooler, Antoine made a fire in the fireplace. Their whispering, touching, kissing had progressed to reclining, Cat lying on top of him. They were content to be close, quiet, breathing easily, sharing the warmth of fondness and perhaps just the need for someone.

From above them, a sudden, frightening, angry, loud voice. "Father, you and this woman are disgusting animals." She focused on Cat who now was standing. "This knife is a warning to you." She was pointing the knife with jerky movements. "Never again entice my father."

Just slightly above her normal tone, Cat said, "Thor."

The boys were unaware of the ruckus, in their room listening to music. Thor heard the angry voice, was up from his bed and outside the boys' room when he caught Cat calling his name. Before Cat's next breath, Thor was in the air, his large mouth full of bared teeth clasped the wrist of the hand holding the knife. He knocked her to the floor, dropping on top of her, growling, drooling in her face. She screamed, "Get this dog off me!" and tried to push Thor away. He bit her other hand.

Red lights were flashing outside in the parking area. Three policemen had spotted her car as they passed the chalet, patrolling the area. They entered the still open door. "Okay, Thor, we have this. Thank you." Two pairs of strong arms stood her up. She was holding her bleeding, hanging, broken wrist with the other arm above her bleeding hand. She was still angry about her father and the woman, mumbling about his disrespect for her mother, but strangely, didn't seem to feel the pain from Thor's attack.

The third policeman picked up the short, narrow-blade knife with a rubber-gloved hand, placed it in a plastic bag.

Cat calmly asked, "Do we need to call an ambulance?"

The officer was concerned about Cat being wounded. "We have called, an ambulance will be here shortly. Were you touched with the knife?"

She shook her head. "No, Thor didn't let her touch me, but I'm so glad you were nearby."

He looked at Thor, who was watching the enemy being dragged away. "You are my champion."

Standing in the dark kitchen, observing the scene, was the housekeeper's husband, the bodyguard Nikolai had sent to Lausanne to protect the family he loved. He had heard the loud, rude voice, stopped in the shadows when the police entered. He was prepared to get rid of the threatening intruder. In his hands he was holding a strong flexible rope, thinking, *Perhaps this distraught woman came to her mother's house to end her life, to put this rope around her own neck, tie the end to the wood railing and step over the balcony. If she comes here again, I will testify to the taking of her own life.*

Antoine put his arms around Cat. "I have endangered your life. I couldn't imagine she would go this far, threaten with a knife. Her mental state has become even more intensified. I will talk to the psychiatrist I took her to years ago, ask for his evaluation, and if he agrees, have her committed."

May stared at her sister. "I didn't know you were leading such an adventurous life." They laughed.

Cat took her sister's hand. "Let's have lunch, a wonderful Nicoise salad with grilled salmon instead of those fishy anchovies. Then you can have a nap."

"As if I could sleep after hearing your saga. Where is Monsieur Bisset today, as we sit in his chalet, eating perfect lunch, looking at a postcard view?"

"He has called every day, told me he spent two hours with his lawyer, revising the trust for his daughters. I think that oldest girl may have a surprise when she discovers the new trust, if the lawyer ever allows her to know about it. If she isn't already in an institution, it would surely send her to one. Yesterday he asked that we please forgive him for not staying in Lausanne to meet you." Cat looked sad. "I think he is so embarrassed."

Antoine rented a villa at a resort in the South of France: two golf courses, tennis courts, a spa, mountain biking, and picnics. He had stayed two weeks last year, liked it, and planned now to stay three or four months. Then he would rent an apartment in Zurich, where his youngest daughter and some cousins lived. He told Cat he would give her a good price if she was interested in buying the chalet.

Cat took her sister to the Château d'Ouchy, the twelfth-century castle near the lake. They toured the castle, had lunch in the Château dining room, walked along Lake Geneva, or Lac Léman as the locals called it. Only the English-speaking people said Lake Geneva.

"May, tell me about your life in Toledo. Does Marco have a job? When we talk on the phone, you don't mention him, I suppose because Monica is nearby."

"When I walk out the door, going to my job, my shoulders relax and I breathe. Getting back home, I stop breathing. Then I feel guilty exposing my daughter to the unhealthy, noxious atmosphere. Monica's a junior in high school now, lucky for her she'll go to college after next year."

Monica had finally realized her father had problems. As a young girl, the stories he told her were captivating: He had lived an enchanted life in South America. His father was President of Chile, they lived in a mansion, he grew up watching his father give speeches to hundreds of people; or: His father was an architect, went to Greece to study, met a Greek girl, brought her home to Chile, married, had eight children, became a famous architect. One day she was with her grandmother and innocently asked if she still could speak Greek.

"Why would I speak Greek?"

"Because you were born in Greece."

"I was not born in Greece, I'm from Chile."

When Monica confronted her father, he cleverly changed the story. "Oh, that was my grandmother, not my mother."

May recapped the Ferrari incident, still distressed, and told her sister the rest of the story. "I already told you he sold the red Ferrari and put the money in his own bank account. He didn't repay the money from my IRA that I had withdrawn to pay off the loan in order to get the title. I related the story to his sisters. One said it was my responsibility to support him because I made more money. Another sister rudely reminded me Marco has raised our daughter since I am never home. Cat, I travel once or sometimes twice a month and I'm never gone for more than three days. Many business people travel every week."

The despair in her voice was painful for Cat. "When Monica goes to college, might be a good time to file for divorce. Then she could choose where home is."

"I told him I am talking to a lawyer and I wanted him to move out of my townhouse. He told me to move out, he will keep the townhouse. Also, with the money he stole from me, he bought a sleek, fast-looking, black Porsche. There's a track outside Toledo, and for a fee, a sports car owner can race around the track. 'Get the feel of your high-performance machine' the ad says. He goes there every weekend."

They were sitting on a bench off the walking path, Cat scooted closer to her sister. "Don't cry, we can handle everything. I will help you buy a new townhouse, you can furnish it the way you want. We'll get a restraining order and he will not be allowed to step one foot into your house."

CHAPTER XXVIII
The Prodigal Father Returns

"Do you live in a modern chalet with a view of Lac Léman and the mountains? Is that Mont Blanc back further with snow on top? If you turn around, look toward the Old City, have you noticed the spires and belfry of the Gothic cathedral rising above Lausanne?" He looked up to the first balcony, perhaps feeling her presence.

Cat would have known his voice without the caller ID. The low pitch, like an introduction on the PA system, the friendly, personal warmth as if he was looking at her, smiling.

She was standing behind a planter of *Pelargonium*, "Angel Eyes," a species of geranium, pale pink around the edges of each petal, deep pink inside. "I'm angry at you, Zack."

"I'm coming up there to explain, so you'll be un-angry." He was on the top of the outdoor steps as she opened the heavy wooden door.

She reached up to put her arms on top of his shoulders. He held her waist with both hands, kissed both cheeks. "The Swiss air agrees with you."

Cat backed away, looking at him, hit his upper arm with her fist. "What took you so long?"

"Could we sit and discuss this?"

"It better be good, Zack," an edge in her voice. He watched her walk to the kitchen, followed. "I have a machine that makes coffee for every mood." She showed him the coffee maker that could be found in fancy cafés. "Latte, cappuccino, caffè mocha, espresso? My boyfriend taught me how to make all those coffees."

"Where is he? I'll challenge him to a duel." He imitated a scowl.

"Actually, he's an ex-boyfriend." That was Cat, she had to be truthful, couldn't continue with deception.

"Lucky for him, he's not around."

He followed her to the all-wood-paneled living room, a floor-to-ceiling stone fireplace, two comfortable sofas, both carrying their mugs. She took a sip of tea, turned to look at him, admired his face, the square jaw, full, sensuous lips, the brawny body in a gray buttoned shirt under a perfectly fitted charcoal, cashmere crewneck. *There is gray mixed in with that thick black hair. Is that new or did I not notice it?*

"I missed you, Zack. No, I needed you, needed to talk to you."

He turned serious. "Cat, Xander left and I felt I had fallen down a hole. I wouldn't have been help for you. When you came in my office that day, told me I was being selfish, but should go to Moscow, be with Nikolai, it turned out to be good advice. We reminisced, talked through our anguish, leaned on each other, and our broken hearts began to heal. And you were right, I was being selfish. I'm sorry I wasn't there for you."

He told her he was aware she had private meetings with Joe. Everyone in The Compound had difficulty dealing with the loss. Before Zack left for Moscow, The Team met for group therapy every morning. Joe led the sessions, which Zack said was helpful for him and that Joe brought in psychiatrist friends for different perspectives. They learned The Team had become so entwined they were dependent on one another like a school of fish, when one turned, all turned. Even though Xander called himself a member, saying all eight men were equal in authority, he was looked up to as the leader. Nikolai was Xander's partner. The Academy was put together and operated for Nikolai, who was authority through Xander. The Team agreed, even though Zack had grown up with him like a brother, all eight had become brothers.

"I'm proud of you, Cat, the way you have taken hold of your life. I know you felt a serious responsibility to your son and that kept you going, still, it took strength of character, a resistance to being overcome with grief. Please forgive me for not being there to offer comfort or support."

Cat wasn't sure if she was ready to forgive him. She was still hurt by his ignoring of her, no offers of help, no encouraging calls. "I'm thankful for my sister and Amelia and Mona. They rescued me out of that first year of despair, boosted me up. Alex suffered from the loss of his dad. He and Oso had always been close, it was Oso's counsel that was most helpful for him. Also, Alex took on an obligation to be responsible for his friend Mikhail's well-being, supported him against the school bullies. That kept him mentally strong to handle both situations. He's intelligent, compassionate, respectful, kind."

She felt it was getting time for the boys to come home from school. The mother of one of their classmates had formed a carpool, Cat only had to drive once a week. She looked at her new gold Swiss watch.

"New watch?"

It had a fine, mesh, eighteen-karat band, mother-of-pearl face, gold hands. "Yes, it's a little showy, but I bought it for myself, to prove my independence. Most watches today are digital, I like the old-fashioned hands." She put her sleeve back over the watch. "The boys will be home from school soon. You can help me get out some juice for them to have with their after-school snacks."

The Ukrainian housekeeper had placed bowls of cut-up carrots, celery, apples, cheese, crackers on a tray, waiting on the granite counter. Cat introduced them.

"Oh, you're Señor Zack, from Mexico. Hello. I will set a place for you at the table for dinner."

He looked at the tray of food. "Is this for the whole class?"

"Only two growing boys," she answered.

In Russian, he asked, "Is that a Russian accent?"

Sometimes, Cat asked the housekeeper if she would like to join her and Thor for a walk when the boys were in school. They would exchange life stories. The housekeeper knew about Zack and wasn't sure she liked him. He hadn't helped this good woman in her sadness, whom she liked very much. But, now, he spoke Russian. *He might not be so bad.*

Alex and Mikhail announced themselves with loud, quick pounding up the wooden steps, then in the front door like they had been pushed by a gust of wind. "Whose car is that? Who's here?" He saw Zack, standing near his mother. "Look, Mikhail, the Prodigal Father returns!" There was something in his tone—anger?

Zack hid his smile. "That's the problem with these Swiss schools, they teach everything from Bible Stories to the Space Program. As I remember, that particular story stresses forgiveness." They silently looked at each other.

Both boys greeted their mom with a kiss on the cheek. "Excuse us, we have homework to do before dinner." Alex picked up the tray, Mikhail took two bottles of apple juice. "*Merci, Madame.* Come on, Thor, it's snack time." There had been no greeting to Zack.

During dinner, the boys politely answered questions about school subjects, activities, teachers. Zack told Alex he would like some private time with him. It wasn't a request with a question mark, it was a statement from father to son.

Zack picked from the several guest rooms where he would be staying. He scooted the desk chair to face Alex in the side chair, knees almost touching. "You have heard an overview of this story, your story. I believe you are ready to know the details of your beginning, yet an extraordinary outcome, due to your mother."

He began telling of the beautiful Russian girl, desperate for a new life. He spoke gently, but honestly, of the events of Alex's life. The guileful but clever way she became pregnant, thinking pregnancy would force him to take her to Mexico. He admitted his anger, feeling deceived, wanting the child to stay in Russia and to only pay for his support.

He watched Alex's face, intent on every word, and continued. Zack told him she was not healthy and explained the respiratory system illness, a fatal pulmonary condition that left her weak with difficulty breathing. He left out the fact that pregnancy strained her system even more, but affirmed she had died soon after giving birth.

Zack got up, went behind Alex, rubbed his shoulders, kissed the top of his head, handed him tissues from the desk.

As he sat again he said, "Please allow me to tell you more."

He was choosing the words carefully, telling that Cat had not been able to get pregnant and wanted a baby to love, raise, complete her family.

Alex interrupted him. "I know—the vasectomy, the low sperm count. Mom explained that years ago and Oso helped me understand." His tone had impatience, as if to say *I already know all this.*

Zack hesitated. *Did I know about vasectomies and sperm at this young age? I think it's a complex situation for a young mind.* He went on to the easier part. "It was Nikolai's suggestion to ask Cat if she would like to adopt the baby. She was ecstatic, carried you with her everywhere she went. We thought you wouldn't learn to walk, she never set you down."

"Mom told me a long time ago that you are my biological father. That's when I started calling you Zack instead of Uncle Zack. I want to tell you this. You are too much like my dad, Mom could love you. Don't stay here unless you're serious, don't hurt my mom."

Alex started to get up, Zack held his hand up. "Here's my confession. I have loved your mom for longer than I want to admit. I'm here. If she will permit me to stay, I will never leave. I'm serious about her and I will never hurt her or you."

Zack put his hand out. Alex stared at him, thoughts circling in his mind. Zack waited. They shook hands, exchanged profound looks. A trust had taken place.

Mornings, after the boys left for school, Zack and Cat exercised in the back room. He used the rowing machine, watching her do yoga, meditate, stretch before folding up the mat and placing it against the wall.

"We need to join a gym club, my biceps, triceps, pecs are shrinking." He flexed his arms, took a breath in, puffed his chest out. He was wearing a tee shirt, stretched across his chest, upper arms.

Cat watched. *Nothing looks shrunken to me.*

On the days she drove the carpool, Zack went along, and after two weeks, he asked if he could drive. They would drop the boys off at school, go to a coffee house for breakfast, then stroll the lakeside promenade, watch the swans or take the walking path along the pier, waving to people on the boats. They sat on the benches, his arm around her, looking across the lake at the mountains. "Let's take the boys skiing when it snows," he said. "There are great winter activities: tobogganing, dogsled rides, snow tubing, plus skiing and ice skating." He said he would like to show her and the boys the boarding school where he, Xander, and Nikolai spent years at young ages. "Cat, we can talk about Xander, tell me when you're missing him, things you want to remember, and I'll do the same. He filled our lives and will always be with us. That day we watched his ashes settle around the bay wasn't the end. He lives in our hearts. We can't pretend he didn't exist."

"It's wonderful of you to say that, Zack." She felt more comfortable. It gave her permission to like the feel of his arm around her. She had known him for so many years. She thought of the times she presumptuously walked into his office, giving her opinion or criticism or asking a favor. *He seems to have finally gotten to the place, after grieving, that he can offer comfort. For me, it's more than comfort. I care for Zack. He was going to leave The Compound when Alex came, but he stayed when I asked him to stay. He didn't want to donate sperm, but agreed when I asked it of him, though we never got to continue with that procedure. I believe Zach has always cared for me. It feels right for us to be together.*

Dinnertime was full of loud talk and laughter. The boys repeated gossip about their teachers. "Mr. Mason fell asleep at his desk while the class was taking a test, really." They asked Zack if he remembered his classes, teachers, headmasters. He bragged about being the Perfect Student and only got in trouble because of Nikolai and Xander. "One amusing incident I remember—we thought it would be quite clever to stand on a desk, naked, in front of the window facing the campus quad. We took turns, one standing nude, while the other two shined flashlights up and down the body."

Through the hysterical laughter, Alex asked, "Whose idea was that?"

Quietly Zack muttered, "I guess I instigated that one, but other than that, I was perfect."

They got the obscure joke and asked, "Did you get caught? What happened?"

"The usual: letters to parents, threats of expulsion, extra assignments including an essay on 'Proper Behavior.'" He said it in a bored tone, like it was a routine happening. "However, we were held in high esteem by our classmates."

Each night at dinner, the boys couldn't get enough of Zack's stories of boarding school. He also charmed them with plans to "get to know" Switzerland. "Saturday night we will have dinner in the Old City near the cathedral. You will learn what the tourists don't know, too hurried to sit and listen. The cathedral is actually named Notre Dame, but the Swiss don't mention that because the world associates Notre Dame with Paris and prefers to call it The Cathé."

Cat sat back, skeptical. "Zack, is that true?"

Alex smirked. "Would Mr. Perfect lie?"

Everyone laughed.

The restaurant in the Old City was hidden on a back street, a locals' favorite, serving typical Swiss food, not listed in the tourist guidebooks. The most popular dish was strips of meat, usually veal, cooked in a sliced mushroom sauce. The side dish was rosti, coarsely grated potatoes, packed in a skillet, fried crisp on the outside, top and bottom. So similar to French fries, maybe even better.

Inside The Cathé, Zack told them to sit where they could look up at the south Rose Window. "Find the images representing four seasons, four elements, four rivers of paradise, four winds, the twelve labors of the months, and the signs of the zodiac." He gave them handwritten lists, sat a few rows back with Cat, letting them play the game without being crowded by parents. He quickly pointed to the images for her, put his arm around her shoulders, pushed back some loose hair, kissed her cheek.

She smiled. *I wouldn't mind if he really kissed me.*

The boys proudly brought their lists, all items with check marks, handed them to Zack who thought, *I must find something that will keep them busy a little longer.*

Mischievously, Alex said, "No PDA in church." He liked teasing Zack. The taunting went back and forth.

Zack hid his smile, loudly whispered to Cat, "Public display of affection. Let's send them to school in Italy. They have no rules against PDA."

He steered them outside. "It's almost 10:00 p.m. Every night, 365 days a year since 1405, the watchman walks the 153 steps to the top of the Lookout Tower. From 10:00 p.m. to 2:00 a.m. on the hour, he calls out to the four directions in French, 'This is the Night Watch, the hour has struck.' Originally, his main purpose, besides calling the hour, was to look for fires."

Mikhail asked, "Did you learn about The Cathé in boarding school, Zack?"

"No, we learned lots of things from Swiss girls we met exploring the Old City." He raised his eyebrows at them, they laughed.

The next weekend Zack hired a car and driver, leaving early morning for an all-day tour. They took pictures of the terraced vineyards of Lavaux carved flawlessly around the hills, empty of grapes now.

Lunch was raclette, a melted cheese served with vegetables and fresh-baked crusty bread. Zack told them next week they would have lunch in an igloo where they specialized in Swiss cheese fondue.

They strolled the market town of Vevey. Cat bought a fondue pot with long-handled forks, Zack said he knew a cheese shop in Lausanne. He bought the boys Swiss army knives. "We'll need these next summer when we go camping." They looked at him with doubting eyes. "What—I know how to camp."

Wherever they were, Zack sat close to Cat, they held hands, he kissed her cheek, whispered he loved her. Every three or four days he told the boys he was taking their mom to "dine in a romantic restaurant."

He has become so romantic and affectionate. It feels right, like I'm in love. She began to initiate the kissing, the closeness, the hand holding. When they kissed, she kept her arms around him, not wanting the end, the separating.

When Zack suggested the lovely, romantic café where Antoine's daughter first surprised them, she told him the story of her doomed friendship.

Zack said he would check with the police, ask if they had seen her car in Lausanne. "I hope her father is cautious. That daughter is impending danger."

Lausanne was a Christmas card picture. Buildings were covered with snow, and icicles clung to overhanging roofs. Store windows were outlined with pine cuttings, embedded with colorful lights, and music poured from opened doors. Cat said, "Christmas in Lausanne is the way I always dreamed Christmas should be."

The boys school ski club took a weekly busload of rambunctious snowboarders on day trips. The club manager asked for parent volunteers to chaperone, and Alex asked Zack to go with them. He taught them rowdy songs to sing on the bus. They teased him, called him "old-fashioned" for using skis, not trying a snowboard. As a group congregated at the top of the mountain after getting off the chairlift, he tightened his boot buckles, adjusted his ski poles, and loudly said, "Observe Artistry." He turned, looked at Alex, smiled, "And perfection." He took off down the slope in brochure form. The boys laughed, followed behind him. "Your dad is fun," a classmate commented.

Amelia called Cat. "I'm inviting a group to spend Christmas at your chalet." Joe, May, and Monica joined Joaquin, Amelia, and the twins and told Oso that Cat would be angry if he didn't go, also. Oso thought, *I miss mi hermana and my godson. A phone call doesn't take the place of being with loved ones in person.*

Cat was busy every day preparing for her family. Zack was sent to get a pine tree for the high-ceiling living room. He came back from the Christmas tree market with a huge mountain spruce and two men to secure it in a stand. They filled the tree with strings of tiny lights, then attached more strings around the balconies and on the railing up to the front door.

Zack, Cat, and the boys went to several Christmas markets in Lausanne and towns nearby collecting decorations and a large white-robed angel for the top. "I'll need to rent a derrick to place that girl up there, or maybe one of you guys could stand on my shoulders." Zack looked at Alex and Mikhail.

"Not me," they said together. "Maybe Mom." And snickered.

They separated and secretly did gift shopping.

The family filled the house like the herd had come into the corral. It was two weeks of laughter, hugging, toasting, sightseeing, skiing, and much eating. Cat served cheese fondue in her new pot and gave everyone a set to take home.

Alex and Mikhail took Emilio to their school. It was closed, but the Headmaster was in his office and let them tour the classrooms. They explained the agenda for each subject. When they got back to the chalet, Emilio asked if he could attend school next fall with his cousins.

Joaquin said it's something they could discuss at home. *Would I be able to let go of my boy at such a young age? Children grow up too fast.*

Cat wanted a full report of the drug rehab clinic The Team was building on the border, which they had named El Gato Clinic. Joaquin had photos and let her know young doctors from all over Mexico gave some of their time. Patients came for help before the clinic opened. A staff and programs were put together, the process of healing began and construction continued.

Joe took all to Moscow in The Team's Gulfstream for three days, which wasn't long enough for Nikolai. He gave them extravagant gifts: diamond bracelets for the ladies, Apple watches for the children, birthstone cuff links for the men.

"How do you know my birthdate?" Joaquin asked.

"It's in the file I keep on you. I'm ex-KGB, remember?" Everyone laughed, Joaquin smiled slightly.

Joe stopped in Lausanne, everyone said good-bye to Cat, Zack, the boys, and continued home to Arizona.

As they returned to the chalet, Alex and Mikhail hugged their mom and Zack. "It was a fab Christmas."

It was snowing, large silent flakes, the best time to sit outside in the steaming hot tub, acknowledge the quiet, peacefulness of snow.

Cat asked Zack if he wanted to join her in the spa. "The water was changed today, not contaminated with the lotions and oils from a herd of people." She wore her usual, conservative one-piece bathing suit, he took off his robe, revealed a sculpted body in tailored swim trunks, stepped in across from her.

I won't sit close, she may feel intimidated with so much bareness. I'm happy to just look at her. They reviewed the visit from their family, the love they brought, the laughter that filled the chalet. Cat felt the years had delivered changes: the friends even more protective, an anxious concern for one another. The children, influenced by the family, given opportunities to grow, were intellectual, independent thinking. They talked about Alex and Mikhail, growing up, their advancement in school. He said the warm weather passed and he hadn't taken them to the fairy-tale Chillon Castle. "That will be our next excursion, a boat up Lac Léman in the spring."

He was planning their family time and she was elated, like finding something lost. *He's a thoughtful father to our boys. I still think of carrying a baby in my body. There should be love between two people to consider having a baby together. I wonder if he thinks about that or remembers we talked about it, seems so long ago. It was right that we never proceeded with the in vitro plans. It would be wonderful to have a baby with a man who loves me.*

She smiled at him. "You can stay longer in the hot, relaxing water if you want, I'm going to shower off these chemicals." *I'm having thoughts and feelings of being intimate. I wonder if he thinks about me like that. Wherever we go he sits close and kisses me. Even says he loves me.*

He watched her wrap the terry robe, tie the sash. "You go ahead, I'll put the cover on the spa." *I wish I knew her thoughts. Should I make the first move? No, I'll wait.*

Zack had showered, put on light-blue cotton pajamas someone had given him, the shirt unbuttoned, hanging open. His door ajar, Cat pushed it open, closed it behind her. She was barefoot, scented of lavender, wearing a floor-length, pale-pink, matching robe/nightie set of fine brushed cotton, delicate lace at the neckline.

He was sitting at his laptop, turned to look at her. Slowly, he got up, walked to her, gazed into her eyes, his hands held her face.

Cat whispered, "Are you sure?"

He smiled, "I've been waiting for you. It had to be your decision."

She put her arms inside the shirt, around to his back, felt the warm, strong body. She lifted her face to him.

He kissed her neck, cheek, lips, firmly, craving. "Let's have our baby, Cat. I have never been so sure of anything. Do you want to think about it?"

"I've thought about it so many times."

He scooped her up in his arms, carried her to his bed.

CHAPTER XXIX

To Live Through The Past Brings You To Sunlight

Joe and Joaquin left the 98-degree dry heat of Arizona, were coming in for landing in the hot 80-percent humidity of Toledo, Ohio.

Joaquin had reserved a 700+ horsepower McLaren 720S Spider, the "Ultimate Sports Car," waiting to be picked up at the airport. They drove to the racecourse outside Toledo where Joaquin could test the car's performance and his driving skill at an arrive-and-drive open track day.

"Are you sure you don't want to ride with me around the track?" Joaquin teased, knowing Joe had never been tempted to ride in his Lamborghini at The Compound or The Oasis.

"I'll stick with rides that go up in the air—much safer."

Joaquin parked at the entrance and they got out to register, using their alternate IDs, since they had to show driver's licenses, pay with credit cards, and sign insurance waivers. Then each received a wristband, different colors for their driver and spectator roles. Once inside the track compound they found the paddock parking area, where other drivers had already gathered and spectators were wandering around, admiring the fancy hardware. All eyes followed the "millennium car" as it cruised in and parked.

Joaquin pushed a button, the top lifted up, stowed itself in the back compartment. They got out, left the doors up in the air like butterfly wings on both sides. People started walking toward them.

Minutes later a sleek, black Porsche arrived and parked at the end of the row beyond the cars that had come in after the McLaren. The Porsche driver got out, walked around the car, opened the passenger door for a lovely young blond woman in skinny jeans and a tight red tee. The driver, slim, a cocky walk, was wearing a zipped-up black shiny racing jacket with a small Porsche emblem on the front and matching leather driving gloves. His eyes were concealed by Porsche Design aviator sunglasses.

Joaquin could tell the driver was observing the McLaren from behind the dark lenses, though his face was angled attentively toward the blond. One of the regular spectators walked up to the driver and clapped him on the shoulder. "Hi, Marco, how's that Porsche running?"

"Perfect. I'm going for ten laps today. My fiancée has come to watch."

Joaquin raised his eyebrows, then sidled around the front of the row as Marco and his fiancée strolled along the backside of the row past a Ferrari, a BMW i8 with gull-wing doors, a Maserati, and a Lamborghini. Nonchalantly they joined the crowd around the McLaren taking photos and asking questions. While their backs were toward him, Joaquin stepped alongside the freshly washed and waxed, shiny black Porsche.

With the touch of a button, the compartment door opened, the hard convertible top of the McLaren moved up and toward the front, locked into place on top of the sports car. Joaquin buckled his helmet and took his turn on the track, flying around it five times, faster than he ever could at home, a grin on his handsome, mischievous face. The ride was a gift he had given himself, and the crowd's whoops and fists punching the air went unheeded. At the end of his laps, not waiting for praise or to discuss the car's handling, he picked up Joe and headed for the Airport Hilton Hotel. The exotic car rental company took back the McLaren and left a Mercedes SUV. They checked into The Hilton, changed into swimming trunks, and went down to the pool to join the water volleyball game.

Tired, they had left Arizona early, they went to their rooms to shower and nap. Joe said, "I'll let you know when I get a call."

Joe had dozed off, the airplane magazine on his chest, his cell woke him. "May, you must have ESP. I'm in Chicago on Team business, was just going to call you."

"He's dead, Joe, an accident at the track." Her voice was full of awe, she was trying to grasp what had just happened.

"Joaquin and I will leave now. It's less than an hour flying time, we'll get a car at the Toledo airport and be at your house in about two hours. Are you and Monica okay?"

Then the dreaded news: "His sisters are on the way over here."

"Lock your doors, that will stall them until we get there. We'll handle the sisters."

May felt strange. *Shouldn't I be crying?* Instead there was a sense of relief, as if she had been lifted from a swirling eddy, now safe and warm and dry.

Joe was anxious to get to May. He and Joaquin were in the SUV, waiting for more time to pass so it would look like they had come from Chicago, weren't near the track where the accident had happened. Parked a block from May's townhouse, they could see three cars in her driveway. "Let's go, she needs help."

Joaquin parked behind the cars, blocking them. One trunk was open, piled with clothes. Coming out the front door, a man and woman were carrying a wood and glass coffee table, one at each end. Joaquin showed a long-blade, thin knife to the man, put it to his throat, some blood dripping from the slight touch. Joaquin growled, "Take that table back in the house."

May and Monica were in the bedroom holding a woman's arms. She was carrying a load of clothes. "You can have his clothes. Put mine down."

Relieved, happy, May saw Joe. "She's stealing my suits for work."

He blocked her at the door, she tried to push past him, stocky, like a sturdy bulk. "This is my Marco's clothes. Get out of my way."

From behind her, Joaquin reached around and showed her his knife, she ignored it, called her sister for help. He scratched a skin wound on each woman's beefy shoulder. They saw blood, screamed, dropped the clothes, threatened to call the police and went out the door, cursing him in Spanish, holding their shoulders. Another woman and man ran to their car, each holding a lamp, tried to lock the car doors, but couldn't manage fast enough. Joe opened the door, she handed the lamps to him.

The motor was running in the car that had the open trunk full of clothes. The Mercedes SUV was blocking it from exiting the driveway. The trunk was down, the doors locked. Joaquin yelled at the driver, "Open the trunk."

The man yelled back, "Fuck you. Move your car."

Joaquin took a step back, kicked a big dent in the door, stepped toward the front, kicked a bigger dent in the fender. The trunk opened. He helped May and Monica take armloads of clothes back into the house. "I would rather give his clothes to The Salvation Army," she murmured.

Joe moved the SUV, the three cars backed out, drove away. Another car stopped in front of May's townhouse. The blond woman in skinny jeans tiptoed across the patch of lawn as if she had seen a sign that said, "Do Not Walk on the Grass." She rang the doorbell, even though the front door was still open.

Monica came to the door, looked at the mascara-smudged face. "Hello."

"I'm Marco's fiancée. I would like to collect his papers."

May walked up, stood next to Monica. "What papers would that be? And who are you?"

"Mom, this is Dad's fiancée."

"I didn't know a man could have a wife and a fiancée at the same time." Joe had stepped up to the small porch.

The blond woman turned to him. "They aren't married. Marco was just living here, separately, until we bought our own house. I want his life insurance policy, I'm the beneficiary."

Joe thought, *She believed his lies, doesn't know the true story, didn't know the real Marco.* Patiently he said, "Give me your name and cell number, we will call you when we have time to go through his desk."

Standing in the small living room, Joe put his arms around May and Monica. In her organized way, collecting her thoughts, aloud to herself, May asked, "What shall I do first?"

Joe, letting her know she had help, answered, "Let's call the morgue, have his body cremated and the ashes sent to the oldest sister, the one in charge of stealing. Then, call Monica's school and your boss, get a few weeks off, and come with us to The Oasis." He held Monica's chin. "I can't wait for you to see my *White Falcon.*"

"A bird?"

"Yes, the biggest and most beautiful bird you have ever seen."

* * * *

The boats that decorated Lac Léman were slowly coming out of hibernation. The high Alps beyond were still totally concealed in white as if they were keeping a secret hidden as long as possible. Spring brought a two-day snowstorm to Lausanne, then the sun appeared and the walking paths were revealed.

Alex had showed Zack the switch that turned on the heated wires, melting the snow on the roof of the chalet, and together they had figured out the mystery for starting fires in the floor-to-ceiling stone fireplace. They thought those two jobs were finished for a few months of warm summer, but not yet.

The boys and two friends from school had dinner with Cat and Zack, then disappeared to their spacious quad suite for male talk and teen music.

Cat changed into her warm flannel robe and nightie, Zack put on sweats, ready for their drowsy evening. They were cuddled on the sofa, Cat's bare feet under a lap robe in front of the crackling flames. "All the shop owners say we're having an unusually cold spring, but it's just a reminder to appreciate the blooming trees, ready to burst into color."

Alex was the messenger. "Mom, could we have ice cream with the chocolate sauce that gets hard like a shell when it's poured on top?"

Zack didn't eat many sweets, but it sounded interesting. "I've never had that."

"Stick with us, kid, we'll show you good stuff." Alex and his friends were teenagers, "the dangerous age" they liked saying. They were aggressive, bold, brazen.

Zack laughed. "Thank you, I intend to. That doesn't sound like Swiss school talk."

"There's some Americans at our school from Louisiana, they call us 'y'all' and tell us we talk funny. They liven up our classes. You should hear them speak French with a Southern accent. We invited two brothers to stay overnight with us next weekend. They wanted to know if we were going to have Southern fried chicken." Alex laughed. "I told them we were going to have rosti. They said 'Okay, we'll come anyway.'"

Cat unfolded her legs to stand, Zack put his hand under her elbow, pulled her up, smiled at her.

"Zack, you use the ice cream scoop, I'll get the hard sauce, Alex, you get four soup bowls and two rice bowls."

Alex carried a tray with four bowls, each with three scoops of ice cream, sliced bananas, shredded coconut, and hard chocolate sauce over all.

Back on the sofa, Zack asked for help.

"Crack the shell with the spoon, then eat bits of hard chocolate with the ice cream," Cat instructed.

The scraped-clean bowls on the end table, Cat settled against his chest. He put his arms around her, both hands on her stomach, whispered, "We have a baby growing in here, my love."

Cat wouldn't go to the doctor until she missed three periods. "I just want to be sure." The pregnancy was confirmed. Every time they glanced at each other, it was a happiness message. Cat passed the nauseous phase undaunted, they laughed at the frequent bathroom calls, and when she felt dizzy or tired, both lay down to nap, close, fitted to each other like two esses.

* * * *

After Marco's death, Joe and Joaquin took May and Monica to The Oasis and they were enveloped by The Team. Monica was introduced to the meaning of a genuine caring family. Hitch made her a Team Phone and explained about electronic communication equipment.

Geoff gave her fundamentals of three languages so she could choose one to start studying. She chose Spanish and was encouraged by her new family, including the students, who greeted her with, "*Hola!*" or "*Cómo está usted?*"

Oso was happy to be Tío again. He let Monica drive the cart to the driving range, taught her the golf swing, and they practiced putting. They had long talks about the struggles and required effort of growing up. He gave her a blank, ruled journal and told her to write about her life, good memories and not-so-good. "Your past will be stored in your journal and you can move forward and make new memories to write about."

Sarge let her lie on the grass with a litter of puppies crawling over her. Then she was presented to Sarge's Dobermans and learned respect for animals for their intelligence. She talked to them, told them she never had a pet. They looked into her eyes, there was an understanding, as if they heard one another's thoughts.

Joaquin made her giggle around the curves in the Lamborghini. Afterward she hugged him. "I never rode in any of my dad's sports cars."

He gave her his effortless, infectious smile. "That's part of your past. Write about those feelings in your journal. Then write about your Uncle Joaquin and the Lamborghini." He lifted his chin, raised his eyebrows. She laughed.

Joe flew with May, Monica, Amelia, Joaquin, the twins, Oso, and three students in *The White Falcon* to LA, then drove in the Hummer to the beach.

"Joe, she's not a real bird," Monica snickered.

"Sure she is, didn't you see her fly?"

Joe took May and Monica back to Toledo in The Team's small jet. Every weekend he returned, helped clean out the townhouse, gave the furniture Marco had selected that was so out of place and May disliked, to The Salvation Army.

Hidden behind clothes in the back of his closet May found a small, plain, white gift box with "PRIVATE" written in black marker on top. Inside were bank envelopes full of receipts showing Marco regularly stashed money in a personal account. A shoebox, also marked "PRIVATE," contained hundreds of dollars in small bills. An insurance policy, on which May paid the premiums, his seven sisters were listed as equal beneficiaries. He had told May it was money for her and Monica. They made a copy and sent it to the blond woman in skinny jeans. He had told her she was the beneficiary, also.

Joe quietly said, "Let's send the policy to the oldest sister, let them collect on it. We don't want or need it. Let Monica open her own bank account with the cash and the money from his private account."

He took them to Aspen, Colorado, rented a condominium, hiked the mountain trails, went to a fancy restaurant every night. On the last night they hurried inside from the mountain-cool evening, sat in front of the bright electric flame in the fireplace. Joe knelt at their feet and proposed marriage, asking May to be his wife, Monica to be his daughter. They stood for a three-way hug, Monica sobbing, May and Joe teary-eyed, all rubbing one another's shoulders.

Joe asked May to give notice at her job and move to The Oasis at the end of Monica's school term. "I will pay my daughter's tuition for senior year at the private school Emilio and Amy attend, then for the college we will help choose."

Excitement at The Oasis included plans of marriage, a triple ceremony: May and Joe, Cat and Zack, Mona and Marshall. The Team reserved the ballroom at a resort in Phoenix. Amelia, May, and Mona picked the menu: white asparagus with a creamy boiled-egg dressing appetizer, *insalata caprese*, choice of salmon or filet mignon, wild rice, grilled vegetables, three different kinds of wedding cake. It was to be cocktail dress and dark suits, dancing and champagne.

Cat talked every morning to May and The Girlfriends. She told them, "I'm wearing a pale-pink silk suit with lots of glittery beads and a very loose jacket."

May and Mona said, "Loose jacket, me, too."

Cat wasn't sure if she was reading something into their answer. "What are you saying?"

Together they announced, "We're pregnant."

They laughed like four high school girls. In awe, Amelia wanted confirmation. "Three pregnant brides?!"

Nikolai called The Team at The Oasis, included Zack and Cat in Lausanne. "I want the triple wedding to be at my residence. You know I can't go to Arizona. How can all of you get married without me?"

Zack answered, assuring Nikolai he was part of their lives. "We aren't excluding you. Here are the plans for your approval: After the wedding, Joe, May, and Monica are stopping in London for a few days of sightseeing, then going to Moscow to be entertained by Uncle Nikolai. Everyone loves this young girl. Joe told her you would arrange tours for her of Moscow and St. Petersburg. Now, she's studying Russian history."

Cat related their plans to The Team and Nikolai, a honeymoon in Australia. He grumbled, but she was so excited, he gave in. "I can't wait to see that incredible Opera House and kangaroos and koalas in person," Cat said.

She detailed the information about the month-long wilderness survival camp in Montana. Alex, Mikhail, and Emilio had gone through the information packet, watched the video, decided it would be their challenge. They would attend after the wedding ceremonies.

"Nikolai, this is for you. After our honeymoon in Australia, we will stop at The Oasis, pick up Alex and Mikhail, and go back to Lausanne. Then we go to Russia and spend the ninth month of my pregnancy with you. The baby will be born in Moscow under her godfather's care."

There was silence, then Nikolai cleared his throat. "I've never been so happy. All the arrangements will be made."

CHAPTER XXX
To Bask In Sunshine

At The Oasis, the call came from Nikolai. "Cat is in the delivery room, all going well." Joe and Joaquin flew The Team's new, luxurious Gulfstream to Moscow, bringing May and Monica, Amelia and the twins, and Oso.

After the baby was born, Cat and Zoey were taken to the President's private hospital suite, where Zack had finished pacing. A dining/living room was connected to the bedroom, a buffet crowded with platters of assorted Russian specialties. Seated at the table, Cat's family was noisily discussing her glow, anxiously waiting their turn to cuddle the new baby.

Two rocking chairs, side by side, were placed at the foot of Cat's bed. Uncle Nikolai was gently rocking a pink-blanketed newborn. Peeking from a pink knit cap were wisps of pale hair. He was singing to her in Russian.

Tío Oso sat next to him in the other rocker. "When my mother would put me to bed, she sang that lullaby to me. It's my turn, give Zoey to me. I want to sing to her. Cat, will you explain to him about two godfathers and equal time with our goddaughter?"

Alex and Mikhail knelt next to Uncle Nikolai. Alex put his finger in the palm of the dainty hand, she curled her miniature fingers around it. "Mikhail, look at the fingernail on her little finger. Isn't it the tiniest fingernail in the whole world?"

Zack sat on Cat's bed leaning into a pile of pillows and gathered her in his arms, she leaned back on his chest. He bent to her ear, whispered, "We have a beautiful baby girl, my love." They were enclosed in their own aura of bliss.

Acknowledgements

I am fortunate to be a member of The World's Greatest Writing Group. The writer brings copies for each listener, then reads aloud and gets an honest, intelligent, helpful encouraging critique. My heartfelt thank you to June Ferrill, MaryAnne Crowe, Meg Lamme, Beverly Byers-Pevitts, and Kate Marck.

I imposed on wonderful friends to read my manuscript and give feedback from a reader's point of view. Sincere thank you to Judith Newton, Millie Evans, Peta Stockdale, Judy Post, Judy Golis and Jerry Ruther.

Without the help of professional editor, Carolyn Haley, this story would be full of commas, assumptions and too many mistakes to mention.

So grateful to Ghislain Viau, Creative Publishing Book Design, for a most imaginative and artistic cover design.

Barbara Jean Ruther, author

CPSIA information can be obtained
at www.ICGtesting.com
Printed in the USA
FSHW010647230721
83408FS